EDWIN
PHILIPS

1988 Salmon High
School Graduate

MissTAKEN

Published by Goldcrest Books International Ltd
www.goldcrestbooks.com
publish@goldcrestbooks.com

ISBN: 978-1-913719-67-8
eISBN: 978-1-913719-68-5

Dedicated to the several mountain-west farm girls I had the privilege to know during my college years. Your examples, of quiet, humble confidence, hard work, kindness, patience, and integrity were the inspiration for Jessica. And I hope she inspires many, as you did.

Chapter One

Jessica Hansen was just starting to awaken. A weird, unnatural grogginess pervaded her mind. It saturated her limbs, leaving them sluggishly lethargic. Her brain obstinately rebuffed her efforts to direct her thoughts. Fragmented memories swirled around in her head, slowly coalescing; her first year at college, her roommates. Spring break in Mexico. Loud music and dancing and drinking. So much alcohol, but not for her—she didn't drink. It kinda made her uncomfortable being around it, but at least her roommates got back to the hotel safe every night.

Except, not tonight.

She'd gone to dinner with her roommates, and when they passed a dance club, they'd insisted on going in for "just a few minutes, to see if anyone famous was there."

The bouncer eyed her critically when the three approached the entrance. She didn't look like she belonged with the other two. Sarah was positively stunning in a forest green, fit and flair mini dress and matching stilettos. Meredith's white halter top and pencil skirt were not quite as bold, but grabbed attention nonetheless, and highlighted her green eyes and her thick red hair, cascading down her back in loose curls.

Jessica was wearing comfortable jeans, a navy t-shirt, and mid-top hiking shoes.

"You're in the wrong club, *señorita*!" the bouncer yelled over the blaring music. "The cowboy bar is down the street!"

"I'm just here to babysit my friends!" she quipped. The corners of his mouth twitched upward into a barely perceptible smile, and he let her in.

They met three boys that night—local guys, kinda cute. They all said they were between nineteen and twenty years old, though Jessica was suspicious they might be a bit older than that. They were all on the tall side. The youngest one had friendly eyes, and a big smile that proudly displayed his perfect teeth. His dark hair was a carefully styled, messy look. His skin was flawlessly smooth, and his eyes had a look of perpetual amusement. He was an easy conversationalist and had a disarming charm. The other two appeared to defer to him, despite his younger age and smaller build. They were more reserved, their gazes more intense, they gave off a definite macho vibe with their close-cut hair and dark stubble.

Her roommates were really into them, but she'd been annoyed. Why?

Her head ached like she'd taken a nosedive off a spooked mare. Her mouth was dry.

Oh yeah, the guys really pressured her to drink. Like, a lot. They badgered her until she was ready to knock one of them out, then they finally backed off, and got her an orange juice. It tasted a bit funny, but not like alcohol.

A voice in the back of her head told her she shouldn't be awake right now, so she lay very still, waiting for the grogginess to go away of its own accord.

The persistent rumble of a roughly running motor, seemingly right behind her head, intensified her headache. Her mind tried to rationalize the presence of the motor noise—she didn't remember leaving the club. She strained her ears trying to pick up the incessant *thump-thump* of the club's techno music. A mild wave of nausea passed over her and her thoughts scattered again.

Voices caught her attention. Somewhere beyond her feet, the boys from the club spoke in Spanish. She'd hung out with the ranch hands a lot and managed to pick up a fair vocabulary. As her head began to clear, more words were recognizable.

One described in crude terms stuff he wanted to do to a girl. Was he talking about her? Then there was another voice—not one of the boys. Older. He was yelling and threatening the boy. He spoke fast. A lot of words she didn't understand, but she caught the word "virgin" and "money". The implication was that she was a virgin and was worth a fortune and he better keep his hands off her or he would lose them along with his head and possibly a few other extremities.

Her head pounded. Something was definitely wrong, but she couldn't keep her thoughts straight long enough to make sense of anything. Someone moaned softly next to her, and her shoulder was jostled as a body next to her shifted.

"One of them is waking up!" a voice said, "Should I dose her again?"

"No, we are only thirty minutes more to the ranch," the older voice said. "Hit her with a shot of the trainer, we'll give her an early start."

There was a sound of shuffling, and something bumped roughly against the bottom of her shoe. Something brushed against the outside of her leg, and there was another soft moan, and more rustling sounds as something next to her was moved. Another bump against her shoulder was followed by a short, soft little cry. Jess carefully opened one eye just a bit. She recognized one fuzzy outline as Sarah, with another fuzzy person holding her up a bit. She risked opening a bit wider, and a syringe came into focus, stuck in Sarah's arm. Sarah's eyes rolled back, and she went limp. The other person set her back down.

Jess fought against the waves of panic breaking over her; she focused on her breathing, keeping it slow, quiet, steady. She concentrated on her limbs, willing them to remain still and relaxed. She diverted her attention away from what happened to Sarah and focused on making sure it didn't happen to her.

The vehicle jolted, throwing her head to the side. She let it happen as smoothly and naturally as she could. She chanced peeking out of her left eye, which was now concealed from above by her nose. Her head was clear now, as was her vision, and she could make out the filthy interior of a van. A small backfire drew her focus to the motor again.

When she was younger her father would play a game with her and her siblings to pass the time whenever they were stuck near a road or parking lot, which they called 'guess the motor'. They would close their eyes, listen for a passing vehicle, and try to guess what it was by the sound of the motor.

As she listened now, she easily identified the distinctive, rhythmic sounds unique to the air-cooled motor used in a Volkswagen Bus. She was on the floor in the back, on the driver's side of the van, with her head near the back. She knew Sarah was directly to the right of her. Was Meredith here as well? On the other side of Sarah perhaps?

Her wrists were bound with rope, in front of her. Her forearms rested over the front pockets on her jeans. A little downward pressure confirmed her pockets were empty—someone had taken her wallet and phone. Her ankles were tied together as well. She surveyed the small section of van floor she could see without moving her head. Several crumpled food wrappers, some dirty rags, lengths of rope, a couple of hypodermic needles—likely used. Near her left hip rested a stray razor blade. A fortunately timed bump rocked her whole body, twisting it to the left and giving her the opportunity to drop her hands to the van floor, directly over the blade.

She hooked her middle fingernail under the edge of the blade on one side, while pressing her ring finger lightly against the top. She eased the blade to vertical and pinched it between her fingers.

Another jarring jolt rolled her to her back again. She managed to keep her grip on the blade, and using the fingers on her other hand, she shifted the blade's position to conceal it better between her index and middle finger.

Jessica remained still as the minutes passed, jostling on a rough, bumpy road, punctuated by an occasional moan from Sarah. Jess focused on keeping her eyes closed and remaining relaxed and ragdoll loose so as not to betray her conscious state.

The vehicle stopped and the motor cut. Doors creaked in protest as they were opened. The muffled sound of men talking and laughing became clearer and the sliding door on the passenger side opened with a rough, scraping sigh. It was much like the banter among the men at the ranch as they moved bales of hay from truck to barn.

"Mer." Sarah's voice was slurred, "Where're you going?"

Sarah's body shifted away from Jessica. When hands grabbed her ankles and pulled her, twisting her body on the floor and dragging her toward the open passenger door, she fought the urge to scream and fight. She forced herself to remain limp as she was hefted onto someone's shoulder like a feed sack.

"Not her," a voice said, "she goes up to the house, put her in Miguel's room. Juan, go with him, tie her to the bed, and stand guard." He spoke louder. "Anybody goes near that room, you shoot them. I'll be up to get her later, and if she isn't still untouched—if I find even a tiny bruise when I get there, I'll take an axe to your *cojones. Entiendes*?"

The man she lay on shifted, spinning her around. Her body bounced under his footfall. After a short walk she heard the click of a latch, followed by the creak of a door opening. The sounds of footsteps on stone changed to footsteps on wood floors. A series of upward jolts punctuated by a faintly hollow sound with each footfall informed Jessica she was being carried upstairs.

Jessica chanced opening her eyes briefly. Juan was apparently leading the way as nobody was behind. Jessica realized if they tied her hands, they would likely see the razor blade. Carefully but quickly, she lifted her hands to her head and gently slipped the blade into her mouth, biting down gently on the edge of the metal to prevent it slipping in her mouth and cutting her. She returned her hands to their dangling posture and closed her eyes just as they reached the top of the stairs. Another door opened, and then she was lowered onto a bed.

One of the men lifted her arms, slid a rope between them, and then wrapped and tied it around the ropes already binding her wrists. He pulled her arms over her head and tied them to what she assumed was the bedpost.

What if they tie my legs to the bed as well? Her stomach tightened in panic. How would she get the razor to her hands if she was trussed up?

A hand skimmed the front of her shirt, and again she fought the instinctive urge to tense up—to scream. The man began to apply pressure when the distinct click of a revolver being cocked reverberated around the room. The hand froze.

"Easy, Juan, it's just you and me."

"Yeah, and if he so much as smells your stink on her clothes, his axe makes me a *eunuco*. Walk out of this room now so I don't have to get yelled at for splattering your brains all over Miguel's bed."

"Okay, Okay, man. Chill."

Jess breathed a quiet sigh of relief as the two men left and the door closed. A lock clicked into place, followed by a dragging sound of wood on wood. She guessed Juan had pulled a chair in front of the door and posted guard.

Cracking her eyes, a bit at a time to confirm she was alone, she surveyed the room. It was a modest-sized room with a door to a balcony and opulent furnishings. The bed frame was a heavy, dark-stained hardwood, with intricate carving work. A small bedside table, a desk and chest of drawers also adorned the room, each of similar material and workmanship, with intricate gold inlays around the edges. She guessed from the décor—posters of rock bands, movies, and scantily clad women in provocative poses, some of which appeared to be autographed—that Miguel was a younger man in his late teens or early twenties.

The room started to go out of focus, and the edges of Jessica's vision darkened. She realized she was panting.

"Oh, good one, Jess," she murmured softly, "first moment you get to yourself and the best idea you can come up with is hyperventilate and pass out."

Jessica closed her eyes and focused on taking slow, deep breaths. *In through the nose, hold it, out through the mouth*, she repeated the mantra in her mind, counting six seconds between each action. She had learned this breathing technique at a workshop the university had set up as part of freshman orientation. It was presented as a means of managing anxiety before an exam. She nearly laughed out loud at the thought of comparing her current predicament to that of taking a test.

Jessica opened her eyes again. She could only see two options open to her at the moment; wait to see what happens next or try to escape.

Might as well work on option two, she thought, *it'll pass the time while I wait for option one.*

She examined the rope around her wrist. It was braided nylon, about a quarter-inch thick, which was wrapped around her wrists five or six times and tied in a square knot. There were no loops between her wrists apart from the thicker rope which tethered her to the bedpost. It was looped once and tied to itself in a slip knot.

She flexed her wrist experimentally. The rope had a little bit of stretch to it, but she couldn't quite wriggle her hand free. Shifting and squirming, Jessica scooted her body toward the head of the bed until her hands could reach her mouth. She gingerly extracted the razor blade. She worked it around to where she could bite down on the back edge, holding it firmly between her teeth with the blade protruding in front of her lips.

She rotated her hands and brought her wrists closer until the nylon ropes about her wrists rested against the exposed blade. She moved her arm side to side, dragging the rope across the razor. She applied a little more pressure and was rewarded with the hiss and pop of tiny nylon threads being severed. She continued slicing at the coils of nylon braid while the minutes ticked by.

A noise came from outside the door, and she froze, holding her breath in dreadful anticipation for the door to open and for Juan to discover her attempting to escape. The door remained closed. Relieved, she resumed cutting.

After cutting through the first few coils, she was able to loosen the bonds sufficiently to pull her hands free. She untied the rope around her ankles, then coiled it and stuffed it into a back pocket of her jeans. She crammed the bits that held her wrist into the other back pocket, and then collected the rope used to tie her to the bed. It was a thicker, twisted rope, maybe twelve feet in length. She coiled it around her waist and tied it off like a belt. A knife and rope were the number one and two items on any survival essentials list. Her family camped a lot, and survival fundamentals were well ingrained, particularly since her brothers fancied themselves as mountain men.

You're alone in enemy territory Jess, a voice in her mind said. *You better look around and gear up for a long, lonely trek.*

She retrieved the razor blade which she had dropped on the bed once she was free, and she placed it in the small waste bin standing next to the desk, taking care not to let it drop or clatter. She quickly explored the room, looking for anything which might help her. Miguel had a liking for cowboy culture. His closet was full of jeans, Western style shirts and cowboy boots, though many of them looked altogether impractical, spattered with sequins and rhinestones and other extravagances.

His collection of cowboy accessories was not limited to clothes. She found a few pairs of garish spurs, which would be useless for actual horse riding. There were also a couple of gaudy cowboy hats. A hat would protect her head from the sun during the day, but these hats were as attention grabbing as a disco ball.

On the corner of the desk rested a familiar looking knife. Her brother Joseph collected knives. One of his favorites was the SOG SEAL Pup. It was nine inches long with a metal handle and five inches of blade, the two inches at the hilt serrated. This one was in a durable nylon sheath with a flexible strap system on the back for attaching comfortably to any variety of belts, harnesses or backpack straps. A small strap with a snap wrapped over one finger guard, holding the knife securely in the sheath.

Jessica picked the knife up to examine it. She tugged at the strap and the snap released with an audible click, which seemed to echo in the room. Jessica winced. She looked at the door, then glanced around the room, frantically looking for a hiding place. The door remained closed.

Stupid! she silently berated herself. She relaxed slightly, and returned to her examination of the knife, removing it from the sheath to observe the condition of the blade.

She would have preferred a standard pocketknife—something light, easy to carry, and easy to conceal, something she could use to cut rope, gut small game, or make tinder shavings. This knife was a bit bulky and not quite as versatile. But any blade was better than no blade. And the large blade would work for batoning, so there were some pluses.

She returned the blade to the sheath and fastened the strap, wrapping it in the hem of her shirt first to muffle the sound of the snap. She fastened the sheath to her belt and continued her search. How long before they came for her? She needed to hurry.

Jessica crept to the drawers, grasped the top-drawer handle and inched it open, keeping the rough rasping of wood against wood as muted as possible. In the drawer she found a pair of socks that looked like they would fit her.

"Wet feet are bad news on a long hike," she recalled her father saying once as they were packing for a weekend family outing, "Always make sure you have an extra pair."

Further rummaging turned up a deep navy bandana. She wove the socks into the rope around her waist, and she tied the bandana around her neck.

As she inched the drawer closed again, she heard the measured thud of footsteps on stairs. Abandoning the drawer, she tiptoed quickly to the balcony doors. She reached for the handle, turning it with measured slowness to avoid the slightest noise. Once the latch retreated into the door, she pulled it open and peeked out.

The balcony was dark, and stretched the length of the house. Several doors led to the balcony—she assumed from other bedrooms. Crouching, she padded softly to the railing and peered through the bars. A couple outbuildings lay to her left, all dark except one. Three or four men with rifles wandered about near the outbuildings, though they seemed less than alert. Given the drive time, they were likely in the middle of nowhere, and their job was more a formality than a need.

Off in the distance to her right she could make out another man, also armed with a rifle. He wasn't a concern, but the dog at his side was. That could complicate things considerably. It was difficult to tell from a distance, but the size and shape reminded her of a pit bull.

On the bright side, it's not a hound, she thought. He'd be trouble if he heard or saw her, but once she was clear of the property and in the trees, he'd be fairly easy to elude. Terriers were fast, ferocious beasts. They were great for protection, and they had been popular among early settlers and pioneers for that reason. They'd rip small varmints to shreds, and they would even face down a cougar or a bear to protect their family. But while they could be decent trackers, she hadn't known anyone to train them for that job.

She skulked left along the balcony, until it wrapped around the house. Carefully she peered around the corner. The van they arrived in—an old Volkswagen bus—and an old pickup truck were parked in an open area, just past a walk, which went around a large fountain and up to the house. Beyond, a narrow road disappeared in the darkness among the trees.

This must be the front of the house, she concluded.

She continued along the front of the house to the other corner. Looking out, she could see only empty, open space for maybe twenty yards, then trees. Peering over the side, she couldn't see or hear anyone below.

If she could get down here, the house would be between her and the dog—at least for now. She assumed they were probably patrolling, so that might change.

She quickly swung a leg over the railing. Grabbing hold of the corner post, she lowered herself down, until she was hanging from the post. Her heart was threatening to break out of her chest.

It's just a game of fugitive, she told herself. She had played fugitive in the dark with her brothers and friends often during the summer. She talked her college roommates and a number of people from other dorms into playing a round last fall as well. It was a cross between tag and hide and seek. A few people were selected to be the fugitives and the rest would be cops. A starting point and a destination were selected. The fugitives got a two-minute head start and raced on foot to the destination. The cops got to use cars—or bikes when she was too young to drive—and their objective was to chase, find and tag the fugitives before they got to the destination.

Her brothers added a twist to the game by giving the cops nerf guns, so they could shoot you from a distance.

"Yeah," Jessica whispered, "you're just playing fugitive." She tried not to think about the real guns the men were holding. She glanced around quickly to be sure she was alone, then released her grip on the post.

She crouched as her feet touched the ground, to absorb the impact and minimize the noise her landing made. She froze briefly, listening for any sound of alarm.

Nothing.

Staying crouched she half walked, half ran across the open ground to the tree line. She picked out the North Star, low on the horizon in front of her. There was something soothing about finding it. Anytime she was outside with her dad after dark, he would always point out the North Star. She habitually looked for it anytime she could see stars in the sky. It was an anchor in the night. She chose north as her direction of travel because America was north. Home was north. It was a fairly stupid reason to pick north, but, she had nothing else to work with.

She picked her way through the vegetation as quickly as was safely possible, constantly checking her bearing against several overhead constellations, to ensure she didn't accidently circle back. The half-moon gave her just enough light to pick out the trees and large bushes, but not enough for her to be easily seen.

After several minutes the terrain in front of her sloped upward. It wasn't terribly steep, but she had to force herself to keep moving, each step becoming harder as the adrenaline coursing through her body diminished. Before long she found herself cresting the ridge of a modest hill, panting and struggling to bring moisture back to her dry throat.

Turning back, she could see the ranch below. There appeared to be a fair amount of activity on the grounds, beams of flashlights flitted about. They must have discovered she was missing. She looked at the small outbuilding and thought of her roommates. She had left them behind.

It wasn't a choice, she reminded herself. Trying to get to them, and then get them out in their drugged state would have only caused her to get caught.

"I'll come back for you..." she promised. Then dropped down the other side of the hill.

Chapter Two

Jessica continued northward through the night. The going was slow, she had to be cautious in the dim light not to step in holes. She had to be careful of the wildlife as well. Snakes were hunting rodents, and scorpions were out and about as well. What other poisonous, venomous, carnivorous or otherwise dangerous creatures lurked in the darkness? Spiders? Wild dogs? Big cats? And what about plants? Was she likely to stumble through a growth of poison ivy, or poison oak? This wasn't her stomping grounds; she didn't know the local flora and fauna.

The sky began to lighten, and a line of red appeared on the horizon, signaling the impending dawn, as she crested another hill, and found herself looking down on a small town.

Jessica wasn't sure if town was really accurate, but that's the word that came to her mind first. It was a cluster of a dozen or so houses scattered in a clear-cut area, sort of surrounding an open space that might pass as a park. A dirt road passed through the central area as well, leading off in both directions. A few of the structures appeared to be concrete blocks, with tile roofs. Most however were a mixture of scrap wood, rusty metal, and thatch.

Jessica considered the rude little village thoughtfully. It wasn't much, but it was civilization. Perhaps she could get some food, or at least some clean water to drink. Maybe she could even find a phone to call the police. If there was no phone available here, someone could surely give her directions to get to one. For some reason though, Jessica couldn't shake off her uneasiness about the place. She worked her way toward the town cautiously, sticking to clusters of trees for cover.

Jess made her way undetected to the edge of the town and watched from a thick growth of brush as the town began to awaken. A young boy emerged from a house, a small dog at his heels. He picked up a stick, and the dog went wild, shivering in ecstasy. The boy threw the stick and the dog raced after it, barking madly. It picked up the stick and thrashed it about for a moment, then raced back to drop the stick at the boy's feet. As the boy picked the stick up, the dog raced off in the anticipated direction the stick would be thrown. After a few moments, the boy was joined by another boy and two girls, engaged in an early morning game of tag.

A tired-looking woman shooed a group of hens out of a doorway with a broom. Two older, weatherworn men greeted each other and sat together on a bench, exchanging stories while sharing a cigarette.

Jessica ducked deeper into the bushes at the sound of a motor approaching. A jeep drove into sight, carrying two men in uniforms. As the jeep stopped, the woman disappeared into her doorway. The passenger exited the jeep and strolled over to the two old men on the bench. He greeted them pleasantly, but the wary return greeting given by one of the old men suggested that this man was known to them, and his pleasant demeanor was a façade.

The reactions of the locals reinforced Jessica's own misgivings. She tucked her head down, making sure her face was covered, and she drew her arms in front of her, covering as much of the bare skin as she could. She modulated her breathing, taking slow, shallow breaths to minimize any sound.

A man—probably the husband—came out from the same doorway the woman had disappeared into moments earlier.

The uniformed gentleman turned and greeted him. "Carlos, *buenos días! Como está*?" His voice carried as he spoke, as though he intended the whole town to hear.

"*Bien.*" Carlos walked slowly toward the uniformed man, his gaze wary and his steps hesitant as though he were approaching a coiled rattlesnake. "What brings you here so early?"

"A young woman is missing. *Gringa*, about five and a half feet, tan, dark hair with a hint of red. Very pretty girl."

Jess froze; the man was describing her.

"No *gringas* here." Carlos shook his head slowly and shrugged his shoulders.

"Oh." The uniformed man looked down, then off to the side, squinting. "If you see her, you will be sure to hold her for me? She is the property of Los Caballeros Templarios. They are very concerned that she be returned to them in perfect condition." He paused. "I am certain there will be a reward for her safe return."

He returned to the jeep and moved to climb in, turning back to Carlos at the last second, his brow furrowed in concern, "Of course, if something happens to her, and they think you are responsible ..." his voice trailed off ominously.

The woman, who had returned to the doorway, gasped and she wrapped her arms protectively around a young girl about nine or ten years of age. Carlos's eyes were wide with terror as he looked to the woman and child, then to the other children.

The man turned his attention to the two old men on the bench. "Good day, gentlemen." He nodded pleasantly, a cruel glint in his eye, as he settled into his seat. His driver started the engine and the jeep continued through the town.

Jessica remained motionless.

"I suppose I should feel flattered. I wonder just how much I am worth to them?" she quipped to herself, in an effort to lighten her mood.

"Actually, it would be helpful to know." It would give her something to use to estimate how wide a radius they would be willing to search—how many resources they would invest in her recovery. She was within the expanding search radius, and it was unlikely she'd be able to outpace it. However, on the upside, her trek to the town suggested she was in rural area with rugged terrain. Lots of forest and mountains would hamper search efforts and make it easier for her to stay out of sight, even with the locals enlisted. The downside; she was ill equipped for an extended trek. Her gear consisted of the clothes she was wearing, and the few sundries she had pilfered from Miguel's room.

What would the weather be like? How hot would it get here? The temperatures on the coast had been pleasant enough, but she had no idea how far they had been moved. Or in which direction. Still north of the equator she supposed, as the North Star was still visible at night. Most likely still in Mexico, but no longer on the coast. Beyond that, it was anybody's guess. She could probably learn the name of the town with a little sleuthing, yet since she didn't know the geography of Mexico, it would bring her no closer to knowing her location.

Ixtapa, the town they had been abducted from was in southern Mexico, which was... what? Something like a thousand miles from the US border? That would take somewhere around a month, assuming the weather was good the whole time, she didn't have to stop to deal with blisters or other injuries, and she was able to consistently find sufficient food and water as she was going.

Water. The thought made her aware of her dry mouth and parched throat. She was going to need water, soon. She was going to need a way to carry it, and a way to purify it. Food would be nice too at some point, though that could wait a while. A few days, maybe even a week or two, if need be, though that would leave her low on energy, which would affect her strength, endurance, mood, and mental acuity.

She thought of her roommates again. Thus far she had kept a good mental note of direction and distance to return to them. The farther she travelled, the harder that would be.

And how long would they remain at that location anyway? Just long enough to get them ready to sell, she reasoned. A value had been affixed to her; she assumed the same applied to them. They were livestock. They were a product—an inventory to be moved. The longer you held on to it, the higher the cost and the lower the profit. She shivered at the thought of it, but that was the way it was. Simple economics.

Jessica clenched and unclenched her fists in indecision. She couldn't leave her roommates, she had to help them. She couldn't help them. How could she help them? She couldn't....

She couldn't stay here any longer. She was too close to the village. The kids, or the dog, would inevitably find her if she stayed put. She had to move.

Move where? Where was she? Where could she go?

Her abductors would watch the roads more closely, she reasoned. A college girl partying in a foreign country finds herself abducted. What would she do? Find civilization. Go to the police. So that was where they would look first. Was the guy in the jeep the police? She had no idea what Mexican police looked like. She had heard they were corrupt, that they could be bribed. She was advised to keep bribe money in her wallet just in case.

A friend had told her about visiting Mexico the year before. On the way back to the airport, they were pulled over and accused of speeding, though her friend was certain the car they were in wasn't capable of exceeding the posted speed limit. The police officer told her friend they would have to come to the station, fill out forms, go to court… It would be very expensive. Two twenty-dollar bills exchanged hands, the police left, and her friend made it to the airport just in time to catch his flight.

"Hey, God," she said softly, glancing skyward as she moved through the brush, away from the village. "I am in a real pickle right now. I am feeling awfully alone, and I don't know what to do. I'd really be grateful if you could give me a little guidance—point me in the right direction. And please, look after my roommates. I don't see how I can help them, but I know you can."

She slowly turned about, facing every direction briefly, hoping for some inspiration or impulse to guide her choice.

Nothing.

She looked back to the town. That would be the place to find supplies. It wasn't very big, fewer than a hundred people. Not likely she could keep her head down and go unnoticed. Besides, she had no money, and even though her circumstances were dire, she still wasn't keen on the idea of stealing.

Rustling sounded in the brush behind her.

She ducked into the thickest brush she could find. A young boy shuffled into view, eyes searching the growth around him.

"*Gringa*?" he said in a voice barely above a whisper, looking around guiltily, "Are you there?"

Jess watched him uncertainly. How had he seen her? She had been so careful. He looked to be no more than ten years old. A stick of a boy, with a thick head of straight, dark hair.

"*Gringa*?" He whispered again, looking around nervously. "I have food for you."

Cautiously she emerged from her hiding place. "How did you know I was here?" she asked.

"*Abuela*," he shrugged, "she said you were here, she told me to bring you this sack, and to make sure nobody sees me."

"So… you won't tell anybody you saw me then?"

He furrowed his brow. "*Abuela* would kill me." He held the sack out to Jessica.

"How did your… *Abuela* know I was here?" she asked as she took the sack from him.

The boy shrugged again. "She knows almost everything." He turned and walked toward the village. "Good luck, *gringa*."

"*Gracias*," she called out to him softly. He didn't look back. He returned to the village and resumed playing as though nothing happened.

Not wanting to take chances, Jessica hurried quickly away from the village—south, more or less—back the way she came. After several minutes she changed direction, moving west, then northwest, to circle the village. Her selected destination was a taller, heavily forested mountain nearby. She reasoned the thick vegetation and rough terrain would prevent vehicle travel, and she hoped that from that vantage point, she might be able to see something which would give her a clue as to where to go, or what to do.

Travel was over rolling ground, with trees growing in thick clusters, separated by areas of grasses. She remained in the trees when possible, and she sprinted in a crouch across open areas when there was no other option. Twice she had to cross narrow roads. Checking carefully for anyone who might be able to see her, she would sprint across and drop to a crouch in the bushes on the opposite side, listening for any indication she had been discovered. Satisfied that her crossing went undetected, she continued onward.

By noon, she was in heavy forest, which appeared to go unbroken now, all the way to the top of the mountain.

She paused at the base of the mountain to rest her legs. Her head ached. How long had she been awake for now? Apart from an hour or two of drug-induced unconsciousness, she guessed it was close to thirty hours since she last slept. That would explain the light-headedness. Her sweat-soaked t-shirt clung unpleasantly to her body. Her exposed arms were sticky with sweat and streaked with dirt. They were covered in small scratches from branches.

Jessica opened the small sack and examined the contents. A loaf of bread, a bottle of water, and a shawl. She broke off a piece of the bread and chewed on it. It had a nice aroma, a hard crust and a spongy middle. It must have been freshly baked that morning, or the night before. The bottle was a typical plastic bottle. The seal was broken. She stared at the water. It looked clean, but there could be parasites in it. Reluctantly she set it aside.

The shawl could help protect her bare arms and neck

from the sun but would probably be too hot to wear. It might come in handy if temperatures dropped at night.

Jess examined her arms; she could see redness of the early stages of sunburn. She needed to do something about that right now. She retrieved the bottle from the sack again, opened it, and poured a small amount on the dirt at her feet. She mixed the dirt and water with her fingers until it was a thick mud, which she spread over the exposed skin of her arms, neck, and face.

Jessica shook her head to clear a wave of dizziness that passed over her. She was beginning to feel the effects of forgoing sleep the previous night now. She would need to find a safe place to rest. She needed to keep a clear head. Sleep would be crucial.

She closed the sack and continued onward, moving carefully through the thick vegetation. She planned to reach the summit a few hours before nightfall, giving her a chance to survey the surrounding area, and plan her next move.

The going was slow, the vegetation was considerably thicker and lusher than the high desert areas she normally hiked with her family. She had covered hundreds, maybe thousands of miles of Utah desert land over the years. Hiking and camping had been part of her life as far back as she could remember.

Halfway up the mountain, she paused to catch her breath. Glancing at the sky through the canopy, she caught a glimpse of the sun. It was lowering already. She bit down on her lip and gazed at the forest in front of her. The chance of her making the summit by nightfall was slim.

Jessica abandoned that effort and began the search for a safe place to sleep. What would be safe here? The area was teeming with life. She had been listening to the cacophony of bugs, birds and who knows what else most of the day. No doubt activity would pick up at night as the various nocturnal dwellers awakened.

The forest had been mostly oak trees. As she climbed higher, there were increasing numbers of pine and fir trees. Not the skinny lodgepole pines she was accustomed to, these were large trees with wide bases, bunched impassably close together. She selected a particularly imposing grouping of such trees which would provide cover and restrict the movement of larger predators. Using the SOG, she began hacking off several smaller branches. She moved enough greenery to create an entry to the base of one of the largest trees in the grouping. Ants scurried up and down the trunk.

Fire ants? She had heard of them on the news and knew they could be deadly but had never seen them. The news reports had been from Texas; would southern Mexico's climate support them? Even if they weren't fire ants, they'd be poor bedmates.

Better find a different place.

She moved to a smaller cluster of trees. Pushing in among them, she found a small clearing. It was mostly bug free. The trees, while smaller, were still large enough and thick enough to impede the passage of larger creatures, she thought. Cutting more branches and using the smaller pieces of rope she had taken, she fashioned a very rough, very makeshift lean-to shelter. It wasn't as good or sturdy or protecting as the ones she and her brothers made when they were camping out on the ranch, but it would serve. She cut several younger boughs and laid them in the bottom to serve as a bed.

Now, what to do about nighttime critters? Fire was a good critter repellant. It would also be a great beacon for anyone looking for her. The surrounding trees might provide a sufficient screen.

Jess poked at the earth with the tip of the knife, testing how easy it would be to excavate. The blade slipped though the ground easily, so she kept going, an idea forming.

She would build what Grandpa Hansen called a Dakota fire hole.

He had showed her how to build them once on a hunting trip. The fire would burn nearly smokeless, and the light would be difficult to see, even from quite close. She had asked how he learned to make it, and he had mumbled something about Indian lore learned from the pioneers and passed down through the generations. That meant it was probably something he had learned, or at least used during the war and didn't want to talk about it.

She hurriedly dug a hole, roughly a foot in diameter and a foot deep. She then moved a foot away and dug another hole, this one a smaller tunnel, angling down to connect with the first hole at the base. She gathered some dry pine needles and small twigs and placed them in the bottom of the larger hole. Scouring the surrounding area, she found several larger, dry twigs which she broke to uniform, one-foot lengths. She constructed a teepee in the hole, centered over the pile of twigs and pine needles.

The needles and small twigs were the tinder—they would catch fire and burn easily. They would generate enough heat and flame to catch the larger twigs—the kindling—on fire, which would then catch larger logs on fire. She collected and cut a few chunks of wood for this purpose, trying to estimate how many it would take to keep the fire going through the night.

Now she needed a way to start a fire. No problem, she had built fire bows before with her dad. She selected a couple of chunks of wood with flat surfaces, and one straight, dry stick roughly one foot long and a little thicker than her finger. She cut a sturdy, but slightly flexible branch, and tied a piece of the smaller rope to each end, like a bow with a loose bowstring.

Jessica used the knife to dig a small divot in the larger piece of flat wood, then dug a similar divot in the smaller piece of wood. She chopped at the edges of the smaller piece, taking off sharper bits and shaping it until she could hold it comfortably in her hand.

She cut a point on one end of the stick and placed the point in the divot on the larger piece of wood. She then looped the rope of the bow around the stick. Gripping the smaller, flat piece in her left hand, she placed it on the top of the stick, with the end in the hole she had carved. She gave a few experimental draws of the bow. The looped rope rolled roughly, turning the stick. A few more practice draws, and Jess began to increase the speed.

The friction wore the ends of the stick and the divots, so the stick moved more smoothly, spinning clockwise and then counterclockwise as Jessica drew the bow back and forth. Before long, small tendrils of smoke began to appear where the stick and divot met. She continued to draw the bow as the smoke increased. In the dimming evening, she could see a small red glow. Quickly she tipped the board, knocking the glowing embers onto a file of dried pine needles and dry grass she had prepared. She scooped up the pile and the embers and gently blew on it. More smoke appeared. The embers glowed brighter with each breath, then between one breath and the next, a flame appeared. She carefully blew a few more times at the base of the flame, feeding it more oxygen, then dropped the burning mass into the hole.

The wood in the hole caught fire, drawing oxygen through the tunnel.

Jess pulled the plastic bottle full of water out of the sack and examined it. She removed the cap and gently squeezed the bottle until the water was right to the rim. She replaced the cap tightly. Examining the bottle once more to be certain there was no air left in the bottle, she placed the bottle into the fire hole.

Her dad had boiled water in a paper cup once.

"The water reaches a temperature of 100 degrees Celsius and stops," he explained. "Paper doesn't burn until over 200 degrees Celsius. The water keeps the paper from reaching that temperature, so the water boils, but the cup doesn't burn."

Sure enough. The top of the cup burned, right down to the water line. And that was it, the water boiled in the cup. Jess didn't know the melting temperature of the plastic, but she was confident it was higher than the boiling point of the water. She would leave it in for an hour or so—that should make it safe to drink. Maybe she'd leave it overnight. Couldn't be too careful.

In the last bit of evening light Jess gathered a few more handfuls of wood to keep the fire going through the night. She ate another piece of bread, and then tied the sack in a tree away from the lean-to, so as not to invite any hungry critters that might smell the bread directly to her bed.

She would have to do something about water tomorrow. That would need to be top priority. She would need about a gallon of water every day to stay hydrated. She lay down under the lean-to and fell asleep.

She dreamed of the day she left for college. Her car was loaded, and she was hugging each member of her family. Joseph, her sixteen-year-old brother, was of two minds. He was sad to see her leaving, but he was also eager to move into her room. Thirteen-year-old Sam and twelve-year-old Elizabeth were bickering with each other—they were always bickering.

Five-year-old Emily, her baby sister, was crying.

Jessica hugged Emily close.

"Don't leave me! Don't leave me!" Emily cried.

"I'll be back to visit, baby," Jessica reassured her. Emily had been a surprise addition to the family, and since Mom had been diagnosed with cancer not long after she was born, Jess had stepped into the role of mom for Emily. "I'll see you soon, I promise."

The image morphed in the dream. Emily began to stretch, her long, straight, blond hair began to curl and turn flame red. Eyes shifted from blue-grey to emerald green. Her voice became deeper, richer, as she repeated, "Don't leave me!"

It was no longer Emily she was holding. It was Meredith, her roommate, pleading.

"I'll see you soon—" Jess woke with a start, her cheeks wet with tears, and her promise echoing in her mind.

"Heavenly Father, please help me," she cried. "Please help me! I don't know what to do. I don't know what to do. I'm so alone."

She buried her face in her hands and sobbed.

Chapter Three

The sobbing was over as quickly as it started. Jessica hardened her eyes and set her jaw as she roughly swiped the tears from her face.

"C'mon, Jess," she chided herself, "This is neither the time nor the place. Pull it together."

Jessica took a few deep breaths, then rose to her feet. The sun was just peeking over the horizon, bringing with it the long shadows and muted colors of early dawn. She dismantled the campsite, reclaiming the bits of rope.

The fire was reduced to a few glowing embers. Jessica retrieved the bottle of water from the fire hole—a bit misshapen in places, but intact. The bottle was warm to the touch, but not unbearably so. She opened the bottle and took a sip. The water was flat and tasteless, as boiled water generally is, and the warm temperature left it even more dissatisfying to the palate. Which was probably a good thing, as it tempered the urge to drink it in great gulps. She recapped the bottle and set it to one side.

Jessica filled the holes in and scattered loose debris over the disturbed earth. In a matter of minutes, the clearing looked as if she had never been there.

She surveyed the area once more to make sure nothing had been missed. Satisfied with her work, she collected the sack and the bottle. Stowing the bottle back in the sack, she continued upward to the summit. She was still tired, but less so than yesterday. Her head no longer ached, and her mind was clearer.

The muscles in her legs were slightly stiff from yesterday's exertion. Fortunately, she had competed in cross-country, and in track as a distance runner in high school since her freshman year. She had continued a relatively consistent training regimen since graduating. In only a few minutes, she was loosened up and striding comfortably up the steep slope. She reached the summit in no more than an hour—maybe two.

The foliage was as dense on top of the mountain as it was elsewhere, frustrating her efforts to get a good view of the region. Craning her head back, she gazed at the treetops. If she could get to the top, she might be able to see everything she needed to.

Jessica continued to walk, studying the bases of trees as she went. She needed to find a tree tall enough to look over the forest, with branches low enough to reach, and also branches up high that would be strong enough to support her weight. Twenty yards away she spied two massive trees growing side by side, contending for dominance on a raised knoll. Both went straight up, with sparse, sturdy branches angling up and away from the trunk. Neither was particularly climbable, but there were enough intersections of branches that between the two of them she was confident she could get to a high perch.

She placed the sack at the base of one trunk. Looking upward, she took a deep breath, then exhaled, her eyes darting from branch to branch, plotting a route. She shook her arms, hands, and fingers, loosening them up. Coiling like a spring, she leaped with a grunt, stretching her arms upward to grasp the first branch. She paused a moment to adjust her grip, then with a quick jerk she pulled herself upward, swinging one leg up and over the branch. She wriggled onto the branch and stood up, leaning against the trunk for balance. The branch was angled more steeply than she thought. Leaning forward and gripping either side firmly, she monkey-walked up the steep incline, struggling to keep her balance as her shoes shifted and slipped on the bark.

Ten feet out from the trunk, she stood up quickly, grabbing a branch crossing above her head from the other tree. She pulled on it gently, testing its strength; it was thinner than the branch she was standing on, and a bit springy, but would hold her weight. She pulled her feet up and wrapped her legs around the branch. It bobbed up and down, but not dangerously so.

Jessica waited for the branch to settle, then she shimmied to the trunk of the second tree. Once she had footing against the trunk, she wormed her way onto the branch. A couple closely spaced branches here gave her purchase to scramble several feet directly upward, then out along another branch to reach a crossing branch from the first tree. Back over to the first tree, pull up to another branch.

Back and forth and up she went. She had to retrace her steps once when the branch she selected began to crack as she moved out onto it. It took several minutes, and a few breaks to shake out the tightness in her arms and fingers, but she finally found herself above the canopy, with an excellent view in all directions.

North, south and west of her looked much the same, lush and mountainous. To the northeast was a rugged, more barren region, lots of scrub brush, and open spaces, interrupted on occasion by large, rocky formations. That would be more familiar territory for her—more like the high deserts of Utah where she grew up, but familiar didn't necessarily mean better. She knew just how challenging it would be to survive. She felt drawn to it, nonetheless. Was that just a trick of her mind? A desire for something familiar? Or was she being guided? She flicked her gaze between the lush, alien tropic and the familiar but treacherous desert.

Then Jessica noticed a line, meandering snake-like through the desert region. It appeared to be a gully, and it was dotted with greener, more dense clusters of foliage. That had to be a stream or a river cutting through the barren area. That settled it. She climbed back down out of the trees and started down the northeast side of the mountain. It was likely to be a long trek, maybe two days to get there. She really needed water sooner, her lips were dry and beginning to crack. Opening the bottle, she took a gulp. She resisted the urge to drink more. Until she had a way to replenish it, she would need to ration it.

It was still morning when Jessica came to a large, open spot in the trees on a flat area near the base of the mountain. It was completely covered with small, red, white, and mauve flowers on tall stems—about waist height. She froze. Nature wasn't big on homogeneity. This had to be cultivated.

She crept to the left, staying in the trees, but near the field, watching and listening for any activity. She was nearly to the northeast corner when the rumble of a vehicle approached from the north. Jessica crouched lower, her heart rate quickening.

A break in the trees lay about fifty yards ahead. A small shack, camouflaged with branches and netting stood near the break. It blended well with the surrounding trees and shrubs.

She moved to heavier cover as a jeep came in sight through the break in the trees.

The jeep stopped near the shack and two men got out. They were talking, but they were too far away for her to make anything out. They strolled casually into the open field. Both men had pistols strapped to their hip. They examined a few of the flowers as they walked through the field. The men were talking, occasionally laughing. Jess strained to hear but couldn't pick anything out.

After several minutes the men returned to the jeep and started the motor. They turned the vehicle around and disappeared into the trees the same way they'd come.

Jess hesitantly moved through the denser vegetation toward the shack, pausing every few steps to listen. She peered intently at the shack, watching for any movement.

The break in the trees was the head of a primitive road. Two worn tracks where wheels kept the vegetation from growing wound through the trees and out of sight. The shack was on the same side of the road as her, so she slipped up to the side. There were no windows, but the construction was rather shoddy. She was able to peer in through one of the many gaps in the boards.

Inside were a few worn and rusty cultivating tools. Among the tools was a hatchet. That would be handy to have.

She paused, considering. She was not inclined to steal. On the other hand, she needed to survive, and that meant gathering resources to make herself reasonably comfortable.

"Comfortable," she chuckled softly. "Good choice of words, Jess." However, it really was her aim.

Her family used to watch survivor reality shows on TV together. Her dad often sighed and shook his head as they watched. "They make the same mistake right at the start," he would always say. "They act as though they are going to be rescued. That whole optimism thing, I guess. But it's wrong.

"You have to assume you aren't going to be rescued. When you assume help is around the corner, you end up doing just enough to get by until the cavalry comes to save the day. Then, if something goes wrong, which it inevitably will, you aren't prepared to handle it, and you fall apart. When you know the cavalry isn't coming, you do what it takes to thrive."

Jessica checked the door; there was no lock, so she inched the door open and reached in to grab the hatchet. Closing the door again, she slipped back into the trees. She paused, crouching, and listening again for any sound of pursuit. All remained quiet.

Breathing a sigh of relief, she slid the hatchet handle into the rope belt. And started off again. She adjusted her direction of travel slightly to the north, running parallel to the road for a while, to see where it led. After two miles, she could make out a small village on a rise in the distance.

Those must be the people farming the flowers, she thought. The jeep with the two men was parked there, and the men were talking to a small group of women.

Jess wiped the back of her hand over her sticky, sweat-covered face and squinted skyward. The sun was directly overhead.

She swung the sack from her shoulder and sat in the shade of a large oak tree, from where she could watch the village. She opened the sack and retrieved the bottle. After taking another gulp of water, she tore off another chunk of bread. Except for the two men in the jeep, all the villagers were women and children.

To her left, she heard a vehicle driving toward the village from the southeast. Another jeep came into view with three men in it.

As it approached the village, the group of women scattered, racing for homes, and the two men ran to their jeep. She watched as they pulled rifles from their vehicle and aimed at the approaching jeep. The new arrivals stopped abruptly and jumped from their vehicle, their own weapons at the ready.

Jess could hear them shouting, though she couldn't make out what they were saying. She scuttled around behind the thick oak tree, for cover.

Peering around the trunk, she saw one of the three newcomers collapse before she heard the first staccato bursts of gunfire. The remaining four men scrambled for cover. The newcomers boarded their jeep while firing wildly into the village. They turned the vehicle around and retreated the way they came.

The other two men gave chase in their own vehicle, kicking up a cloud of dust in their wake. Jessica stayed low, hugging the base of the big oak until the sounds of motors and gunfire were gone. She looked back to the village. She could hear screaming. A woman was crouched over a small form.

"Oh, Jess, this is a bad idea!" she mumbled to herself.

Staying low she raced toward the village. As Jessica approached, she could see the small form was a young girl, no older than nine. Blood stained her dress.

Jess dropped down next to the little girl. The growing spot of blood was near the base of the girl's neck, just above her heart.

Jessica grabbed the fabric and pulled hard, enlarging the small hole made by the entering bullet. She could see the hole in the girl's shoulder. Dark blood was oozing out. A lot of dark blood was oozing out!

Jessica pressed her hand firmly against the hole to stop the flow of blood.

But then what? Two memories flooded her mind simultaneously, each competing for her attention. She closed her eyes, inhaled sharply, and exhaled slowly, fighting the panic welling up in her.

The first memory was from a first aid class she had attended with a group of her friends as a church activity in her teens.

"Arteries pump. Veins dump." The instructor repeated the rhyme several times, trying to fix it in the youths' minds. The girl's wound was oozing, not spurting. The bullet must have hit a vein.

Jessica fought to steady her trembling hands as she shifted her focus to the second memory. She was with her father and her older brother. They were deer hunting. Her brother had just shot a deer, and her father was examining the wound.

"Bullet entered here," he said, examining the small whole high in the creature's neck, close to the head. He rolled the deer over, exposing a much larger hole on the opposite side. The bullet deformed and expanded as it travelled through the deer.

Jessica briefly removed her hand from the wound to examine it, then applied pressure again. There were tears in the flesh around the wound. That meant this was probably where the bullet came out. The hole wasn't very large though, and exit wounds are bigger than entry wounds. She'd been on enough successful deer hunts with her family to know that.

Jessica slipped her free hand behind the girl's back. More blood, then her finger found another small hole. Jessica breathed a hopeful sigh. That suggested the bullet had passed right through the tiny body, without even expanding. Other than nicking a vein, this wound might not be so bad. She pressed her hand against the second hole.

"I need clean rags and water! *Trapos limpios y agua*!" Jessica said, mostly to give the panicked women something to do for a few minutes, other than screaming and waving their arms.

Her confidence cut through their fear, and they set about searching for water and rags. It took a few minutes for the requested items to be gathered, which gave Jessica a moment of quiet to think.

"Direct pressure for a vein," Jessica rehearsed to herself reviewing again the instructor's direction from the first aid course, "It shouldn't take more than about five minutes to get it stopped." Of course, holding pressure for five minutes was not an easy task.

When the women returned with the rags and water, Jessica quickly pressed a clean rag against the wound and instructed one of the women to hold it tightly in place. She did the same for the wound on the girl's back. She used some of the water to clean the blood from her hands, then using another rag, she worked to clean away the blood from the little girl.

The girl regained consciousness as she was finishing up. She cried, complaining of pain in her shoulder, but otherwise she seemed okay.

Under Jessica's direction, the women slowly removed the rags. Blood was seeping, but no longer oozing from the wound. Jessica's shoulders sagged and she breathed a sigh of relief. She instructed the women to continue pressure with clean rags.

"Is there a doctor?" Jessica queried in Spanish. There was a quick discussion, and one older woman raced off to bring her car, to take the girl to a nearby town where a doctor could be found. The remaining women continued to fuss over the little girl.

Jess quietly took a few steps backward. She was uncertain what to do now. She ran both hands through her hair, pulling it up off her neck, then letting it drop. She could feel the slight trembling in her fingers. She continued to take slow, deep breaths as she turned about, looking this way and that.

"The men who were just here," a voice startled her. Jessica whirled about, facing back toward the group of women. One younger woman had followed Jessica away from the group and was studying her closely.

"They were looking for a girl. A *gringa* with dark hair. They offered a reward."

Jess fought to keep her face passive. Her fists clenched tightly and the muscles in her legs tensed. She glanced to the group of women around the little girl, then back to the young woman.

"I don't think they will turn you in. Not after what you just did." The woman held Jess's gaze. "But it won't be safe for you to stay here. They will be back, soon."

"What just happened?" Jess asked.

The woman shrugged. "Rival cartels. Los Zetas and Los Caballeros Templarios. Sometimes they fight."

"Where are the men?" Jess looked around and then back to the woman inquisitively.

The woman glanced away. "Some are dead, some join the cartels. The rest try to get to America." She looked northward, wistfully. "They send money when they can, and they will send for us if they can find a way to get us there safely."

She paused for a moment, then turned back to Jessica. "You must go, it isn't safe here. They will be back."

Jessica reached out and gently touched the woman on the shoulder. She nodded soberly, then turned northward.

"Be careful!" the woman called after her. "Don't trust the police. Don't trust anyone."

Jessica slipped into the trees and out of sight.

As the day progressed the trees began to thin. By late evening, Jessica could see only small clusters of trees and scrub brush ahead of her. She had used nearly all the water in the bottle, even with careful rationing. She might be able to push on and reach the river before morning.

No. Better to make camp here in one of the small clusters of oak trees. She selected a spot with good cover, constructed another Dakota fire hole, and got a fire going.

Propping herself against a tree, she tilted her head back to the night sky and stared at the stars. Were her family looking at the same sky? Did they even realize she was missing? It had been only three days after all. Even though she called them every night to check in, maybe they thought she was having such a good time she forgot.

With a weighted breath, she lowered her head and rummaged in the sack for the last scrap of bread. It was small—not enough to stave off the loud growls coming from her stomach—but it was enough to keep her going until she got to the river.

Biting down on the crust, her thoughts turned to the little girl. Had the women got her to the doctor in time? She hoped so. She'd done all she could for her under the circumstances anyway.

Not wanting to use the last of her water, she finished the bread and settled in for the night. Leaning back against the trunk, she wriggled to find a more comfortable spot and pulled the shawl over her as a makeshift blanket. Her eyes heavy, she gave up trying to fight them and let sleep take her.

She had the same dream that night, her baby sister morphing into Meredith, begging her not to leave.

She startled awake as before then froze the second she heard the unmistakable buzz of a rattlesnake nearby.

Turning her head slowly, Jess could just make out the coiled shape in the pre-dawn light, not more than two feet away, near the fire hole. It must have come during the night, drawn by the warmth. It was difficult to judge the snake's length, but it looked like a timber rattler. She had seen those as long as five feet back home. Best guess, this one was between three and four feet long, which meant sitting two feet away she was likely within striking distance.

Not taking her gaze off the snake, Jessica moved ever so slowly, ever so imperceptibly away from the snake. First one leg, a mere fraction of an inch, then the other. She pressed her palms against the ground just enough to allow her body to shift, then she slowly slid her hands. It seemed as though an hour had passed before she managed to widen the gap by a foot, her arms trembling from the exertion. She continued until she had placed five feet between her and the snake, ensuring she was out of striking range.

She stood, and looking around spied a fallen branch, roughly five feet long, with a sturdy, forked end. Keeping a close eye on the rattler and using the hatchet, she quickly shortened the ends of the fork to just over an inch.

The snake ceased rattling and began to uncoil, preparing to move on. Jessica walked slowly toward the snake, stepping deliberately heel to toe to avoid making any sudden movements or sounds. When she was close enough, she lifted the stick up, and taking careful aim, brought the fork-end down just behind the snake's head, pinning the head to the ground. In a swift motion she raised the hatchet and swung, striking the body hard directly behind the stick. The blow severed the head cleanly. The decapitated body coiled and uncoiled, dropping small spatters of blood as it flopped about aimlessly.

Jessica used the stick to push the head away from her campsite. Eagerly, she rekindled the remaining embers of the fire. Once the fire was refueled and burning well, she took the still writhing snake body, and placing her boot on the tail just above the still buzzing rattles, she stretched the body out. Using the SOG, she cut a slit down the belly of the snake from end to end. She spread the skin apart near the top of the neck and located the esophagus and gripping it, she began pulling the innards out of the body.

Once the entrails were free of the body, she peeled the skin off, leaving her holding a creepy, twitching, naked snake body.

Using the remaining water, she cleaned out the body cavity and rinsed her hands. The fire was a hot pile of embers now. She gathered a few green branches and fashioned a grill grate over the hole. She cut a green branch from the tree and skewered the snake body at several locations, to keep the still twitching body in check. She then placed the skewered snake on the makeshift grate.

While it cooked, she attended to the head, gouging a hole in the dirt with the SOG and burying it, to reduce the chances of someone or something unintentionally coming in contact with the still venomous fangs.

Jessica removed the snake from the fire, peeled open the crisped outside, and proceeded to pick out and eat the stringy meat.

Some people said snake was good and tasted like chicken. Jessica didn't agree. She thought it might be edible with enough barbeque sauce. But plain, it tasted to her the like result of an unholy pairing of a chicken and an oyster. Still, it was meat. There was probably close to a pound of good, lean protein, which would satisfy her hunger and give her a much-needed boost.

With her belly filled and her spirits lifted, Jess filled in the fire hole and as before, cleared all traces of her having been there. She spied a nice, long, straight stick which would serve well as a walking pole as she was preparing to move on. Things were definitely looking up.

She gathered her meager supplies and began the day's trek hoping to reach the river before dark.

The ground had changed now, less grass and more gravel. There were fewer trees as well. She began to reconsider the wisdom of her decision, as there were few places where she wasn't exposed. Still there would be water ahead, and she needed water.

The sun was beating down now. Jessica used the bandana to cover as much of her face as she could to protect her skin. She wished she had a little water left, to mix with dirt and then rub the resulting mud on to serve as sunblock, as she had done the previous day. Much more of this exposure would likely leave her burned, peeling, and perhaps even blistering,

"Standing outside the fire," Jess sang the words from the country song by Garth Brooks softly to herself, "Life is not tried it is merely survived if you're standing outside the fire."

She took comfort from the words. It was a reminder that most things worth doing were hard. She felt energized as she continued to hum the music, her pace quickening to match the rhythm.

Ducking into the next shady spot she found, Jessica took a break for several minutes. She'd been limiting her exposure as much as she dared while still making progress across the barren landscape, and the pauses gave her a chance to assess the situation.

The sun was getting close to the horizon now. She held her hand up between the sun and horizon to count the number of fingers between the two. Six fingers. It was a primitive way to measure time, each finger representing about fifteen minutes. She had roughly an hour and a half until sunset.

She had hoped to be at the river by now. Could she chance getting over one more hill? She wasn't desperately dehydrated yet. She had a goal and didn't want to miss it. Gripping her walking stick firmly, and setting her jaw, she plodded forward.

As she crested the rise, she flashed a celebratory smile. There was definitely running water down there. She could see the shimmer and sparkle, could hear the distant gurgle and splash of it against rocks. She could almost feel its coolness in her throat. Using the high ground, she began scouting out potential campsite locations. She looked for an open area, free of any tall grass, logs, large rocks or other debris that might attract critters. She spotted a location about halfway down the hill, still some seventy yards from the water.

She hurried down the hill as quickly as she dared, eager to reach the campsite and set up for the night. She covered the distance in just a few minutes.

Jessica set to work, using the stick she had fashioned into a trekking pole that morning to scratch out a small circle to serve as her campsite. She had needed to pee for several hours but had been holding it until the campsite was selected. Now she squatted at spots every couple of feet and released a small amount of urine, working her way around the circle to create a pee fence. Hopefully that would help discourage any snakes or other critters from snuggling up to her tonight. She had heard once that most critters avoid human urine scent. It was worth a try anyway.

She used the hatchet to cut a few branches from the trees down by the river and erected another marginal lean-to. Grandpa Hansen would likely chastise her if he saw it. There really wasn't time to do a good job though. With any luck it would be enough to keep her mostly dry, should it decide to rain that night.

Chapter Four

Jessica woke in the morning chilled, stiff and sore. She moved to the fire hole, threw some fresh fuel in, and gently blew the embers back to life. Huddling over the fire, she let it warm and loosen up cramped muscles.

A memory came unbidden to her mind, of camping with her family. Of waking in the morning and warming herself by the campfire her father had built—he was always the first one up. She could hear the sizzling of bacon and eggs on the cast-iron griddle and smell the aroma of the bacon mixed with wood smoke. Her mouth watered, and her stomach growled.

Jessica shook her head, clearing away the memory. The pleasant aroma faded, but the pinch of hunger in her stomach remained. She stretched, took a few deep breaths of the morning air, then took a moment to orient herself.

She was at the bottom of a ravine which wound its way

down through the mountainous terrain from northeast to southwest. She could see smoke to the northwest, maybe ten or so miles away, beyond the edges of the valley that she could see. Possibly a village on or above the river. Or maybe a valley or two over. Difficult to tell what the terrain might do between here and there. No road close to where she was though. Nothing could be seen to the south that looked like people. Her exploration did find a better place to use as base camp. Up one of the draws just north of where she had camped was a steep hill, almost a cliff. At one point the cliff turned sharply, and in that corner was a small pocket. It was difficult to see, difficult to reach, and provided good cover, shade, and shelter. It seemed a good spot to lay low for a while.

How long would be long enough? How long before they tired of hunting her? For now, she needed to focus on thriving.

She made several trips back and forth from a wooded area near the water to her new hideout, hauling pine branches and dry wood.

Jessica used some of the branches to fashion a roof in the one exposed opening. This would prevent anyone seeing a fire from above, and it would let any rain run off the edge, rather than pooling in the sheltered area. She used more branches to create a soft bed.

Satisfied with her creations, Jess stepped out of her small pocket in the rock face. She squinted against the burning light. She shielded her eyes from the sun and pursed her lips. In all the excitement over the finding and setting up the new location, she'd neglected to make water her priority. Now she would have to handle that in the midday heat.

Reckless, Jess. How could you forget something so vital?

Unable to wait for cooler temperatures, she made her way down to the river again, bottle in hand. The water was clear, which was good. She filled the empty bottle, then collected one more load of dry wood and returned to the new base camp.

As Jess got a fire going and dropped the bottle in, she realized she needed to come up with a different solution for sanitizing the water, as the bottle wasn't likely to take much more of this treatment.

She peered out of the opening, scanning the area near the river. Dirt, rocks, brush, and trees. What could she do with any of those? She recalled a show she had watched on making clay. Could she do that? She would need to find dirt with good clay in it. Then extract the clay, shape it, dry it. Were there other steps she didn't recall? How long would it take to find a clay deposit? Would she even be able to identify it on her own?

C'mon, Jess, Keep it simple. What else would work? She sifted through other survival tricks she had learned or read about. She remembered a book she'd read explaining how native Americans made dugout canoes, by using fire to hollow out a log to make the sitting area. If it could keep water out, it could also keep water in, right? Fill a small canoe with water and it is a cistern.

Down to the river she went once more, searching for a log. It wasn't long before she spied a recently felled evergreen tree. It appeared to have taken root on an unstable hillside, which had sloughed off. There were still green needles, but it was beginning to dry out. The base of the tree was roughly ten inches in diameter.

She set to work with the hatchet, clearing away branches, then chopping a section out at the base, she hefted the two-foot log in her arms and made her way back.

The log was too heavy and awkward to carry while climbing to the new hideout. She removed the rope from her waist and tied a loop around the log. Looping the remaining end around her waist, she tied it off. She then began the climb, allowing the rope to drag the log up behind her. She winced as the rope dug into her hips, but she continued upward. Once she cleared the ledge, she pulled the rope hand over hand to drag the log the remaining distance. Exhausted from the exertion, she lay on her back, breathing heavily.

"C'mon, Jess," she murmured encouragingly after a few moments' rest, "You got this." She needed water. She needed calories.

Using the hatchet Jessica cut away wood from the log to flatten one side, to keep it from rolling. Once she had a stable base, she began chopping at the top, roughly carving out a trough. The going was slow, and the inside was very rough.

She piled the shavings in the trough, and using a hot coal from the fire, she set the shavings ablaze. The fire was hot, so she backed away a couple steps and shielded her face with her hands. As the burn progressed, the fire crept up toward the top of the trough. Jessica quickly grabbed a long stick and beat at the flames, keeping the fire back from the edges.

After the fire had burned out, she used the blade of the hatchet to scrape out the burnt wood. The inside of the trough was now deeper, and considerably smoother. She made one more trip to the water to collect a large handful of mud, which she applied to the edges of the trough, to keep them from burning. Then she filled the trough with more shavings and lit them.

She repeated the process again and again, forming a smooth, deep trough. She continued to work into the evening. As the sun set, she opened the bottle she had removed from the fire a few hours earlier and drank deeply. Then she settled down on her pine bed and slept.

Next morning Jessica continued burning, cleaning, and deepening the trough in the log. By late morning, she estimated the trough was large enough to hold a little over a gallon of water. Now it was time to try out another trick her father had told her about on one of their family camping trips.

Jess made several trips back and forth, collecting water in the bottle and pouring it into her wooden cistern. She collected handfuls of smooth, clean, roughly golf-ball-sized rocks on each trip also, which she piled in the fire. Once the rocks were well heated, she used a couple of sticks to fish a few at a time out of the fire and into the cistern. After a few minutes she removed those rocks from the cistern and replaced them with a few more fresh rocks from the fire. In time, the water in the wooden cistern began to boil. Jessica grinned. It was working. She continued swapping rocks, keeping the water boiling for ten minutes.

Jessica smiled contentedly, giving herself a mental pat on the back. She had a process for producing a gallon of clean water—enough to keep her hydrated for a day. Next, she needed to work out a better way than the little bottle to transport the water. She would waste a lot of time and energy making so many trips to the river every day.

Another wooden cistern or bowl would be easy to make, but it would be heavy and awkward to carry. Jess chewed on her bottom lip as she considered clay pots again. She'd only seen how to do it, and it seemed like a lot of work, and they would probably be fragile.

She recalled seeing a jug made from rope, in a museum once. The placard had explained how they used pitch to make it watertight. She didn't have enough rope to make a jug with, but she knew how to make rope from trees. She had done that with one of the old ranch hands once. He had stripped the cambium layer just under the bark from a tree and laid it out to dry. A few days later, he separated it into little strands, and then twisted the strands together to make cordage.

Of course, she needed to work out food also. That would probably need to come before more efficient water transport. Then again, perhaps she would be killing two birds with one stone by trekking back down to the oak trees she had gone through on her way to this spot.

A nice straight oak branch could be fashioned into a longbow, and a bowstring could be crafted from some of the cordage made from the cambium layer. She had watched her father and brother do that one summer.

Jessica's brow furrowed as she chewed on her lower lip. It would take most of a day to get to the oaks. Finding a good piece of wood for a bow stave and collecting cambium would likely consume a day. Three days of walking, with no food, and very little water. She frowned, scanning the horizon.

There were clusters of evergreen trees here and there, just a few minutes' walk from where she stood. She could collect cambium for cordage from them, which would work as well as oak, maybe better. And she was certain to find pitch on them as well. It would likely be harder to find a good, straight, knot-free piece of wood for a bow stave, and the softer wood was almost certain to produce an inferior bow, but perhaps good enough.

She grimaced, frustrated by the indecisiveness she felt. In survival situations, the margin for error was often slim. She didn't want to make the wrong choice.

She wasn't even sure what there was available to hunt in Mexico. Probably deer. There were deer practically everywhere in the world. Some form of big cat no doubt, and some type of canine—wolf or coyote of some sort. Deer would be preferable. She wrinkled her nose at the thought of eating dog or cat. She wasn't in a position to be picky just now, however.

There were probably plenty of smaller critters around as well—rabbits or squirrels or something. Maybe that was the place to start.

She spent the rest of the day building a few primitive figure-four deadfall traps using larger logs or big rocks for the deadfall, and smaller twigs and sticks for the trigger system. It was quick work notching them, and they were fairly easy to set up on worn areas near and leading to the river. She found herself increasingly grateful for her childhood on the ranch, and her father's broad knowledge of bush craft.

That night, once it was dark, she threw a handful of green material on the fire to produce smoke. Holding her breath and closing her eyes, she stepped into the billowing cloud to take a smoke bath. The smoke would kill the bacteria that had been colonizing all over her body for the past few shower-less days; not as nice as a hot shower and clean clothes from the dryer, but better than stewing in her own sweaty stench for who knows how much longer. It would also mask her human odors from animals.

Early next morning, Jessica checked the traps. She found a half-eaten rabbit in one trap, and nearby tracks that looked like coyote. She collected what meat she could and took it back to roast over the fire.

A quick, unsatisfying meal, a big drink of clean water, and she made her way to the nearest cluster of evergreens.

Jess set to work peeling away bark and stripping out large sections of cambium. She was careful to take only one vertical strip from each tree, leaving the bark mostly intact and running the full length of the tree. She didn't want to kill the trees.

Jessica was also pleasantly surprised to discover a few oak trees among the conifers. She found a stout, unblemished branch about five feet in length, and roughly as thick as her wrist—an acceptable piece to fashion a bow from.

Jess shouldered the strips of cambium along with the branch, and made a hasty return trip, arriving at her camp just before dark. She stoked up the fire, drank most of the water remaining in the cistern, and spread the cambium out to dry before settling into to her bed, exhausted.

Over the next couple days, the traps provided a couple of unrecognizable, partially eaten rodents. Jess scowled, as she collected the scraps.

"Stupid, lazy, good-for-nothing welfare coyote," she grumbled as she stomped back to camp to cook the remnants. She ate the meager meal in two bites, and she wondered if she used more calories collecting and preparing it than she received from eating it. This coyote was making her life ten times harder than it needed to be with its opportunistic scavenging.

Jessica worked on shaping the branch into a bow, and on separating the cambium into long, thin strips, which she then twisted together to form cordage. She had to take frequent, short breaks to rest her weary eyes and sluggish fingers. Her mind was less focused with every hour that passed. She tried to keep her movements to a minimum to conserve calories as she worked, but her sparse diet was beginning to take its toll.

Selecting one of the best lengths of cordage, she fashioned a bowstring. She had also found a few stray feathers in a nest while poking around in trees, and she had managed to locate a chunk of obsidian, from which she had broken off a couple decent, flat, triangle-shaped pieces. Using various shaped rocks, she experimented chipping and flaking off material to put a good edge on the triangles and to add notches at the bases to attach the newly made arrowheads to straight sticks. She used some of the finer cordage she had created to fix the arrowheads and the feathers firmly in place.

She was able to manufacture a half-dozen satisfactory arrows with the materials she collected. She had a few more arrowheads and there was more obsidian left. Sticks were readily available—straight sticks somewhat less so, but enough time looking would turn them up. Feathers were a trickier problem. She saw birds occasionally, but she didn't have a good way to catch them. The bow was not the ideal weapon for bird hunting.

Perhaps she could make a sling? She grimaced, remembering the time she had tried using a sling her brother had made a few years ago. Hitting the broad side of a barn required luck—for her at least. She would have to give the feather idea more thought.

For now, she took the bow and arrows out to the open space by the river and made several practice shots at a cluster of bushes, getting a feel for where to aim at various distances. She broke one of her arrows in the process but managed to recover the fletching and arrowhead for re-use.

After an hour or so of practice, she picked a good observation spot near one of her frequently pilfered traps and kept watch as night fell. There was good moonlight, so she had excellent visibility of the trail.

It must have been close to midnight when a rabbit came up the trail, triggered the trap, and let out an abbreviated squeal as the large boulder dropped, crushing the head. The body protruding from the rock convulsed briefly, then went still. Jess remained watchful from her post. Not more than an hour later, a coyote came into view. It made its way boldly over to the rabbit and began picking at it.

Jess nocked an arrow, drew, and fired. The arrow left with a *twang*, and she made a mental note to do something to dampen the string. An instant later the coyote yelped as the arrow struck. The coyote turned and made to flee; the arrow had struck its hindquarter in a glancing blow, tearing flesh, but not sticking. The coyote stumbled, trying to get its legs, then took off. Jess scowled.

"Oh well," she muttered, and she walked down to the trap. "At least he's not likely to mess with my traps again soon." She collected and field-dressed the rabbit, found the arrow, and returned to camp.

She slept well that night after a good, filling meal and dreamt of her home. She was sitting on the couch. Nobody else was there, save an old woman, sitting in an old rocking chair, knitting. She didn't recognize the chair, but she'd seen the woman in a family history book. It was her three times great-grandmother. Or was it four greats? Maybe five? She couldn't remember. Her father's mother's something-something.

At any rate, she was definitely great. A frontiersman's wife, she had lived on the ragged edge of civilization. Her husband had been a scrapper, family lore said he would have his horse walk on his back to loosen up tense muscles. Grandma Dalton was by all counts his equal in sheer strength of will, though not so rowdy, nor short tempered.

"Nice evening" Grandma Dalton observed, not looking up from her knitting.

"Yes, ma'am," Jessica responded. For some reason, she felt the 'ma'am' was important. This gentle, yet solid matriarch deserved respect, though she did not command it. "The stars are beautiful tonight."

"How are you feeling?"

"A little tired," Jess replied, "It's a lot of hard work—lots to do around the farm."

"Yes, dear, it is." Grandma Dalton looked her over critically. "Hard work keeping a house in order. You should get some rest, child."

"Yes, ma'am."

"Off to bed with you, and don't forget to say your prayers. Don't let yourself get so busy running about that you forget to talk to God."

"Yes, ma'am."

As soon as Jessica woke the next morning, she got on her knees. "Dear God, I'm sorry I haven't been taking time to pray lately. I guess I wasn't thinking straight. I promise I will do better. Anyway, thanks for all your help. Thanks for that snake when I needed food, and for that perfect branch I made my bow from."

Jess paused. "Please bless my family and let them know I am okay," she paused again, "and please keep my roommates safe," she whispered. She tried to find the right words to ask for a way for them to escape, her mind turning over a dozen implausibly miraculous scenarios, she finally settled for, "Please help them, amen."

Chapter Five

Jessica spent the next few days making rope baskets from the cordage. She coiled and shaped thicker cordage while she used thinner cordage to bind the coils together. She narrowed the openings and added rope handles to a couple of the smaller baskets, so she would be able to use them like canteens. She gathered some lumps of pitch and dropped them into the rope jugs with hot rocks from the fire, shaking them about until the rocks cooled. After doing this a few times, she filled them with water and checked for leaks. She repeated the process until she was satisfied the smaller two containers were watertight. The larger container leaked a little bit, but as she intended to use it only to carry dirty water from the river to the cistern, minor leaking wasn't a serious concern.

Jessica also made a couple baskets by weaving together thin, flexible branches, to be used for storing extra meat or other sundries. She used the last bit of cordage and some sticks to build a basket fish trap. She placed this in the river, hoping to add a little variety to her sparse diet of mostly tiny, somewhat crushed rodents caught in the deadfall traps.

Jessica also spent time working on the bow, adjusting the limbs, and shaping the arrow rest until she was able to hit a two-inch target consistently at twenty yards.

As the sun went down, she decided to try her hand at catching birds. Many birds would sleep, or at least rest in the trees at night. Maybe she could sneak up on one in the darkness and catch it.

She made her way back to the cluster of trees and discovered the first flaw in her plan. Even with the moonlight, the treetops were shrouded in darkness, making it difficult to pick out the shapes of roosting fowl.

She did manage to locate a few birds, but no matter how slowly or carefully she moved, they always seemed to sense her approach and took flight before she was close enough to make a grab at them.

After a dozen disappointing attempts, she abandoned the effort and returned to camp. She lay down and drifted off to sleep.

"What plans tomorrow?" Grandma Dalton asked. She was in her home again, sitting on the couch, while Grandma Dalton knitted in her rocking chair as in the previous dream.

"I think I'll head down the draw tomorrow," Jessica said, "I saw deer sign when I was down there a few days ago, checking the fences."

Grandma stopped knitting, looked skyward, then turned her gaze to Jess. "You know, dear," she said, "I think you should try north instead. I think you will find the hunting more productive."

"Grandma-great?" Jess was puzzled by this suggestion. "North is higher up into the mountains and high desert. I don't think I am more likely to find deer there, and with less cover, it will be much harder to get a good shot."

The old woman returned to her knitting. "You do as you like. But I really do think you should go north tomorrow."

Jessica woke early the next morning, and in spite of the late night, she felt well rested. "A full belly, enough water and a soft place to sleep," she reasoned.

She hurried through the morning routine of checking the traps, refilling and sterilizing the cistern, and making breakfast. The traps were empty this morning, but for one rodent a bit bigger than a mouse or a rat. It wasn't especially tasty, but it was food, and she wasn't in a place where she could be picky. She needed to start working out some vegetation that would be safe to eat. An all-meat diet would get old after a while. The only non-protein nutrition she had taken in over the past few days had been some pine needle tea she brewed, just for a break from drinking boiled water.

Her dream from the night before kept slipping to the front of her mind. She had definitely been in her home, talking to her ancestor. However, the geography of the conversation didn't fit with anything at home. It did fit with her current geography and plan of action, though.

She intended to go south to hunt deer, so the description of "north" in the dream fit here.

Nevertheless, just as in the dream, she couldn't figure the sense of going north instead of south to hunt and gather more cambium for rope making.

But Grandma Dalton seemed quite insistent that she should go north.

Why? She couldn't shake the feeling it was more than just a random, meaningless dream.

What if the feeling was her gut trying to tell her something? Was it worth the risk of following the pull north? She really needed to establish a better food supply. It was the next key step in thriving: first shelter and fire, then water, then food, then conveniences.

Without shelter, you could die in a matter of hours. Without water you died in a matter of days, and without food you died in a matter of weeks. Once you were solid on those, the sky was the limit.

She had constructed a primitive "cooler" to store surplus meat in—she had piled rocks at a secluded point on the river to create a circular fence where she could sink any meat in her woven baskets. Water flowed through it to keep it cool and extend its life for a few days, yet fish and other scavengers wouldn't be able to get in. Not as effective as the ice-cold mountain streams where she spent her summers, but still better than open exposure. Now she just needed a surplus of meat to put in her "cooler". A haunch of venison would definitely supply that, and it would be considerably more enjoyable than her present rat or squirrel diet.

Using a small piece of rope, she tied the loops of one of her water bottles to her belt. She stuffed her arrows and the hatchet into her sack, gathered it and her bow, and slipped out of the cave. She stood, looking north, then south. She heaved a deep sigh of resignation, shook her head, and turned north to start following the river upstream.

She had traveled no more than an hour when she came to a shallow gravel-bottomed area that was an ideal crossing. The water was clear, and the stones in the stream bed were worn smooth by centuries—or perhaps millennia—of water flowing over them, grinding and polishing them. She took off her boots and socks. While she had the second, pilfered pair of socks, she only had the one pair of boots. The resulting blisters wet boots would likely create were something she preferred to avoid if possible.

She made her way across, gingerly placing each footfall after a tentative exploration with her toes to make certain the rocks she was stepping on were as smooth as they appeared, and that they were solidly in place and wouldn't slip, revealing unpleasant surprises underneath.

Jessica made a mental note to make a pair of moccasins from some of the animal pelts or cordage, just so she would at least have a backup pair of shoes if hers got wet.

She made it across without incident, dried her feet against her jeans, then replaced her socks and boots. She moved away from the river a bit and continued to parallel it as it wandered in a north-northwest direction. The ground began to steepen and climb in front of her as she moved forward over the rocky terrain, dotted with the occasional squat bush which had somehow managed to send roots into the barren soil and find enough nutrients to survive.

Above her, Jessica saw a high point with a stand of evergreen trees. She could scout the area from higher ground if she made the climb.

It was slow going, the ground mainly slide rock, which shifted treacherously underfoot.

As she neared a crest, she thought she could hear voices in the distance. She stopped walking and listened. The ragged sound of her own panting filled the air around her, muffling any other sounds. She held her breath, and cocked her head, straining to hear. She could pick out two male voices now. They sounded like they were yelling.

Jessica expelled her breath as an icy tingle shot down her spine. Should she turn back? It would mean losing all her progress and needing to start afresh the next morning. A waste of time if the voices didn't belong to her captors. She needed to at least check the situation out before retreating.

Jess slowed her pace, and moved more carefully over the loose rock, to limit noise as much as possible. She came over the crest onto a dirt road cut into the side of the mountain.

The voices were coming from farther up the road to the north, around a bend.

Jessica crossed the road, hurrying into the stand of evergreens on the other side. Crouching, she slunk toward the sound of the voices. She scanned the trees for any sign of movement, anything that looked out of place, while monitoring the terrain to avoid dry branches or other debris likely to make a noise under her footfall.

She plotted her course forward, favoring areas with darker shadow and thicker cover. She was getting close enough to make out words. The two distinct male voices were angry. They were trying to get their car running and were arguing about what they should do next.

"Angel's gonna be pissed if we don't have these four to the mine by tomorrow night. He was already threatening to feed us to his dogs for losing the other one, we can't afford another slip up."

"Hey, don't blame me, man!"

Jessica froze. She knew those voices. The first was Juan, and the second belonged to the one Juan had threated to kill for groping her. Jess fought to control the wave of panic threatening to overwhelm her. She dug her nails into her sweaty palms and inhaled, counting slowly to five in her head. She held her breath for five counts, then slowly exhaled for ten. She couldn't afford to crumble now. They hadn't found her yet. And they weren't going to. Maybe she could use this to her advantage, by gathering information to stay one step ahead of them.

She willed herself to take another step forward, crouching lower.

"Look, we can't be more than six or seven miles from Ixlayotla," Juan said. "I'll walk to the village and get a car. If we hurry, we can still catch our ride tonight. You stay here and watch the girls."

"What, you want me to just sit here for hours?"

"Yes, I do. Keep your eyes on the girls, and keep your hands off them. They end up hurt or missing, it's your head, Marcos."

Jess peered through the branches of the shrub she was using for cover. She saw Juan walking away up the road. Marcos stood, pointing his handgun at Juan's retreating back.

"Point that *pistola* at me again, and I'll cut your hands off," Juan shouted without looking back. Marcos lowered the gun and kicked at the road, sending up a small dust cloud.

Jess remained motionless, staring at the beat-up van. Were her roommates in there? The image of Meredith from her dream returned. She looked from the van to Marcos who was pacing randomly, kicking at the dirt, and muttering expletives under his breath. He stabbed his pistol at the air occasionally to punctuate a particularly acid phrase. She noted that while he spoke Spanish, he seemed to favor English expletives.

She shifted her gaze from Marcos to the gun in his hand, then back to the van. What was she going to do? What could she do? She looked at Marcos and the gun again.

Jessica considered the bow in her hand. She had taken a four-point buck two years ago. She had located it in a meadow in the early evening when she was getting ready to return to camp. She spent an hour carefully slinking around the edge of the meadow to the downwind side, slipping quietly from bush to bush. She had moved to within twenty yards of the deer when she posted up, drew, and released. The slap of the bow startled the buck, but the arrow had already found its mark. It went cleanly through the buck's side, hitting the lungs and heart. The animal jumped once in surprise then dropped, lifeless, to the ground.

She was no more than twenty yards away from Marcos. The thought of firing an arrow at a human being, even one as disgusting as Marcos, caused her stomach to twist and her throat to tighten. She could feel the adrenaline shakes in her hands and arms. She had felt that with the deer as well, but then it was with a sense of anticipation. Now it was pure dread.

Marcos kicked at the ground again, muttering more expletives. He stomped across the road, looking down toward the river. He paused mid-curse, staring at something out of Jessica's view. He glanced around, as if to make sure nobody was watching him, then began to work his way down the slope and disappeared out of sight.

Don't just sit there, Jess, move, a voice hissed in her mind.

Jessica scrambled forward, uncertain what she should, or could do. The hood was up, and the driver's side door was open. She peeked at the engine—she couldn't see anything obvious, but she really didn't expect to. She had done a little work on tractor engines back home, but she was no mechanic. She had felt pushed by an otherworldly power to move; would divine providence smile on her again? Would the engine start for her, when it hadn't for them?

Listening, she could still hear Marcos descending. He wasn't particularly agile, given all the slipping, stumbling and stomping sounds she heard. He wasn't moving very quickly, yet he was moving farther away. She listened for a minute more to his retreating sounds, then slipped into the driver's seat. Looking in the back, she could see four girls on the floor, hands tied.

One looked like a native. She had dark skin and dark hair. Her features reminded her a little of Native Americans. The second was a tall, striking, athletic-looking blonde with exotic features and full lips.

Her throat caught as she examined the other two. They were her roommates.

"Sarah? Mer?" she whispered. Meredith opened her eyes slowly; she moaned and tried to focus on Jessica.

"Jess?"

"Yeah, Mer," Jess said, "It's me."

Meredith tried to rub her face, but her movements were slow and uncoordinated. "Why are you here?" The words came out slurred, a bit like she was drunk, but not quite the same.

"I'm gonna get you outta here." Jessica said with quiet conviction. She twisted around to face forward. She slipped out of the van, and carefully lowered the hood without latching it—that would have to wait until after they were away.

Jessica slid back into the driver's seat and checked the radio to make sure it was off. She turned the ignition key one click, and the lights came on. The battery was probably good, then. She took a deep confident breath, set her jaw, pressed the clutch to the floor and turned the ignition. The starter emitted an unpleasant screech. The engine didn't turn over.

Chapter Six

Jess heard the surprised yell from Marcos, and the sound of scrambling boots on loose rock. Her eyes went wide. "Oh crap!"

Thinking quickly, she released the emergency brake and moved the gearshift to neutral. The van began to roll backwards, and she turned so she could watch out the rear window as the vehicle picked up speed.

"This should be interesting," she murmured. "What were you thinking, Jess?"

The van was gaining speed. She glanced forward as Marcos clambered back onto the road. He was fifty yards or so away. He raced forward, brandishing his pistol. He fired wildly at the van but didn't connect once. The van rounded a corner in reverse, and she could no longer see Marcos.

Jessica tapped the brakes to keep the speed manageable

on the narrow, winding road. But not so much that Marcos was likely to catch up. It was difficult to maneuver the van in reverse. The high, narrow rear window obstructed her field of vision, making it difficult to time the turns properly. She did her best to hug the uphill side of the road—better to bump it than to go careening over the edge.

She was navigating a sharp inside bend, when she realized there was an abrupt outside bend and a steep drop-off; she hit the brakes hard to shed speed, then released them as she jerked the wheel to make the bend, The left-side front wheel was nearly over the edge, breaking off loose dirt and rocks and sending them tumbling below. The body of the van tilted precariously outward, the right-side wheels almost lifting off.

Jess heaved a sigh of relief as the vehicle moved away from the edge. She continued down the winding road in a backwards descent for another ten or fifteen minutes, but the effort of managing the vehicle in reverse was fatiguing her. She was also becoming concerned about their ex-captors. How much longer before Juan returned with a vehicle? It wouldn't take long to catch a VW bus, coasting in reverse.

Also, sooner or later they would run out of mountain. Probably sooner than later. The road was mostly following the river, and they were getting very close to the same elevation as the river now. There had been a few brief stretches of level and uphill on the road, but Jess had managed to build up enough speed to coast through them to the next downhill run. However, there was one uphill section that had her worried. Steeper and longer than the rest, it loomed before her in the back window.

The van began its way up the incline, tilting Jess forward in the driver's seat enough she had to push back against the steering-wheel to keep her back against the backrest. Sky appeared out of the rear window as they neared the top of the hill. They were getting closer, but their speed lessened with every second. They had slowed to maybe five miles an hour as they reached the top and cleared the hump.

Jess exhaled, her shoulders sagging as the van started picking up speed again.

Ahead the road curved with an outside bend to follow the mountainside away from the river. Then an inside bend, then another outside bend. As she rounded the first bend, she looked out the side window at the second upcoming outside bend. The slope of the hill was relatively gradual. Roughly twenty yards down, a grove of oak trees started, and the river was another twenty or so yards beyond that.

She bit her bottom lip. Would rolling over the side work? What if she hit a tree or rolled and crushed them all? She couldn't continue to coast forever, hoping for a better opportunity. She maneuvered through the inside turn, applying the brakes lightly to shed speed. Out the back window the next outside bend was approaching. Now was the time to do it if she was going to.

"Hang on, ladies!" she shouted. "The ride's about to get bumpy!"

Jess turned the wheel to the right to follow the bend, then twenty feet into the turn she spun the wheel hard left. The rear wheels were almost perpendicular to the road when they went off the edge. The bottom of the van scraped ground, then the front wheels reached the edge of the road. Jess straightened the wheels and tapped the brakes, trying to control the rate of descent down the slope, which seemed considerably steeper now she was on it. She was worried if she gave it too much brake, the bus might just end-over and cartwheel down the hill.

The ground was also bumpier than it had seemed from a distance. The van bounced, tilted and careened its way down the slope as Jess fought the wheel, trying to maintain at least the illusion of control over the bucking vehicle. Her half-conscious cargo, thrown about like store mannequins, were heaped in an awkward pile of arms and legs at the very back of the van.

The trees were coming up fast. Jessica gritted her teeth and applied more brake, fighting the wheel to guide the van between two large trees, now looming on either side. As she passed those, she pulled hard right to thread between another cluster of large trees. She caught a smaller tree nearly dead center, snapping it off and sending splinters of wood flying. Jessica yelped but fought the instinct to close her eyes as she jerked the wheel to the left, panting under the exertion. They traveled deeper into the woods, a few lower branches slapping the sides.

There was nowhere left to go. A large tree loomed directly behind; Jess slammed on the brakes. Moments later the back of the van hit the tree, and the van came to an abrupt halt. There were cries, more of surprise than pain, from the tangle of girls. Jessica felt the breath forced out of her, and she was driven into the backrest by the force of the sudden stop.

Jessica lay still for a moment, catching her breath and letting her arms stop shaking from the exertion of fighting the unruly van.

"Is everybody okay?" Jess asked. "Is anything broken?"

The number of distinct groans she heard reassured her that everyone was still alive and conscious. Looking at the pile of arms and legs, nothing seemed particularly out of place, and no blood was visible, so it didn't appear there were any serious injuries.

She slipped out of the van on trembling legs and braced a hand against the side of the vehicle to steady herself as she looked around. They were fairly deep in the trees, but better not to take chances.

Removing the hatchet from her sack, she hurried to lop off a number of smaller branches and arrange them over the hood and sides of the van, in an effort to camouflage it. Looking up the hill, she could see several small but discernable indicators of their path down the hill. She couldn't do anything about the dislodged rocks, broken branches and exposed tracks in the softer earth leading to them except pray her captors didn't notice.

Jessica was arranging the last branch when she heard an engine.

She slipped behind a large tree trunk for cover and peered around. A car came into view around the first outside bend, moving fast and kicking up a large dust cloud behind it. She followed its progress, shifting to keep the tree trunk between her and the vehicle as it advanced, then passed the point where she had left the road. The car continued out of sight around the next bend.

Breathing a sigh of relief, Jessica returned to the van to check on her companions again. She climbed back into the driver's seat and peered over the backrest. They all seemed okay—relatively speaking. They were too out of it to be especially coherent, but they had managed to disentangle themselves from each other, so everyone was at least semi-conscious, and arms and legs appeared to be functioning. She'd have to wait for them to sober up to be certain. She twisted in the seat and stuck her head out the driver's side window, looking at the sky speculatively. They were probably going to be spending the night here. Oh well. The van was shelter at least.

Jessica began an inspection of the van interior, looking for items that would be of use. She found a couple of empty beer bottles, a half-eaten sandwich, and a pack of cigarettes on the floor of the passenger side. In the glove compartment she found some loose papers, a handgun, two spare magazines, several loose rounds, and a few shotgun shells.

She removed and examined the pistol. It was a dull gunmetal gray with brown, plastic grips. The word "Colt" was engraved on the side, followed by "Super 38 Automatic" in smaller print. To the right of the text was an engraving of a rearing horse. Her daddy had a similar Colt 1911 38 Super, only his was shiny silver, with pearl handles. His was well cared for, whereas this one looked neglected.

She checked the safety, removed the magazine and cleared the chamber, then inspected the gun. The slide seemed to run smoothly enough; the trigger had more play than it should have. She dry-fired the gun. The hammer snapped forward powerfully. There was no holster to be found, so she stuffed the gun, spare magazines and loose shells into her sack.

Jessica crawled between the front seats into the back of the van to continue her exploration. Behind the passenger seat she struck gold. A weathered rucksack lay on the floor. She opened it up and emptied out the contents for inspection: a piece of camo netting, a pair of binoculars, a small first aid kit, a roll of electrical tape, flashlight, Swedish fire steel, and a metal canteen. The canteen was empty but smelled of something alcoholic.

She returned the items to the rucksack and transferred the gun and shells she had just deposited into her bag as well. She slipped the handle of the hatchet into a loop on the back of the rucksack, designed for that purpose. She tucked the arrows into an open side pocket, and the now empty bag into the main compartment of the rucksack.

Jessica peered out the window. The light was fading fast. She crawled back to the front seats and rolled up the two side windows. Back at her camp she would be huddled next to a campfire now, hopefully with something to eat. Since they had the van for shelter, and nothing to cook, a fire was pointless; they were close to the road, and she didn't want to risk being seen.

A glance over her shoulder confirmed the girls were asleep. She sat in the passenger seat and thought over the details of the dream the previous night.

"I think you should try north instead. I think you will find the hunting more productive," her great-grandma had said. Lucky coincidence? Jess wasn't much of a believer in luck. She adjusted the backrest as far down as it would, settled in as comfortably as she could, and closed her eyes.

"Grandma Dalton," Jess mumbled, sleep taking hold of her, "If you can hear me, thanks. For rescuing my friends."

Jess was awakened at some point in the night by a panicked whisper.

"Jess," came the hiss from Meredith again. Her words were still slurred, but the tone of panic suggested soberness was returning.

Jess snapped to attention at the rustling sounds outside.

"I hear it, Mer," she whispered back, keeping her voice low. Jess reached into the rucksack and withdrew the pistol. Using it would be a last resort. The report of a fired handgun would give away their position, and her rescued companions were still in no shape to run for it.

The sounds drew closer, the sounds of something rustling through the leaves and grass on the ground. She heard no whispers or footfalls. Slowly, Jessica raised her head in order to peer out of the window. She couldn't see anything from the passenger side of the van. The sound seemed to be coming from the driver's side of the vehicle.

The sounds stopped. Jessica tightened her grip on the gun as she flicked her gaze about in the darkness searching for some clue to what was out there.

Jessica lowered her head and slithered from the passenger seat to the driver's seat. She worked her way up so she could peer out. Still nothing. The small sliver of moonlight passing through the dense foliage provided little help in separating shadow from darkness.

Then she caught a faint movement of blackness against blackness, close to the ground. She looked to the side of the movement, to use her peripheral vision. It helped a little, but not enough to identify anything. Too close to the ground to be a person—unless they were crawling. However, the movement wasn't right for that. It wasn't going anywhere. The motion was in place. It reminded her of something she had seen before. A memory of the ranch flashed in her mind. A late evening, with heavy shadows on the northeast-facing slope. She was riding a horse, next to her father, looking for a missing calf. He father stopped abruptly and pointed up the slope. In the deepening shadows she could make out the carcass of the calf, being dragged up the mountainside by a cougar. The movement and sounds outside were similar enough to ease her worry. She relaxed her grip on the gun.

"It's just a big cat, Mer," Jessica whispered, returning the gun to the rucksack. "Go back to sleep."

"Okay." Meredith rolled over to sleep, and Jess did likewise.

Grandma Dalton was in her rocker again. It seemed strange, since they were sitting by a campfire, next to an olive green, square, canvas tent. The stars above her were unfamiliar. Beside her, a coal-black cat was curled up, purring softly with an unusually large mouse carcass between her front paws. She examined Jessica with cool, uninterested eyes.

"This is a pretty spot," Grandma said.

Jessica looked around. It was dark, but she could still make out tall, inviting trees and hear the soft babble of a nearby stream. The grass under her was cool and soft. The air smelled of lilacs and roses. Jessica breathed deeply and sighed.

"Can't stay though," Grandma said, her tone stern. "Storm's a comin'. Need to get moving at first light if we're to stay ahead of it."

The cat stretched, yawned, then casually swatted at its prize a few times.

Chapter Seven

Jessica was awake before the first faint hint of dawn began to lighten the sky. She peered out of the window; the coal-black cat was still there. A panther? She couldn't remember if they were just in Africa, or if they were a South American creature too. Maybe it was a black jaguar, or maybe panther was another name for a black jaguar.

Oh, well, it wasn't all that important just now. Quietly, to avoid disturbing the cat, Jessica grabbed the pack and slipped between the seats into the back of the VW Bus.

"Mer," she whispered, shaking her, "Sarah, time to wake up."

Both girls groaned.

"Hey," Jessica said as she gently shook the other two girls, "time to wake up, we need to go."

It took several minutes and a considerable amount of shaking and urging to get the four girls to a semi-awake state. Meredith looked out of the van windows with glassy eyes. The second her gaze fell on the large cat, she sat up, her spine ramrod straight and her mouth agape. Her eyes now wide and clear, she gasped and pointed. "We can't leave the van! There's a lion out there!"

"Perhaps not fully sober," Jessica said to herself, reconsidering her evaluation of her friend's state.

"Don't be silly, Mer," Jessica said, without looking up from her examination of the pack. "This is Mexico, not Africa."

The dark-skinned girl gasped, fully awake as well. "*Pantera,*" she hissed. All four girls were awake and panicking.

"Aah, so a panther then?" Jessica asked in a barely interested tone.

The four girls ignored her, all talking at once, to everyone and no one.

"It's. Just. A cat!" Jessica said, raising her voice and cutting off their gibbering. They all stopped and stared at her, as if unsure they had heard her correctly. "It's just a cat," she repeated, softer this time. "They chase mice, play with string, lie around a lot..."

"Uhh, Jess," Meredith said, "pretty sure that is a deer. It's definitely not a mouse."

"Yeah, it's a deer.' Jessica glanced out the window. "A bit bigger than a mouse, but not that much different. A rodent really. They sneak around at night, get into your garden, damage your trees. They're a bigger, more destructive... tastier rodent."

All four girls stared at her, brows furrowed, trying to decide if she was teasing them, or if she had lost her mind.

"Look," Jessica continued, "It was out hunting last night, it has a nice, big, tasty snack, so it's probably ready for a nap. It has no reason to chase after us. We are going to get out of the van on the opposite side, and we are going to walk slowly toward the river over there while staying close together. We aren't going to go near the big cat, we aren't going to stare at the cat, and we aren't going to run. It may be big, but it is still a cat, if we aren't threatening it or its meal, and we don't look like we might be fun to chase, it won't have any reason to take any interest in us, okay?"

Jessica opened the side door and stepped out. She paused for a moment, then turned, addressing the two strangers. "Oh, by the way, hi. My Name's Jessica, Jessica Hansen. My friends call me Jess." She extended a hand to the blonde, who was the closer of the two.

The blonde girl stared at her hand for a moment, then up to her face. Her eyes hardened and she lifted her chin proudly as she stepped from the van. "My name is Alyona Kostenko," she said. She stared challengingly at Jessica as though inviting a confrontation.

"Alyona," Jess repeated, grabbing Alyona's hand and shaking it vigorously, "pleasure to make your acquaintance! Love your accent! Where are you from?"

"Ukraine," Alyona responded tersely, maintaining her posture of challenge. She was a full head taller than Jessica, and by her grip and her stance, this fashion model of a girl could hold her own if it came to a fight.

"Ukraine? You're a long way from home! How'd you end up here?"

"Long story," she quipped, "After introductions, perhaps." Alyona then stepped confidently past Jessica, walking in the direction of the river.

Jessica turned her attention to the dark-skinned girl as she exited the bus. "Hi," she said with a smile, extending her hand again.

"Leticia Mora," the girl said, shaking hands with Jessica.

"*Habla ingles?*" Jess queried.

"I hear some," the girl nodded, then smiled timidly, "I speak… no so good."

Jessica nodded. "You understand we are going?" Jess pointed toward Alyona.

"*Si*," Leticia nodded. Then she looked back at Sarah and Meredith, still huddled together in the van. Timidly, they climbed out to join the others.

Jessica smiled reassuringly. "Let's go," she said, gesturing with her head. She started forward, and the other three followed.

Jessica could feel a palpable rise in collective anxiety as they moved to where the van was no longer between them and the panther. She slowed her pace slightly and moved to the side to place herself between the cat and the three girls.

"Just keep your eyes on the river and keep walking," she said. "Let me worry about the kitty cat." The three girls quickened their pace, closing the gap between them and Alyona. Jess glanced over her shoulder. The cat lay with its front paws wrapped around the small deer carcass. It eyed her with a look of half-interest, its tongue lolling out, almost like a panting dog.

Alyona stopped at the edge of the river and turned to watch the progress of the others. "Where to from here?"

"About twenty feet farther down," Jessica pointed, "where that slide of rock runs right into the river. We'll cross the river there.

Alyona looked at her dubiously, then at the river. "The other side is rock, maybe taller than me."

"Yup."

"Ten feet farther down is sand. We can just walk out."

"We could," Jessica agreed, "but we'd leave a trail."

"You think they will try to find us?"

"Yup. Probably find the van later today." Jess stepped gently on the loose rock, so as not to disturb it, and made her way down to the water's edge. She took off her shoes and socks. The water was relatively clear, and the bottom seemed smooth and free of sharp objects. "Doesn't look like we'll get more than knee deep. I'd recommend you keep your shoes and socks dry. Less likely to get blisters that way."

Alyona arched an eyebrow. Then, shrugging, she pulled off her heels and stepped gingerly into the water.

Jess took note of her other companions' footwear. Their shoes were all of the semi-provocative variety. Unlike Sarah and Meredith, the shoes Alyona and Leticia were wearing must have been supplied by their captors, judging from the poor condition and fit. Still, even the best fitting heels were no good for back-country hiking.

Although the slow-moving section of water was no more than twenty feet wide and got only slightly deeper than mid-calf it took a long time to cross. The other girls moved slowly, halting often to probe the smooth rocks and occasional squishy spot of mud. Up ahead, Meredith froze, every muscle in her body tensed as she stared at Jessica over her shoulder with petrified eyes.

"What's wrong?" Jessica asked.

"Something touched my leg." She clenched and unclenched her fists at her sides.

"Oh my gosh, what if it's a leech, or a piranha, or… or a crocodile?" Sarah whimpered, searching the river.

"It's none of those things." Jessica pinched the bridge of her nose. "It was more than likely a leaf."

Meredith didn't look convinced. "But—"

"Meredith, keep moving. You're fine, I promise."

Meredith grimaced, but she lifted her foot and continued across the river.

Jessica sighed. One crisis averted, how many more would she have to face? Hopefully they'd all be as minor and easy to solve.

They stopped under the small cliff face on the other side as Jessica assessed it. It wasn't really that daunting—maybe one foot higher than she could reach with her feet flat. She turned and appraised Alyona. Then, she turned to Leticia. "You know how to tie a good knot in a rope?"

Leticia nodded affirmatively.

"Okay." Jessica pulled a length of rope from the pack. "I have a rope here. If Alyona and I boost you up, do you think you could tie it off to a sturdy tree and throw the end down to us?"

Another nod.

"Give your shoes to Meredith. She'll toss them to you once you are up."

Jessica looked at Alyona as she positioned herself at the base of the rock. Alyona moved forward beside her and bent her leg slightly, creating a stepping point. With help from Alyona and Jessica, Leticia climbed from knees to hips to shoulders. The two then used their hands under Leticia's feet to push her up onto the top of the rock. She disappeared from view for a minute, then they heard a grunt, and a rustling of leaves. A bundle of rope appeared, uncoiling as it dropped, the end coming to a stop about three feet above the water.

Meredith tossed Leticia's shoes up to her, then one by one, they each tossed their own shoes up to Leticia.

"Sarah, how about you go up next?" She glanced at her friend and performed a double take, frowning. Beads of sweat dripped down Sarah's forehead, and her face was pale with dark circles beneath her eyes.

"Sarah, are you okay?"

"I think so," Sarah responded feebly.

"Withdrawal." Meredith eyed her with compassion. "They've been drugging us for the past several days. Heroin, probably. We are all likely to be a mess in the next day or so. Hope you have a good hiding place in mind, not too much farther from here."

"I'm okay," Sarah insisted unconvincingly, her voice weak and her legs unsteady. She took the rope, preparing to climb.

Alyona stepped next to her and braced her knee again. "I'm easier to climb than rock wall, save your strength."

Jessica braced herself on Sarah's other side, smiling encouragingly. "Nice and easy."

Sarah struggled, but, with the help of Jessica and Alyona from below, and Leticia from above, she managed to get onto the rock. Meredith followed her.

Jessica bent, extending her arms down and interlacing her fingers to form a step, "Your turn, Alyona."

Alyona placed one foot on Jess's hands. She reached as high as she could and grabbed the rope. Then, kicking off Jessica's hand and pulling at the same time, she launched herself up. She released with one hand and placed it on the top of the rock. Her knees connected with the flat of the rock and she smoothly shifted forward and up to her feet, all in one smooth graceful motion, like an Olympic gymnast.

Jessica removed the rucksack from her back and tied it to the rope. She instructed the girls to raise it. They quickly did so, then the end of the rope returned.

Jessica took a deep breath, exhaled, wiped her hand on her hips, then reached up and grabbed the rope. Jumping would be less effective, as she would have to launch directly out of the water. Instead, she placed one foot against the rock, leaned back, then placed the other foot.

"No, no!" Alyona shouted down, "too much effort! Just hold the rope, and we'll pull."

"Okay." Jess wrapped her arm in the rope and let it relax. She heard Alyona bark an order, then was pulled upward; she walked up the rock wall, then shifted forward at the top placing her palms on the top, where Alyona grabbed her shoulder and helped pull her the final distance.

"Thanks." Jessica said.

Alyona waved her hand. “Which way?”

“Upstream. We’ll stay close to the water, so we can use the trees and bushes for cover.” Jessica gestured with her eyes toward the strip of green. As the forest area they were in thinned, giving way to the rock and scrub of the desert, the greenery marked the river’s path through the otherwise barren hills ahead. She estimated they were better than a half day’s hike from her base camp at a fast pace. She knew that was out of the question, yet she hoped they could make it before nightfall.

Feet were dried as best they could against clothes, and shoes were collected.

“I think we have a problem,” Alyona said, holding her shoes in front of her.

“She’s right,” Meredith said, “These shoes can be tricky to walk in on flat ground. They are likely to be lethal out here. Somebody will wind up with a broken ankle.”

“Pass me your shoes,” Jess said, holding her hand out to Sarah.

Sarah passed them to Jessica, who snapped the heel off before handing them back.

“It’s not perfect, but it’s better than walking barefoot.”

The other girls did likewise and slipped the now flat shoes back on their feet.

It was slow going. The route was rough, with heavy vegetation as they followed the winding, upward path of the river. Sarah needed frequent stops to catch her breath; she was sweating, shaking and feverish. The other girls started to struggle as well as the day progressed.

“How long does withdrawal last?” Jessica asked

Meredith later in the day, as they walked side by side through the scrub.

"Several days to a few months," Meredith said. "Worst of it will be over in a couple days."

Jessica looked back at Sarah, who had stopped again and was leaning against a tree.

"I'm worried about her." Meredith looked back as well. "I don't know if she will be able to go much farther."

"Let's stop here for a few minutes," Jessica said, "and rest our feet."

Leticia smiled gratefully as she sat down, her back against a tree. She peeled off her shoes and began massaging her feet.

"You were right," Alyona whispered to Jess, pointing through the small cluster of trees they were presently using for shade. From their current position they could see down to where they had crossed the river from the Volkswagen. Five men stood right about where they had entered the water.

"Everyone get down and stay still and quiet," Jessica hissed, and the girls obediently crouched beside her. It was noon, and they had come quite a way from their starting point, but it was better not to take chances. An accidental reflection, or a flash of bright color might catch an eye; a careless conversation might carry farther than expected. The men might have binoculars, or a gun with a scope.

She watched the men through the foliage. The men stood close to one spot for a minute, looking around. One of them pointed across the river. The men conversed for a while, and another man pointed downstream. Then, two of the men began to make their way across the river while the other three fanned out into the trees. One of the two in the water waved his arm and then pointed into the water. The second man joined him as the others walked back to the water's edge.

Jessica's heart sank. Had he found a patch of disturbed mud? She thought of her climb up the rock face. Her feet had been clean of mud before she started the climb, and surely by now the wet footprints would have dried, leaving no trace. Still, she found herself holding her breath as the men continued across the river, eyes intently searching the water in front of them. They were below the rock face now, searching the bank, and then the water farther downstream.

They turned back to the three on the far bank, and one raised his arms in a gesture of frustration before exiting the river and moving downstream.

So far so good, Jess thought. Although she felt only slight less worried. The smallest thing—a broken branch, a shoe print—could give them away. She had been careful to lead them where the ground was hard, or where there was enough random clutter on the ground that any disturbances they made while crossing would blend in with the rest of the noise.

"I'm thinkin' maybe we shouldn't stay here," Jess whispered, "in case they start searching back this way. Better to get moving now, while we have some distance. If we stay right near the water, and stay low until we get around that bend, we should be okay. We'll have the hills for cover after that. We'll go one at a time, and I'll go last and try to cover our tracks."

Chapter Eight

One girl after the other, crouching or crawling to stay below the level of the various scrub and brush, they made their way around the bend. Jessica checked the position of the sun. They weren't going to make it to her camp. She'd been sleeping in the shelter of a cave, with a fire. Nighttime without a fire or cover was likely to be miserable.

Finally, Jessica began her journey. She searched and smoothed out any shoe prints left by the girls, and she redistributed leaves and debris where crawling girls had cleared spots. As she disappeared around the bend, she made one final check for any obvious sings of human passage. Satisfied, she turned and hurried to catch up with the girls walking together in a group ahead of her.

"My parents died in automobile crash when I was fifteen," Alyona said as Jessica joined the group. "I was sent to live with my aunt and her husband. They were very poor. She was always very sad and quiet. He was always very drunk and *vyrodzhennya*.

"One day, about two years after the accident, he came home after midnight, and came into my bedroom. I woke up to him groping me and trying to kiss me." She narrowed her eyes, and the corners of her mouth turned up in a vicious grin. "I clawed his eyes with my fingers, and I bit the tip of his tongue off."

The girls gasped.

"What did he do then?" Meredith asked.

"He screamed and bled." Alyona shrugged. "Not long after, he sold me to the son of a mobster, who was trying to make his reputation in the crime business. I found this out from him after two of his thugs kidnapped me and brought me to his mansion." She snorted.

"I really think he believed I would just go along with his plans once he told me he had purchased me."

"What did you do?"

"I bit the first thing he tried to put in my mouth too." She paused and looked at the others, her eyes gleaming wickedly as she gave them time to consider the implications of what she said. "He also bled and screamed. Then he passed out, I think. I'm not quite certain, because one of his minions came into the room when he started screaming. I don't really remember much after that until I woke up in the hospital with a broken jaw and a few cracked ribs."

Alyona rubbed her jaw, as if in memory. "His father heard the screaming too, apparently, and he came and saved me from being beaten to death. From him I learned he didn't care for his son—he thought he was a spoiled, selfish idiot. I also learned he wasn't fond of the slave trade. He felt it was demeaning. He stuck to drugs, guns, the occasional extortion."

Jessica gaped at Alyona as they kept walking. Alyona spoke so casually about her experiences.

"He was actually very polite to me. But he couldn't just let me go. 'Bad for business,' he said. Although, he actually sounded like he regretted it when he explained it to me," She snorted disdainfully, "So he sold me to a group who worked out of Amsterdam."

"I thought prostitution was legal there," Meredith interjected.

"It is." Alyona shrugged. "But that doesn't mean the… willing supply… is enough to satisfy the demand. I was too unwilling though. A few cuts and bruises later, and I was sold to these Templarios. They said it was my last chance. I would either work for them, or they would kill me. So far, they are not making good on that promise." Alyona smiled a small, grim smile.

"I'm so sorry," Jess said.

Alyona waved her hand, as if chasing away an annoying fly. "And what about you? How did you come to be here?"

"I came here for spring break, with them." She nodded toward Sarah and Meredith. "They slipped us some drugs and kidnapped us."

Alyona looked puzzled. "How then were you not with them? With us?"

Jess shook her head. "Don't quite know for sure. When they took us out of the car, they took me to the house instead, and put me in a room alone. I managed to get loose and made a break for it." She looked back to the others, apologetically. "I wanted to get y'all loose but..."

"But," Alyona continued," If you had tried, you would have most likely been caught again, and would be with us now recovering from our first day... on the job... Or you would be dead."

They all walked in silence for a while, considering Alyona's prediction. Jess knew Alyona was right, but every glance at Sarah struggling along sent a stab of guilt through her gut. But trying and failing wouldn't have changed that. The important thing was they were with her now, and she could keep them safe.

"You're virgin?" Alyona queried, snapping Jess from her thoughts.

"Why do you ask?" Jessica asked cautiously.

"They took you to house, away from others. So, I'm guessing you're special—more valuable. Virgin, yes?"

"Yes, but I don't see how they would have known. They didn't ask, and I didn't offer. I guess I can't be a hundred percent certain, but... I really don't think they... Checked..."

Alyona stared at the ground, lost in thought. "The drugs, how did they give them to you?"

"They bought us all drinks," Meredith offered, "They almost didn't get Jess."

"Oh?" Alyona looked at Meredith, eyebrow raised.

"Jess doesn't drink," Meredith explained, "They tried for a long time and finally persuaded her to accept some orange juice."

"I should have been suspicious of that," Jessica said, mostly to herself, "given how hard they were trying."

Alyona pointed at Jessica. "Maybe they assumed you were virgin. If you don't drink, you probably don't party."

"Oh my gosh!" Meredith looked horrified, the color draining from her face. "It's my fault. Jess, I'm so sorry."

"What, Mer?" Jessica stared blankly at Meredith, puzzled.

"I was a little buzzed, but I remember them asking why you wouldn't accept a drink. I told them you didn't ever drink, and they made some jokes about you being a prude. They said, 'she's probably a virgin, too, isn't she?' I said you were. Oh, Jess, I'm so sorry—"

"Don't be." Jess placed a hand on Meredith's shoulder and squeezed. "Them separating me is what allowed me to escape. It's why I was able to rescue you guys."

"If I hadn't said anything, maybe they wouldn't have thought to give you orange juice, though. Maybe they would have given up."

"Maybe. Or maybe they would have taken you anyway, and I wouldn't have known where to find you. Or maybe they would have found another way to get me, and there wouldn't have been a way for me to escape, or maybe..." Jess looked skyward, "Maybe an asteroid would have crashed into the ocean causing a tidal wave that sank Australia, and a lawyer would have come and informed you that you were adopted and that your real parents were the King and Queen of Siam, and they were visiting Australia when it sank, so now you are the heir to the throne."

Meredith furrowed her brow and opened her mouth to speak, but Jess cut her off.

"You can play the maybe game all day, Mer," Jess explained, "You're just guessing at what might have happened. You can't know for sure because it didn't happen. And since it didn't happen, it doesn't matter."

"If it makes you feel any better," Alyona said, smirking, "Leticia and I are very grateful to you for throwing your friend under the bus."

Leticia looked confused, but smiled and nodded at the mention of her name.

Jessica chuckled, then grew serious as she looked at the sky again.

"How much farther?" Leticia asked.

"Too far," Jessica said. "We've covered maybe two-thirds the total distance today."

"What'll we do?" Meredith asked, her voice tinged with fear.

"See that big boulder up ahead? We'll shelter under it. Everybody pick up a few dry pieces of wood and carry them with you."

"Fire?" Alyona raised an eyebrow skeptically, then looked downstream.

"Small and concealed," Jess replied reassuringly. Alyona's gaze maintained its skepticism, but she veered off toward a cluster of trees and collected several dry branches from the ground.

The boulder was about four feet high, with a flat face on the downhill side. Jessica directed the girls to move the dirt at the base of the boulder outward, to create a flat area where they could huddle together.

"Why don't you take a break, Sarah," Jessica suggested when the work was finished. She then set the rest of the girls to gathering more wood and some medium-sized rocks, while she pulled the netting out of the pack. She anchored one side on and over the boulder with some heavy stones, then she stretched the corners of the other side out over the flattened area, creating a makeshift lean-to shelter.

Under the shelter, she quickly set about digging a fire hole right at the base of the boulder.

The sky was starting to darken as she struck a spark into a handful of tinder with the fire steel. Using gentle breaths, she nursed the spark into a small flame, then dropped the burning mass into the hole, along with several small twigs. She added fuel to the fire until it was as big as she dared make it. She dropped several of the rocks into the pit next to the fire.

Jess pointed to the flat area. "Let's use a couple of these heaver sticks to dig out a couple trenches."

"Where we just smoothed?" Leticia questioned.

Jessica nodded. "We're going to get some of these rocks hot, then we'll push them into the trench, bury them, and smooth it all out again. That way we'll have a cozy spot to sleep on."

The girls set to work, digging down until Jessica was satisfied the holes were deep enough to cover the hot rocks. She used a couple of heavier sticks to push the hot rocks into the trenches, spacing them evenly, then the girls filled in the trenches and smoothed everything out again.

They huddled together on the warm ground, most of them exhausted from exertion and from the effects of withdrawal. Alyona seemed mostly unaffected; she was intimidatingly stoic. Sarah was hit the worst. She was shivering violently, and the vomiting began before the night was fully black. She would make it no more than a couple of feet clear of the shelter before she would drop to her hands and knees, retching.

Before long the air in the shelter began to carry the faint aroma of stomach acid. Nobody complained though.

Then the diarrhea started. The vomiting was definitely preferable under current circumstances. Leaves just aren't as gentle or effective as toilet paper.

Jessica wished there was something she could do to help. She knew blackberry root tea could help with diarrhea. Witch hazel could help with the inevitable rash. Did either of those grow in Mexico? She hadn't seen any in her travels so far. Maybe Leticia would know of something. Nothing could be done now though. They couldn't forage in the dark.

As the darkness began to recede in the early morning, Jessica helped Sarah down to the river's edge to clean up as best she could. Sarah was weak and unstable, and she leaned heavily on Jessica for support.

"Rough night, eh?" Jessica cast her a sympathetic glance.

Sarah was quiet as she crouched in the river and sluggishly splashed water on her face, washing away dried bits of vomit from her face.

"I was a virgin too," Sarah said. It was barely more than a whisper.

"What?" Jessica asked.

"I was a virgin too." Sarah stopped washing and stared at the water directly in front of her. Jess stared at the ground and shifted uncomfortably, uncertain how to respond.

"I mean, I've made out with guys before," Sarah continued, "but, most *normal* girls do." Jessica detected an almost accusatory tone in the way Sarah emphasized the word 'normal'. She decided it would be best to ignore it.

"Why didn't they take me with you?" Sarah fixed her gaze on Jessica, her eyes a storm of emotions; grief, anger, pain.

"They probably didn't know ..." Jess started. "They were probably about the same age as us, and they were guys. They only knew I was 'cause Meredith said so."

"They asked," Sarah corrected, a tear escaping from the corner of her eye.

"Well... yeah..." Jessica slid a hand under her hair to rub the back of her neck, "after they were making jokes about me being straitlaced and all. Maybe it's like Alyona said. Because I didn't drink, which was strange to them, they thought to ask."

"They just assumed because I was drinking, I was loose," Sarah spat.

Jess felt a twinge of guilt, vowing to herself to never again make those assumptions about anyone. "I'm so sorry, Sarah."

"And now I'm worthless."

"What? No! Why would you say that?"

Sarah rolled her eyes. "I've read the bible. People

who drink do that too, you know. It says something like 'a virtuous woman is worth more than rubies,'" she paraphrased in a sarcastic, sing-song voice. "It says something about some guys stealing 'their most precious possession; their virtue.'" A fit of coughing interrupted her train of thought.

"I don't think it means that," Jess said.

Sarah shot Jessica a hard look and snorted. "*Really.*"

"Do you remember my Uncle Daxon? He visited our apartment just before Thanksgiving."

Sarah thought for a minute. "Yeah, he was really quiet."

"Yeah," Jessica said sadly, "He wasn't always that way. He used to be super outgoing before he joined the army. He got stationed in the Middle East and wound up in an area where there was heavy fighting. Now he hides in his basement on New Year's Eve and for a week around the Fourth of July. The fireworks remind him of the gunfire and mortars and stuff. He's a wreck a week or so before, just anticipating it. It's heartbreaking to see."

"PTSD." Sarah nodded.

"I think that's what the scripture means. It's not what they took from your body, it's what they took from your mind." Jessica placed a hand on Sarah's shoulder. "I imagine it would be hard to be trusting and open after something like that. Seems to me that everything and everyone would seem a bit more… sinister."

"I suppose that makes sense," Sarah acknowledged.

"Makes more sense than God kicking you to the curb because of something that wasn't in your control." Jess checked the sky. The sun was well above the horizon. "C'mon, we need to get moving."

As she helped Sarah back up to the shelter, Alyona and Meredith's voices carried through the air, the conversation becoming heated.

"We need to rest for a while," Meredith said firmly. "At least for a day or two until we get over the worst of the withdrawal symptoms. We need to rest, and we need to hydrate."

"We can't stay here," Alyona replied through gritted teeth, "We are still too close to where they are searching for us. This is not a good place to hide."

"Jess," Meredith asked as she approached, "What do you think?"

"Sorry, Mer," Jessica responded, "we have to keep going. Another half-day to a day, depending on how fast we can move. There's a place in the rock where we can hunker down for a while. There's some food there, and a way to get safe water. There's shelter from the sun too," she added, noting the bright red skin on exposed arms, shoulders and backs.

Meredith looked around desperately. "What about Sarah? She's completely trashed."

Jessica glanced to Sarah. She was struggling to keep her eyes open, let alone stand. Could she make it?

"We carry her," Alyona said.

Meredith furrowed her brow. "How far are we going?"

"We carry her, or we drag her," Alyona responded without the faintest hint of humor. There was an awkward pause as the others stared blankly, trying to decide if she was serious.

"Let's clean up the campsite," Jessica sighed, as she started taking down the netting. "We need to cover up the campfire and the piles of sick, and we need to re-landscape the sleeping area. Leave no trace. Nothing that will give them a clue we were ever here."

Chapter Nine

It was quiet as they continued following the river. The going was slow, and the girls were miserable. They all took turns helping Sarah, but they were struggling and needed frequent breaks. Their energy was depleted because of the lack of food, water, and sleep. Apart from Jessica, their shoes and clothes were inappropriate for hiking. Their shoes hindered their steps and their feet and ankles ached. Their clothes exposed their skin to burning sun. Even Jessica struggled to remain calm and optimistic as the day wore on. They desperately needed to make it to the cave. They needed clean water and food.

After a few hours of walking in silence, Alyona started singing, to pass the time.

"What language is that?" Jessica asked.

"Russian," Alyona said. "It is an old folk song."

"It's pretty. Do you speak Russian?"

"Yes, it's pretty common in Ukraine. Maybe half the population can speak it."

"What does the song mean?"

"It's about a clumsy little bear walking through the forest. He's picking up pinecones, and one hits him on the head, so he gets angry and stamps his foot."

"That doesn't make sense," Sarah said.

"It's for little children," Alyona replied, "like 'this little piggy went to market, this little piggy stayed home?'"

"Oh," Sarah flushed, "sorry."

Alyona smirked and waved it off. "Eh. Lots of things don't make sense in this world."

"That's the truth," Sarah muttered.

Leticia pointed to a tall peak in the distance. "Are we... are we going, all the way to there?"

"No, not that far, about half that distance."

Leticia sighed in relief.

"Why do you ask?" Jessica asked.

"So far!" Leticia exclaimed, casting Sarah a concerned glance. She slumped her shoulders and fanned her face. "So hot. So tired."

"Does this river go there?" Alyona asked.

"No." Leticia pointed to the right of the peak. "There."

Alyona looked puzzled. "Why then you think we're going there?"

Leticia squinted, trying to think of the right word. "Mine."

"Your what? The mountain? You own the mountain?"

Leticia shook her head vigorously, then turned to Jessica again. "Is...mine? *Mina*?"

Jessica chuckled, "Yes, 'mine' is correct. The word has more than one meaning. Mine can mean something that belongs to me, so *mía* in Spanish, or it can also mean a place where you look for gold, or diamonds or other valuable minerals—*mina*."

Leticia smiled and nodded.

"What are the words in Russian?" Jessica asked Alyona.

Alyona pointed at herself. "*Moy*," then she pointed toward the mountain peak, "*shakhta*." She chuckled and shook her head. "English is very tricky."

"Oh right." Jessica smirked. "You don't have any Russian words with two meanings?"

"Many," Alyona conceded, "For instance *kosa*, means braid, or... what's the word? It's a farm tool for cutting grain. Grim Reaper carries it."

"Scythe," Jessica said.

"Yes, scythe."

Jessica chuckled. "The Grim Reaper carrying a braid."

"And in Spanish, *papa* is potato and also pope!" Leticia offered, giggling.

"I had a friend," Jessica began, "He was learning Spanish—his whole family was. His dad was a leader of a congregation for his church, and there was this Spanish family—they invited them over for dinner.

"So, they are getting ready to eat and the dad turns to one of the daughters, and he decides to try out his Spanish. He goes to ask her if she is hungry but instead of saying '*tengas hambre*?'—do you have hunger—he says '*tengas hombre*?'—do you have a man!"

Leticia gasped, then giggled, covering her mouth and blushing. The other girls laughed as well. For the next hour everyone seemed in much better spirits, and they managed to cover almost as much distance as the previous two hours.

The sun was brushing the tops of the mountains when the girls reached the bottom of the hill leading to Jessica's cave. Sarah had all but collapsed in the last hour, so Meredith, Alyona and Jessica took turns carrying her piggyback. Leticia repeatedly apologized to the others for being too small to take a turn. Jessica let her carry the backpack, which seemed to make her feel better.

It took all four girls working together to hoist Sarah up the steep face and into the cave. They collapsed, sweaty, dusty, and exhausted on the cave floor, moments before the last sliver of the sun dropped behind the mountains.

*

The sound of retching woke Jessica early the next morning. Sarah was curled in a ball at the cave entrance, dry heaving.

"Is there any clean water?" Meredith asked groggily. "She's dehydrated, we need to get fluids in her."

"I will get some boiling in a few minutes," Jessica said. She grabbed her dirty water container and started to the entrance. As she looked out, she froze.

"What is it?" Meredith asked, eyes wide with fear.

Jess whipped her head around and raised a finger to her lips. Dropping the water container, she grabbed the bow and a couple arrows which were leaning against the wall near the cave entrance, and slipped stealthily out.

What a stroke of luck! There, right at the base of her hideout near the river was a lone deer.

"Settle down, Jess," she muttered under her breath. "Now is not the time to get buck fever." She moved to the drop and crouched for stability. She nocked an arrow on the string and placed it against the bow, using her left hand to keep the arrow in place. She inhaled deeply and drew the string back with her right hand, anchoring the arrow gently to her cheekbone. Exhaling, she sighted in on her target—an area just above and slightly behind the visible front leg. She held her breath near the end of the exhale and released the string.

The deer raised up and looked toward her, startled by the slap of the bow string. By the time it registered danger, the arrow had found its mark, cutting through the side and sinking into the animal's heart and lungs. The deer sprang into the river, leaping towards the other side. One jump. Two. Three. It collapsed, motionless on the other side of the water.

Elated, Jessica scrambled down the hill, nocking another arrow. She approached the downed animal, feeling the exhilarating shakes from the adrenaline surge, and fired into the heart again at point blank range to ensure the animal was dead. It would be a terrible day for her if it jumped up and started thrashing around while she was in the middle of slitting its throat.

Satisfied it was dead, she reached to her belt, feeling for the sheath containing the SOG. Her hand found the hilt, and she flicked the release on the sheath with her thumb. Gripping the handle of the SOG firmly, she withdrew it, dropped to one knee, and set to work field dressing the carcass. Using the tip of the blade, she cut the anus loose. Then she cut open the abdomen from the hole she had created around the anus up to the middle of the front legs. Reaching into the opened cavity, she pulled the gut sack loose and out of the body. She reached deep into the cavity with the knife and severed the esophagus, separating the innards from the body.

Jessica froze, regarding the gut pile with chagrin. "Maybe I should have hauled this deer somewhere I could easily bury and dispose of the guts, instead of just dumping them out on the rocks ..."

She shrugged. Too late now. She pulled the backstraps out of the cavity and set them aside, then she set herself to the task of skinning the deer. The hide would be useful. She had made a pair of moccasins from the hide of her first deer. She and her dad had tanned the hide. She tried to recall the items they'd used in the process. She could use the deer's brain to tan it. She'd need lye as well. She could make some with wood ash. She'd need an acid too—urine would probably be the easy option—but that would have to wait. The current goal was to get the hide off and get the meat chilled. She'd break it down and put it in the baskets she'd made to sink it in the river. The girls would at least have a few good meals now. And maybe Leticia could help identify some edible vegetation. Jessica felt the corners of her mouth rising in a genuine smile. She began to hum to herself as she worked.

"How can I help?" Alyona came up beside her, walking barefoot on the rough ground.

"Oh, rats, I totally forgot about the water." Jessica looked at Alyona and grimaced. "Poor Sarah. "Did you see that container I had? I think I dropped it on the cave floor."

"This one?" Alyona held up the container Jessica had failed to notice in her hand.

Jessica nodded sheepishly. "Would you please fill that with water from the creek and dump it into the log with the hollow in it? Do that two or three times, until the cistern is ...two-thirds or three-quarters full."

"Okay." Alyona set to work gathering water while Jessica finished butchering the deer.

Jessica loaded the basket with the skinned meat and was just getting ready to sink it in the river when she paused. The backstraps she had set aside were going to make a nice meal this morning, and she'd pull some more out in the evening to cook, but it would be nice to have something to snack on between meals. Was there anything could she do for that? Maybe if she dried some out, she could create a rough form of jerky. That would serve well if they needed to leave the camp as well.

She pulled one hind quarter back out, setting it with the backstraps. The rest she sank in the river. It was worth a try.

Jessica hauled skin, hindquarter and backstraps to the cave. She placed the backstraps on a rock near the fire to cook. Then she began cutting the hindquarter into thin strips, which she hung over the fire to dry. She added a bit of green material to the fire to create some smoke. That would help keep flies off until the outside was dry enough.

She could sun dry it the rest of the way. Not jerky exactly, but it would keep well enough.

All the girls were awake and staring hungrily at the sizzling meat.

"Patience, ladies. Let it finish cooking." She left them staring at the venison while she went out to rinse her hands and the knife in the river.

When she returned, she sterilized the water in the cistern using her collection of hot rocks, then she cut the backstraps into equal portions and divided them among the girls.

"There's no seasoning," she apologized, "and it is likely to be pretty gamey, but it's protein." The girls ignored her as they devoured the chunks of charred flesh. Had they been fed by their captors, or was starving them also a part of the 'breaking in' process?

"How do people get to that point?" she pondered aloud.

"To what point?" Alyona asked, her mouth full of meat.

"Sorry. Didn't realize I said that out loud. I was just wondering how people get to the point that they are okay with treating other human beings so terribly. Something to be used, abused, exploited, and discarded."

Alyona shrugged. "It's just business, no?"

"It's people. Their own kind!"

"Most people are like wolves."

"Wolves?" Jessica frowned.

"How you say… predators. Survival of fittest. If a wolf is hungry enough it will eat its own pups. For these men, we are their food, nothing more. They catch us and sell us. Other men pay them so they can use us to satisfy… another kind of hunger. Is all about hunger, yes? Hunger for food, hunger for breeding, hunger for hunting. You enjoy hunting, yes? It excites you?"

"I don't hunt people!" Jessica scowled.

Alyona shrugged. "Your parents taught you not to. Some parents don't teach. Some learn life has higher meaning, and for others, life is survival of strongest. You protect yourself; you protect your pack. Everything else is food or enemy."

"People are different," Meredith disagreed, "They can choose, they don't have to be driven by instinct."

"Bah!" Alyona snorted, "People are different in that they can belong to more than one pack at a time."

An uncomfortable silence fell, and the girls turned their attention back to satisfying their hunger, consuming the last bites of meat with subdued eagerness.

Jessica distracted herself from the conversation by grabbing several of the thicker pieces of cordage she had made and began coiling them in a flat oval. She used thread-thin pieces of cordage to bind the structure. Holding it to the bottom of her foot, she shaped it and used more thread to fix the shape. Once satisfied, she started another one, using the first one as a template.

Leticia watched her curiously, "What is it?"

"It's a sole for a shoe." Jessica held it to the bottom of her foot again to demonstrate. "I'll make some straps, probably from the rabbit pelt I have back there. So, I guess they'll be sandals, not shoes."

Leticia nodded and continued to watch as Jessica worked.

"You want to try?" Jess offered, pointing to the small pile of cordage. Leticia looked at the pile, then back to Jessica, Jessica nodded and pointed again. "Go ahead. You try. *Intentas.*"

Leticia took some pieces of the cordage and began shaping them the way she had watched Jessica do. It took a few tries, and a little coaching from Jessica, but soon Leticia had a pair of soles fit to her feet.

The rest of the day passed quietly, Meredith nursed Sarah, who looked on the verge of death, too weak to move. While working on the sandals for the girls with Leticia, Jessica had taken a break to roughly carve a small crude bowl, which Sarah could vomit into. Alyona assigned herself the job of shuttling it down to the river to empty it. She would also occasionally make short trips to a vantage point where she could see downriver, looking for any sign the men might be following them.

In spite of the relatively lazy way the girls spent the day, sleep came easily when night fell.

Chapter Ten

A howl rang out, startling Jessica. She looked around. She recognized her surroundings as a small slot canyon, a few miles southwest of her home. At her feet were four tiny newborn lambs, shivering in the cold night air. The moon was less than a week from a new moon, and the Milky Way galaxy cut a bright strip of white across the starry sky.

Another howl echoed through the canyon.

"Those wolves sound hungry." Grandma Dalton sat next to the glowing remains of a campfire. She glanced toward the lambs at Jess's feet then gazed into the darkness. "Persistent devils, aren't they?"

"I can't move all these lambs by myself—not fast enough. They're too tiny. They shouldn't even be away from their mama yet."

"Well, the wolves have the scent, so you really only have two options. Chase them away or lead them away."

Jessica's eyes snapped open as she was jolted awake by a groan. She sat bolt upright, gazing around the cave for the source. It was Sarah; she didn't look good. Her skin looked ashen, and her cheeks were sunken. Meredith was awake too, anxiously hovering over Sarah.

Jessica rose and moved to the mouth of the cave. She stared out into the predawn darkness, looking for any sign of people moving—any lights or fires. She listened intently for any out of the ordinary sounds. There was nothing other than the occasional slap or gurgle of water from the river.

She stood, lost in thought. Her recent dreams had been too spot-on to ignore. But what did it mean? What should she do? What could she do?

She could start getting more water. She grabbed her dirty water container, climbed down to the stream to fill it, and returned to the cave. She started a fire, being careful to make sure it was a clean, hot fire with no visible smoke. Once the fire was satisfactory, she made another trip to the river to collect more water.

She stopped to check her fish trap after filling the water container, and she was delighted to see two decent-sized fish. They weren't a species she recognized, but they resembled some sort of catfish. They wouldn't provide much meat, yet not much was better than none.

She extracted them from the trap, killed them, cleaned them, then took them and her second haul of water back to the cave. She placed the fish on a flat rock next to the fire and set to work sterilizing water. Leticia was awake and watching intently.

"*Diez minutos*," Jessica said, pointing to the boiling water, "*mantenlo hirviendo*. Keep it boiling."

Leticia nodded. After a moment, she stood up and reached out, as if to take the wooden utensils Jessica had fashioned for moving the hot rocks back and forth.

"You want to try?" Jessica asked. Leticia nodded. Jessica handed her the tools and watched for a while. Leticia was an excellent study and mimicked Jessica's actions and timing precisely. When it was clear Leticia had a firm handle on the process, Jessica decided she would take some of the venison from the submerged basket and cook it to supplement the fish.

"What you want me to do?" Alyona followed her out of the cave.

"I could use a dozen or so sticks. Sturdy, a little thicker than your finger, and about as long as your forearm." She pulled the SOG from its sheath, grabbed the back of the blade and offered the hilt to Alyona. "Pointy sticks."

Alyona's brow furrowed as she cocked her head to one side, but she obediently took the knife and went in search of the desired sticks. Jessica continued to her baskets and collected a chunk of venison before returning to the cave. She instructed Leticia how to cook the meat, in between stuffing a couple bites of the cooked fish into her mouth.

Leaving Leticia to tend the fire and food, and Meredith to tend Sarah, Jessica grabbed the axe and started up the game trail in the narrow gulley that ran away from the river, under the cave and up into the mountains to the northwest of the river. About fifty yards up, she came over a crest. The trail flattened briefly as the gulley widened out, then it dropped slightly, following the contour and winding through a cluster of trees. Beyond the trees, the trail climbed up again and disappeared over another crest fifty or so yards away.

Jessica selected a spot on the trail in the trees and began digging, using the axe blade to speed up the work. Jess worked late into the night enlarging and deepening the hole. When the hole was about four feet long, two feet wide and a foot deep, she stood up, stretched, and retraced her steps.

Jessica arrived back at the cave and was greeted by four worried faces.

"Where were you?" Meredith's tone was anxious and accusatory. "We were afraid you were hurt, or you had been found, or ..."

"I'm sorry," Jessica said, "I got busy working, and lost track of time."

Alyona stepped forward, holding a bundle out in front of her. "Your pointy sticks," she said, offering the bundle.

The girls stared at Jessica expectantly, waiting for an explanation.

"They're coming," Jessica said after a long pause. "They are going to come this way before long—probably in the next couple days. We can't fight them off, and Sarah is still in no shape to run, so we need to lead them away."

"Okay, so what is plan?" Alyona asked.

"You girls will hunker down, stay quiet and out of sight, and I will lead them off."

"By yourself?" Alyona asked, arching one eyebrow.

"I'll leave a false trail and stay ahead of them."

"I don't think you will convince them you are five girls." Alyona paused. "I will go with you. It will be more believable that way."

"It's going to be dangerous," Jessica protested. "There's a lot that will be improvised."

"If I am slowing you down, then you leave me to the wolves."

Jessica winced, recalling the sound of the howling in her dream.

Alyona continued, "One set of footprints will never convince them of the herd, but two sets of footprints might."

Jessica chewed on her lower lip. She turned to gaze out into the darkness. "Okay, that makes sense," she conceded.

"What do we need? What are we taking with us? What are we leaving here? Do we need to prepare anything? When are we leaving?"

"Slow down!" Jessica raised a hand to ward off the barrage of questions. We'll take the pack and the gear in it. If we have time, we'll make another water bottle like these, that will give us three to share. The canteen we'll leave here—the lid leaks, and we don't have a holder to carry it anyway. We'll take the knife, but leave the axe, I think. We'll take some of the dried meat, but we'll leave some behind too, in case the others have to hole up in here for a while."

Jessica turned to Leticia. "You might have to stay hidden in the cave for a few days without going out at all.

No fire. Nothing to call attention to you. Ration the water and the dried meat."

Leticia nodded.

"We'll clear tracks around the area below, so it doesn't look like anyone camped here—nothing that will draw their eyes to this hollow. Maybe make a fake, short-term campsite near the water, then we'll make a few trips up this game trail I walked today, to give them a nice easy-to-find track to follow. Not so much it looks like we're trying to be found; just enough to look like we got a little sloppy."

Alyona chuckled, "You think of so many little details, are you American commando? American spy? Or Maybe American ninja?"

Jessica smirked, "I think command-ette is the term you are looking for."

"As you wish, *Polkovnik*!" Alyona saluted, grinning.

"At ease, soldier!" Jessica grinned back.

The next day was a flurry of activity. Jessica and Alyona returned to the hole she dug. They set the sharpened stakes in the hole, standing vertically, the points a few inches below the level of the rim.

Alyona watched curiously as Jess constructed a delicate cover over the hole using thin branches and leaves, and then extended the pattern of branches and leaves several yards in front of the hole and a few yards beyond.

"You're thinking of leading them into this trap?" Alyona asked. "I don't think it is big enough for them to fall into. And not enough sticks."

"It's mostly meant as a deterrent," Jessica said. "Most likely they will see it, or one of them will stumble through it. But once they have discovered one trap, they will likely be more cautious—move more slowly. At least for a while. It will buy us some time to get farther ahead of them."

"How come you're so sure they will come back this way and that we need to lead them away?"

Jessica inhaled, then exhaled deeply. "I guess I don't know for certain. Let's call it a premonition."

"Premonition?" Alyona asked, her voice laced with doubt.

"I rescued you because of one. Got us away from the van just in time to keep from getting caught again, too." Jessica shrugged, "They've been right too many times to ignore."

Once Jessica was satisfied with the trap, she and Alyona continued up the trail until it dropped down over the other side of the mountain and into a valley. As the trail reached the bottom of the valley, it crossed a small stream with muddy banks. The girls crossed through the mud to an open grassy area on the other side, cleaned their boots on the grass, then walked thirty paces out into the grassy meadow, until the grasses covered their passage.

Jessica removed the pack, opened the top and pulled out another pair of shoes.

"Sarah's shoes?" Alyona asked.

"I borrowed them," Jessica replied. "Since she's not going anywhere today, I figured I'd put them to good use." She took her shoes off, tied the laces together and hung them about her neck. Slipping Sarah's shoes on, she grinned at Alyona.

"Now we walk backward." Jessica instructed, stepping backward through the grass and into the mud.

"Aaaah!" Alyona beamed, "It looks like lots of tracks. And Sarah's shoes are so it's more than two shoes?"

"Yes, ma'am." Jessica smiled, then scowled, "Hopefully that will be enough to convince them we're all together."

"Very clever," Alyona complimented Jessica.

It was late in the afternoon when they returned to the cave. Leticia had been busy collecting and boiling water; the various containers and the cistern were all topped off. She had also collected the strips of venison which had been hung on a makeshift rack to sun dry and placed them in a neat pile on a clean flat rock. The sticks which were used for the drying rack she had also brought in and stacked in a corner out of the way.

Meredith was tending to Sarah, who still looked like death warmed over. Meredith had torn a strip of fabric from her shirt waist and was using it to coax drops of water onto Sarah's cracked lips, and into her mouth.

Jessica nodded to the girls, who returned the silent, somber greeting. She dropped the rucksack on the cave floor, removed Sarah's shoes, and put her own boots back on. She grabbed a handful of the dried venison and stuffed it in the small bag given to her by the boy from the village. As she stored the bag of dried meat and the water containers in the rucksack, her hand brushed the cool metal of the gun. She circled the handle with her fingers and withdrew it, along with the ammo, offering them to Meredith. "You should keep these here," she said, "Just in case."

"But you're making them chase you," Meredith shook her head vigorously, "shouldn't you have it?"

"We'll have a lead on them," Jessica smiled, "and we plan to stay ahead of them. I'm not planning on there being any last-stand, guns-blazing, battle-to-the-death. The gun is just in case they don't follow us. It isn't very likely, this spot is fairly well concealed and uninteresting, but… you know. Be prepared, and all."

Meredith looked at Jess, then at the gun, biting her lip. She nodded and took the weapon. "You know I'm not very good with these," she said. "You remember that time we went with those guys to the gun range?"

"You only had two shots that didn't hit paper. And you quickly picked up all the rules for properly handling a firearm," Jessica said. "Plus, you didn't flinch, and you had good control. You do just fine."

Jessica hunched over to close the rucksack. "Seriously, I don't think you will need to use it. If you do, it is because something has gone horribly wrong, and… well…"

Meredith nodded, staring into the distance with haunted eyes. "If it comes to it, it beats going back to… that."

Jessica reached out, touching Meredith's shoulder. Meredith looked at her through tear-laced eyes. Suddenly she reached out, grabbing Jess in a fierce hug. "Be careful."

Jessica hugged her back. "It's gonna be okay, Mer."

"They're coming!" Alyona burst into the cave panting, her eyes wide and her arms scratched up from an incautious ascent. "I hear a dog barking. We have little time."

Jessica stuffed her arrows into the side pouch of the rucksack. She snugged the compression strap around the arrows, tight enough to hold them in place, but not so tight that she couldn't slip them out—not as good as a quiver, but it would do. She slipped the pack on her back, clicking the sternum strap into place, then grabbed the bow.

"Stay inside and quiet," she ordered. "And smother that fire quickly and thoroughly, so it doesn't smoke."

She bolted out of the cave; Alyona was already sliding down the steep face. As soon as she was clear, Jessica started running down the face. She pushed off hard at the bottom and landed heavily, but she remained upright. The two girls sprinted up the ravine, following the path.

Jessica looked back to make a quick survey of the area. At a quick glance, it looked as if the girls had camped near the river, then made a hasty effort to break up the camp and move into the ravine. Their mad scramble added to that narrative.

Hopefully their pursuers would interpret it that way as well.

Looking forward again, she saw that Alyona was several paces ahead of her, thanks to her long legs and impressive stride. Jessica could tell Alyona was holding back somewhat to keep from leaving Jessica behind.

Jessica was about thirty yards from the first rise when she heard the dog's excited barking and snarling. It was starting up the ravine. She didn't hear people yet. The dog must have been released to run them down. It was closing the gap fast.

Fifty yards away. Forty yards, thirty, twenty.

In one fluid motion, Jessica brought an arrow to the bow. She turned, planted her feet, drew to her cheek, exhaled and released. The dog emitted a horrible yelp of anguish as the arrow sank deep into its chest, just inside the right shoulder. It dropped, flailing as its yelps of pain filled the air.

Dirt exploded several feet to the left and downhill from Jessica, and the explosion of dirt was followed by an ominous crack. Jessica looked at the man with a pistol, firing in her direction. She turned and bolted, racing up the remaining ten yards of hill and over the crest.

Once she was certain she was out of sight, she stopped and nocked another arrow.

"What are you doing?" Alyona hissed, sliding to a stop.

"Keep going." Jessica motioned her away then, in a crouch, she crept back to where she could see over the crest. Four men sprinted up the ravine, their heads down, so they didn't see her. She drew and fired toward them. The wild shot hit one of the men in the arm. She couldn't tell if the man cried out—the dog was making so much noise—but he grabbed at his arm, and the men scattered for cover. She turned and ran out of sight again, as gunfire erupted behind her.

Ahead of her, Alyona neared the grouping of trees.

"Stop, stop, stop!" Jess yelled, bringing Alyona skidding to a halt just before the strewn sticks and leaves on the trail. "Go around!" Jess hissed, gesturing with her hand as she continued to run.

Alyona looked at her, back at the trail, then she took off running again to the left side of the debris. Jessica followed her, sprinting through the trees. Once past the trap, the girls returned to the trail and continued to the second rise.

They were fifteen yards from the crest when a rock shattered near Alyona.

"*Bleen*!" she hissed, ducking as the crack of the gunshot reached them.

"Run!" Jessica yelled, "They're lousy shots; they are no more likely to hit you running straight than zig-zagging, and you'll get to cover faster!"

Alyona straightened her path, heading directly to the rise. Jessica glanced back as she cleared the rise. The first man approached the cluster of trees, and moments later the girls heard a scream.

Alyona looked at Jessica. "Your trap worked?"

"Sounds like," Jess panted. They had been running hard, and mostly uphill. "Hopefully, it will slow them down."

The girls slowed their own pace to catch their breath. Jessica strained her ears and frequently looked over her shoulder, checking for their pursuers. None came into view as they continued following the ravine's upward path.

The shadows were lengthening. Jessica looked for the sun and took a quick measurement of its height above the horizon.

"We have about fifteen minutes of daylight left," she said as she scanned the path ahead. "We'll break out of the ravine there, in those trees." She pointed a finger. "We can use them for cover and go up toward the peak. We'll have good cover there and a good view."

Alyona nodded, panting. "Good plan."

The forest was a mix of oak and pine trees. They weren't quite as dense as they had first seemed, yet Jessica was confident they would provide enough cover. The ground was thick with green, springy grass and shrubbery, which covered all traces of their passage, even with their faster, less cautious pace. As the incline became steeper, there were places they were nearly crawling rather than walking. They slipped and stumbled, struggling upward, as the thick ground cover also hid the uneven places in the terrain.

As the sun began to slip from sight, the path became more difficult. The ground seemed more treacherous, and details washed to gray in the growing darkness.

"It is going to get cold at this altitude when the sun is gone," Alyona said, "We can't keep walking in the dark. There are too many little drop-offs. There isn't much chance of finding good shelter." She squinted, looking around. "Chopping branches will be too noisy so close."

"Yup," Jessica confirmed, "Fire's out of the question too."

"What are we going to do?"

Jessica reached back and patted the rucksack on her back. "We have the netting, and we have each other. Hope you like to cuddle." She smirked. Alyona regarded her curiously.

"Up there." Jessica pointed to a small grouping of old trees beyond a thick cluster of bushes.

"Won't those bushes hide us better?"

"Yes," Jess agreed, "but, they are also a better hiding

place for bugs and spiders and the things that eat the bugs and spiders. And that will probably also attract whatever eats them. I'm thinking those couple of big trees will strike a happy medium. Somewhere in between getting caught and getting bit."

Alyona considered Jessica's plan for a moment, scowling, her gaze flicking from the trees to the bushes. "Okay."

They selected a spot under one of the trees that, as best they could tell in the darkness, was reasonably smooth, free of rocks, and bore no obvious signs of animal or insect traffic.

Jess pulled the netting out of the pack and spread it out over the chosen spot. "This'll be a moderately crumby blanket. Won't do much to trap heat."

"Better than sleeping in a freezer though, yes?"

"Why yes. Kudos to you for the positive attitude."

Alyona snorted. "You must be rubbing off on me. Your attitude is contagious, hopefully is not terminal."

"Not terminal, but maybe chronic."

"Ugh, you mean I might spend the rest of my life surrounded by rainbows and unicorns? Dreadful."

"All right, come here," she chuckled as she sat down on the netting. The ground was firm, but not rock hard, and the grass provided a small amount of cushion. "We'll use this half for a mattress and fold the other half over us for a blanket."

Alyona lay down next to her. "Just like happy couple, eh?"

"Something like that."

"You don't snore, do you? I'm a light sleeper."

"Not to my knowledge, no."

Neither of them snored. Neither of them slept well either. Both were on edge; every click, chirp, and snap had them listening for men's voices. As the night wore on, the temperature dropped. Not to freezing, yet enough to be uncomfortable. The girls huddled together, shivering as the hours passed.

Then it began raining. The raindrops pattered lightly on the trees and the ground around them, masking many of the other night sounds. The thick foliage overhead served as an umbrella, keeping them dry. The hypnotic sound of the rain soon overcame the girls' wariness, and they reluctantly surrendered to slumber.

Chapter Eleven

Jessica and Alyona awoke as the world around them shifted from black to gray. The rain was still falling, and the tree which had so valiantly protected them from the water during the night was beginning to lose the battle. The persistent rain penetrated the canopy drop by drop. It worked its way down the labyrinth of leaves and began to drip on them.

Alyona groaned and stretched.

"Good morning, sunshine," Jessica said cheerily from behind Alyona. She had awakened a few minutes earlier, and was sitting with her back against the tree, watching the rain. Alyona turned her head and scowled.

"Yes, we are probably going to get wet," Jessica responded to the unspoken statement. "On the bright side, it will be much harder for them to find us, what with the reduced visibility."

Alyona grunted.

"And," Jessica continued, "we'll get a refreshing shower, and our clothes will get washed while we enjoy a nice hike."

Alyona fixed Jessica with a hard stare. "Good. You need a shower. You're starting to smell."

Jessica gasped, eyes wide, with an open-mouthed smile. "I think you need some protein."

She dug into the pack, fished out two strips of dried venison, and offered one to Alyona. Alyona grunted again but took the meat and began gnawing on it. Jessica tore off a bite of her strip and chewed on it.

She stood and stretched, shaking out her arms and legs to get her blood flowing. Her calves were tight from the impromptu cross-country race they'd run yesterday. She rubbed and stretched them to loosen them up.

"How long until we go back?" Alyona was up too, working out the kinks in her muscles.

Jess considered a moment, tilting and twisting her head to stretch her neck. "A few days, maybe a week at most. I think by then they ought to have moved on or given up." She cocked her head, looking upward. She shrugged, then proceeded to pack up the slightly damp netting, stuffing it into the pack.

"How far are we going to go?"

"I think we'll continue up this way to the peak. That should give us a good view, and hopefully, we'll be able to spy out what they are doing and where they are going. We can go in whatever direction makes the most sense from there, depending on their actions."

"Aah, very strategic, *Polkovnik*."

Jessica shot her a half smirk. "Let's go get wet."

Wet was an understatement, the clouds descended to meet them as they ascended the slope. The rain drenched them from above, and the air soaked them everywhere else. It wasn't cold, but it wasn't warm either—a sort of unpleasant, clammy coolness, that left their skin feeling numb and almost corpse-like to the touch. Their damp clothes clung to their damp skin, adding to their discomfort.

The ground was treacherously slippery in places, slowing their progress. More than once, Jessica misjudged it. A loose rock, or a patch of slippery ground cover, would send her foot shooting out from beneath her and her heart into a gallop. However, each time she caught herself a split-second before landing face down in the mud. Alyona snickered every time. Jess didn't mind though. Alyona's chortling lifted their moods.

One upside to the weather was the bad guys wouldn't be able to see them since visibility was less than forty feet. Of course, it meant the high ground wasn't going to help them keep tabs on their hunters either.

"Weather can change," Jessica mumbled to herself. This might even work out better for them; the clouds were giving them excellent cover for the climb. Maybe the weather would clear after they got on top and situated in good cover.

"What about the weather?" From Jessica's left side, Alyona turned her head to fix Jessica with a querulous gaze.

"Oh, I uh, just thinking this is a nice change from all the sunshine."

Alyona rolled her eyes and groaned. "How does your optimism not cause you to strangle yourself?"

Jessica chuckled. "C'mon. You must admit this is giving a little relief from the sunburn." Jess gazed at the bright red, peeling skin on the tops of Alyona's arms and hands, then raised her own arm next to Alyona's, comparing their burns.

Alyona scowled, then sighed. "Yes, is nice."

All of the sudden, a tall rock face emerged from within the fog, blocking their path and forcing them to a halt. It stretched above them, disappearing into the clouds.

Jessica studied the rugged wall. "I don't recall seeing that. To be fair, I doubt we came straight up. Hard to keep direction straight in weather like this, and we've been back and forth."

"You think we walked around the mountain?" Alyona asked.

"A little more than a quarter of the way around. That's all it would take to get to a part we hadn't seen."

"Do you think we went more left or more right?"

"Not sure, that's the tricky part. Pick the wrong one and we may end up walking around the whole mountain."

"Well, at least we are closer to top, so is short distance to walk." Alyona grimaced, "*Ugh,* your optimism is getting into my brain!"

Jessica smiled, "Feels good, doesn't it?" She turned serious as she scanned the rock in front of her for some sign or clue to tell her which way to go. "I'm thinkin' we probably went more to the right than left, 'cause we were favoring right to avoid the trail."

Alyona grunted.

Jess stared at the cliff again, second-guessing her instinctive choice. "Climbing is a bad idea in this weather. Rocks'll be slippery. Yeah, let's follow the cliff to the left."

Alyona nodded and fell in beside Jessica as they started walking to the left, along the base of the cliff.

They had walked for no more than ten minutes when they came to the end of the rock face and began working their way up the steep slope again.

"Wait a minute." Alyona paused. "Won't we be trapping ourselves if we go up?"

"Yeah, it's a risk, but I think it is worth taking the chance to get the view." She looked up into the impenetrable fog. "Not much of a risk at all if the weather stays like this."

It was a surprisingly short climb to the summit. The cliff disappearing into the fog gave the impression it was much taller than it really was—probably only thirty or forty feet tall in reality. The top was a small, tree-covered dome, roughly thirty feet in diameter. The sides sloped steeply after that. Off to the right of where they climbed up, the slope abruptly ended in a rocky edge marking the top of the cliff they had been below earlier.

"What now?" Alyona asked as they peered into the damp fog.

"Let's hang for a while, see if it clears up."

They sat on a dry patch of ground under a group of large trees with a thick canopy for a moment, to rest their legs and to enjoy a brief respite from the constant drizzle on their heads, running into their eyes.

The weather finally broke in the late afternoon. The drizzle stopped, and the clouds melted away. The temperature rose quickly, leaving the girls uncomfortably warm in their wet clothes.

Staying low and watching their step, they worked their way to the edges to peer down at the areas below. Several men were fanned out in the meadow they had made tracks to the day before, searching it and the perimeter.

"Looks like they are trying to find our trail that isn't there." Alyona's voice was smug.

"Yup," Jessica smiled grimly, "Wonder if we should've crossed the meadow, broke a few branches or something."

"If we had, right now you would be wondering if we should have gone another hundred feet to break some more branches."

Jessica smiled. "True."

The girls watched the men continue their fruitless search for an hour or so, frequently scanning the rest of the valley to make sure nobody else snuck up on them. For Jess, it was a bit like reconnaissance before the hunting season—watching animal movement, figuring where they were likely to be, and where the best cover for approaches would be. It was a game of patience, and one which she enjoyed. It was relaxing, just sitting, watching, enjoying the beauty of the natural world.

Alyona was not enjoying it quite as much. She fidgeted. "Shouldn't we be doing something?"

"We are doing something," Jess said, focused on the activity below.

"What are we doing?"

"Waiting for black to make their move."

"What?"

"Chess." Jess took her gaze off the men to stare at Alyona. "We made our move, now it's their turn. We'll see what they do, how are they going to play it? Cautious? Aggressive? How much energy are they going to invest? Are they going to just throw a few pawns at us? Or will they break out the queen and knights?"

"I am not following." Alyona shook her head, drawing her brows low over her eyes.

"I count seven men down there. Is this the whole hunting group or are there others looking for us elsewhere? It was hard to count while we were running from them last night, but I think I counted five, maybe six. One or two more aren't exactly reinforcements. I would expect if there were several groups working from a base camp, the other groups would have been called in to help here, since we had been sighted, but nobody has shown up. So, are they going to keep tracking us or are they about to give up and go back? Is a fresh group going to arrive soon? How careful will we have to be? And for how long?"

Jessica shifted her weight from side to side in her crouch to ease the stiffness in her joints.

"You see those two guys on the far end of the field?" Jess pointed at two figures standing close together. "They've spent most of the day standing or sitting around. They only act busy when those three in the middle of the field," she closed one eye as she pointed, "get too close. One or more of them appear to be in charge."

Alyona followed her hand, gazing between the groups of men and nodding along to her explanation.

Jessica turned her focus to Alyona. "The other thing I've noticed is they keep searching the same spots over and over again. They aren't methodical at all. One of the guys will search a spot, then a while later another guy will search it. Sometimes the same guy will come back and search it again. These guys aren't particularly good at this, and they don't really want to be here. Hopefully, it means they will move on soon, and that we are hitting the limits of what they are willing to invest to get us back. Maybe the hunt will be over soon, and we will be able to move with less caution."

The two were quiet again for a while as they watched the men pace in circles around the field.

"So, what is plan after?" Alyona glanced across at Jessica.

Jessica thought for a moment. "First, we get everyone over the withdrawal stuff—get everybody healthy. Then we'll hang here for long enough to pull together enough food, water, and containers to be able to travel—"

"And where are we traveling to?"

"Still working on that," Jessica said. "Probably the closest option is the city they took us from."

"Risky, perhaps."

"Yeah, at one point before I found you, I was outside a village, and overheard some guys mentioning a reward, so it might not be safe to go back there."

"What other options?"

Jessica shrugged. "I think Mexico City is east of here, or maybe northeast—bit more of a hike." Jess stared off in the direction of the cave. "Not sure everyone is really up for that." She glanced back to Alyona. "Of course, another option is north to the border. That's gotta be something like ...maybe a thousand miles, I guess? Be next year by the time we get there."

"We could drive," Alyona suggested.

"We don't have a car." Jessica paused, then remembered. "Oh yeah, the van. I wonder if they will retrieve it or just leave it? It was pretty beat-up; they might just abandon it. Of course, I don't know if I can get it running or not."

"That van isn't the only vehicle in Mexico, you know."

Jessica shook her head. "We don't have any money. How we gonna get a car?"

"How did you get the van?"

Jessica bit down on her lip and scowled. "I suppose that might be an option. I'd rather not steal though. Maybe we could hitch a ride ..."

"And how you know who to trust not to take us for the reward?"

Jess sighed, twisting her fingers together in her lap. "There is probably a radius of effectiveness for the reward. Hike far enough north and we should be clear of it, then hitch a ride."

"But how far is far enough?"

"Don't know," Jessica shrugged.

"Sometimes you know," Alyona said, "you can do wrong thing for right reason."

"Said every villain ever," Jess retorted.

Alyona cocked her head to one side, confusion shining in her eyes.

"Nobody picks bad guy as their career choice," Jess

said. "Every villain sees himself as the good guy—the hero whose means are justified by the end."

Alyona rolled her eyes. "I'm talking about 'borrowing' a car, not committing genocide."

Jessica opened her mouth to respond, but the words died on her lips in a croak, and she shut it. She opened it again, raising a finger, then closed it again. Was Alyona right? Was there perhaps a circumstance where stealing became justified?

She shook her head. "We'll find another way."

Alyona stared at her for a moment, then sighed and shook her head. "*Uprjámyj,*" she muttered to herself as she stalked away.

Jessica continued her patient vigil, watching for an arrival of reinforcements, trying to gauge the mood and morale of the men below. Nobody else came into view, and the men continued going over the same area.

The sun was low when the men finally gathered and started back along the trail. Jessica watched as they crested the ridge, then started down toward the river. It was dark by the time they reached the clump of trees where she dug the pit on the trail, but the flicker of flashlights gave her an easy way to track the men as they continued down the path.

The lights disappeared for a while as the men traversed the steeper part of the canyon near the base, then they came into view again as they neared the black ribbon of river. They were close to her fish traps, and the submerged basket full of venison. Would they find it? She contemplated whether leaving it in place had been a good idea. It wasn't easy to see, and the girls needed the food. Although, with the men camped right next to it, they couldn't access it anyway.

Before long she saw flickering light and shadow, indicating a fire had been built. It looked like they were going to be there for the night anyway.

Jessica frowned. She really didn't like that they were so close to the cave. If somebody sneezed, or coughed, or even snored too loud it would give them away.

A bright flash to her left caught her attention. It was followed by an ominous rumble. The grass rustled around them.

"Jessica!" Alyona hissed.

"Here!" Jessica whispered back. The rustling continued, moving directly toward Jess. Alyona's face came into view out of the darkness. "You saw that, yes?"

"Saw and heard it."

"I think on top of tall mountain, under tallest trees is not so good place to be right now."

"Yeah, I think you're probably right. Let's work our way down and find someplace to shelter." Jessica stood, brushing and straightening her clothes.

"Difficult in the dark."

"Yep. And remember the cliff. Let's not go down that."

Alyona grunted. "Yeah, no trying flying tonight."

Chapter Twelve

The two girls worked their way carefully down the slope in the darkness, staying close to the cliff edge—to use it as a reference, but far enough away to avoid the risk of a fall. They reached the base of the cliff when the rain started.

Jessica was worried. A cool and wet night could still be enough to cause hypothermia. They really needed to find a place to stay dry.

She followed the cliff, looking and feeling for a large, recessed area she recalled seeing earlier in the day. It didn't take long before she found it. She was walking, her hand brushing lightly against the rock, when abruptly her hand rubbed over a sharp edge and lost contact. She stopped and stretched her arm into the darkness to check the depth. It would be crowded, yet there was enough room for the two of them to squeeze in together and be protected on three sides. A bit of an overhang at the top created a drip line not more than a foot from the back. Not enough to keep more than their heads dry, but it would keep the water from running down the back.

"This should work for tonight," Jessica said, "but we need a better roof. I think there are some evergreens just below. Wait here, I'll be right back."

She scanned the darkness, trying to use her peripheral vision to detect a clump of deeper darkness that would signal a tree. Picking a spot that looked promising, she moved forward, counting her steps as she went. At thirty paces she could make out the dark, conical shape of a fir tree just ahead and to her left.

Pulling the SOG from the sheath, she began hacking at branches. She reconsidered the wisdom of leaving the hatchet behind. The SOG had a good edge, however, and it didn't take long to hack off a dozen or so branches, all between four and six feet in length. She hauled them back up the hill, counting paces again, until she found the cliff. Feeling her way along, she found the crack where Alyona was standing, pressed against the back as far as she could to keep herself dry.

"Crouch down," Jessica instructed. "We'll pile these on top of us to make a slope for the water to run down and away."

Alyona obeyed, and Jessica backed in with the bundle of branches. She jammed the cut ends of the branches against the back of the crack above their heads, forming a primitive lean-to shelter. She shifted the branches around until she was confident they were tightly in place, then she snuggled herself into the empty part of the floor.

"You're wet!" Alyona complained.

"Sorry." Jessica struggled awkwardly in the small space to remove the pack. "Shoulda done that before I got down."

She opened the pack and pulled out the netting.

"Here," she said, touching Alyona with the netting in the dark, "let's work this under us so we are sitting on something a bit softer than dirt and rocks."

With considerable contortion in the confined space, the two managed to work the folded netting underneath their legs.

"Jerky?" Jessica asked, reaching into the pack again to fish out a couple strips of meat.

"Sure," Alyona said glumly, placing her hand palm up on Jessica's lap.

Jessica pressed a strip of dried venison onto Alyona's waiting hand, then began gnawing on the tough strip of deer flesh. It was dry enough that even without salt it would keep for a while. A lot of work to eat though.

"Oh, I didn't think about anything for a pillow," she said as she leaned her head back against the rocks.

"I'll probably sleep with my head on my knees," Alyona replied.

"Can't really lean back in here anyway."

"Yeah," Alyona sighed.

"Hang in there." Jess covered Alyona's free hand with hers and gave it a gentle squeeze. "Sun'll come out again."

Alyona continued chewing, and they finished their meager meal in silence. The thin branch roof served as effective insulation. With the two of them cramped together in the snug space, the combination of body heat and breathing brought the temperature up to muggy in short order. Jessica was uncertain if the moisture covering her body was still just rainwater, or if perspiration had come into the equation.

Jessica leaned forward to stretch her back. Alyona shifted forward next to her. Her breathing began to slow, and her body relaxed. Alyona's forehead came to rest on Jessica's shoulder.

Jessica held still, not wanting to disturb Alyona. She didn't mind being used as a pillow, but the current position was going to be uncomfortable in a few hours.

For now, it was okay—nice even—just sitting there in the quiet, dark night listening to and feeling the rhythm of her new friend's breathing. Alyona was an impressive girl. The things she had been through… It was overwhelming to consider. But she was solid. A little angry perhaps, but solid. So stoic in the face of so much hardship and pain.

How much more hardship would they have to endure before they would be able to get clear of this? And where would Alyona go after? She had no family, it seemed. Would she want to go back to Ukraine? Would she have a choice?

Jessica's thoughts turned to Sarah. How was she doing? Jessica wished there had been some improvement in her condition before they had left. She was worried about her. Sarah probably needed to be in a hospital. But where could they take her?

Jessica took a couple of deep breaths to slow her racing mind. "One problem at a time, Jess," she murmured to herself. "Can't do anything about it now. Stay focused on what is in your control. Don't waste your energy chasing shadows."

Alyona murmured in her sleep and shifted, moving her head from Jessica's shoulder to her own lap. Jessica shifted and stretched, then settled her head against her knees. She closed her eyes and listened to the sounds of the rain falling on the evergreen roof. She liked the sound of the rain. It calmed her. She enjoyed the occasional deep rumbling thunder also, though it was less calming. There was still a kind of reassurance in the ominous boom. The demonstration of nature's superior power. Something simply beyond human control.

She pondered this strange thought, trying to put words to her reasoning. No words came, and she slipped into a dreamless slumber.

Rustling outside woke Jessica. The tiniest bit of light penetrated the thick evergreen thatch in a few places. Something—or someone—was moving out there. She listened for any sounds which would allow her to identify their creator. It was muffled, yet sounded like it could be slow, measured footfalls. She wanted to move the branches and take a peek but didn't dare for fear of making a noise which might draw the attention of unwanted visitors.

Jessica turned her head and slowed her breathing, straining to pick out sounds through the thick, insulating mass of branches. *Shuffle*. Pause. *Shuffle*. Pause. No other sounds could be heard. She slipped her hands into the branches, quietly working to open a slit to peer through. After several tries, it became obvious the branches were too thickly bunched to create a peephole without some substantial moving.

She examined the sides, evaluating the chances of shifting them away from the rock enough to be able to peer out. Then she looked at the base. There the branches were irregularly placed and extended beyond the face of the rock. Several relatively large openings presented a potential viewing portal.

She walked her feet back as close to her butt as she could get them. She worked her hands down to the ground on either side of her hips, one scraping against rock wall on her left side, the other squeezing between her and Alyona's sleeping form.

Pushing up with her hands, she rocked forward from sitting into a crouch on her feet. She moved her hands around in front of her. She had rocked forward so far that her head touched the branches. Shifting her weight onto her hands, she walked her feet back until they touched rock and she was far enough forward for her knees to touch the ground.

Jessica lowered her head to the ground and stretched forward, moving her face toward one of the gaps at the base of the shelter. As her eyes adjusted to the brightness, she scanned the area, watching for any movement, shifting left, then right to see more area.

Rustle. Pause. *Rustle*. Pause.

A leg came into view, and Jessica breathed a sigh of relief. It was a small doe and a faun grazing along the hillside.

"What are you doing?" Alyona's voice broke the silence. The startled deer bolted, and Jessica jumped and gasped.

"I was trying to *quietly* peek out and find out who was moving around out there."

Alyona stared, mouth open for a moment. Regaining her composure, she asked, "And who is moving around out there?"

Jessica released an exasperated sigh and shook her head. "A couple of deer."

"Ah, you think they will rat us out?"

Jessica rolled her eyes and smiled, "Let's get back to work."

"Oh boy, another exciting day hiding in trees, watching nothing happen."

"Nothing happening is good, in this case."

"Yeah, yeah."

The girls slowly moved the branches out of the way, giving their eyes time to adjust to the light. The sun was just above the mountain tops, but still bright in the clear blue sky. After ensuring there was no immediate risk of being spotted, they moved the branches down to the clump of firs, pushing them into the trees to make them less conspicuous.

They each ate another strip of dried venison as they started back up the hilltop. The same group from the previous day had just cleared the ridge and were working their way down to the meadow again. The girls crept up the slope, staying out of sight, and they reached the top of the peak at the same time the men reached the meadow.

Scouting around the peak, Jessica could see no other

search groups. It was the same small group of men, who continued their aimless search.

The rest of the morning passed uneventfully, watching the men wander around and through the meadow. They traced out from the meadow in several directions going a hundred yards or so, then returning.

By late afternoon clouds were rolling in again, and the men beat a hasty retreat to their camp. The girls raced down as quickly as they could too, once it was safe to do so. They collected their branches, plus a few extra to use as a mattress, and crowded back into their crack in the cliff. They settled in just before the deluge began.

After yet another meager dinner consisting of a strip of dried venison, and a couple swallows of water, Jessica fished out the water bottles, removed the lids, and placed them out in the rain. They wouldn't collect much without a funnel, but even a little would help.

They had been on starvation rations for the past couple days, and it was starting to take its toll. Alyona was becoming moody—Jessica was struggling to control her emotions as well.

Fortunately, they had been relatively inactive, but they couldn't keep going like this much longer. They needed more calories, they needed a more diverse diet, and they desperately needed more clean water.

The girls woke before sunrise the next morning. They stored their shelter and packed up their gear. They were rounding the edge of the cliff to start the climb to the top when the sun cleared the horizon. They had ascended less than half the distance to the top when Jessica paused, an uneasy feeling settling in the pit of her stomach. Alyona looked at her quizzically but remained silent and still.

Jessica could make out voices of men. They sounded close.

Jess crouched low and motioned Alyona back down the hill. Alyona moved without questioning this time. They scurried quickly down, staying right against the edge of the cliff. Jess peered over her shoulder as a hat appeared over the crest of the slope. They were still twenty feet from the bottom. She motioned Alyona over the cliff edge.

They scrambled over, trying to avoid knocking any rocks loose. Fortunately, the rock face was solid and well weathered, providing numerous foot and handholds. As the two lowered themselves below the top, two heads came into view. The men were looking uphill, putting the girls at their right rear quarter, just out of peripheral vision. All it would have taken was for one of the men to look back over his shoulder.

Jessica took a moment to collect herself, then began a slow descent.

"What are they doing?" Alyona hissed.

"Probably same as us," Jessica said in a barely audible whisper, "using the peak as a lookout point."

"What are we going to do?"

"Get to the crack and stay out of sight."

They rushed back to their crevice, Jessica scouting for other options as they went. Could they hide in a thick clump of bushes or the cluster of fir trees? Could they make it to them without being seen? Were the men already at the summit? The crevice was likely the best choice at this point.

The girls slipped into the crevice and huddled at the back, statue-still. The sun cast a dark shadow which helped to obscure them, so even looking directly over the edge, the men likely wouldn't be able to see to the back. When they started to ache from standing, they slid down the rock to sit with their knees hugged close to their bodies.

They had just gotten comfortable when they heard faint sounds above them. The men were talking, but at this distance, Jessica couldn't even begin to make out what they were saying. Not far from them there was a small *thud*. Alyona started, and Jessica peered out. Another *thud*.

"They're throwing rocks." Jess whispered.

A dozen or so more rocks rained down. There was a pause, then a spattering of small droplets of water fell to the left of the entrance. The two girls looked at each other.

"Are they peeing off the cliff?" Alyona asked.

Jessica wrinkled her nose and grimaced. "Boys."

Alyona nodded in agreement, then as an afterthought said, "Still, is handy for camping, no?"

Jessica gave Alyona a sidelong glance, then she rolled her eyes and shook her head. What a weird conversation, especially given the current circumstance.

The voices above them ceased, and the girls returned to waiting silently. They waited until it was growing dark, then quickly gathered their shelter branches and returned to the crevice for the night. But sleep did not come to them.

"What are we doing tomorrow?" Alyona finally broke the silence.

"Dunno," Jessica responded

"I don't want to sit here again tomorrow."

"Me neither. How do you feel about a walk in the moonlight?"

"Now?"

"We're awake, right?"

"Where?" Alyona shuffled around in the dark.

"Down the hill a bit, toward the cave."

"Isn't that where they are staying?"

"I think so." Jessica pulled herself into a crouch. "Kinda hoping we can find out something—anything. Today was kind of a bust."

"What if the dog is there?"

"I doubt the dog is still alive. It wasn't a clean kill, but it wasn't a shot that dog was likely to survive."

"What if there are more dogs?"

"Then we probably won't be able to get very close." Jessica scooted some branches aside to make an opening and stepped out of the shelter.

Chapter Thirteen

The sky was clear, and there was a quarter moon, giving them enough light to safely make their way back to the trail. They were cautious moving through the grove of trees where the pit was. The foliage above blocked the moonlight enough to obscure the path.

Jessica shuffled, transferring her weight gingerly from one foot to the next, feeling for a change in ground elevation which would signal the edge of the hole they had dug.

She found it, stepped to and along the side, keeping track of the hole's position until she reached the other end. Once they were comfortably past it, they increased their pace until they approached the final rise. There were no sounds from below.

"No lights," Jessica said, slowing and bending to a crouch.

"It's late. They are probably all sleeping."

"Yeah, but no light? Not even a hot coal from a dying fire?"

"Maybe they put it out."

"Maybe." Jessica wasn't convinced.

She squinted at the dark area below, trying to find any indication of a structure, tent or even dark shapes that might be people in sleeping bags.

"Should we go closer?" Alyona asked.

Jessica shook her head. "I don't think so. We'll be too easy to spot going down the trail if someone is awake and lying in a bag down there. This is about as close as we can get."

Jessica turned her head from side to side, straining to hear or see anything. She was unable to penetrate the darkness, and all she could hear was wind through foliage, the murmur of the river, and Alyona shuffling nervously next to her.

"What if they are still on top of the mountain?" There was a hint of alarm in Alyona's voice.

"Probably not," Jessica said, though she was less certain than her tone implied. "The sounds stopped fairly early for them to have stayed up there."

"Should we find cover? Just in case?"

"Actually, how about we go back to the top? We can confirm they aren't there, then we can watch for them at first light, which will give us time to get to cover when they start up."

"What if they are up there?" Alyona asked, scanning the dark shape of the mountain.

"Back to our hidey hole then, I guess."

"Okay, let's go."

They paced back up the trail, and then up the slope toward the peak. They moved slowly to avoid any stumbles or other abrupt movements which might generate noise. The closer they got to the top the more they slowed their pace. A light breeze, which was on the verge of uncomfortably chilly without a jacket, rustled the leaves on the trees and bushes, creating enough ambient noise to cover the sound of their footsteps through the foliage.

As they reached the crest they crouched and scanned the hilltop for any signs of human activity. Jessica could see nothing out of place.

"Where are they?" Jessica murmured, shivering in the cool night breeze.

"You think they left?"

"Maybe. Been a few days of fruitless searching now. How much time and money can they really justify wasting on us?" She rubbed her hands up and down her arms, trying to generate some warmth.

"It may be more than money though, yes? It may be reputation."

"Reputation?"

Alyona expelled a forceful breath. "Maybe some local people saw something. Stories about little girls getting away aren't good for a tough gang's reputation. No?"

"Yeah, I suppose so," Jessica mused.

"So, what's next?"

Jessica continued studying the area below them.

"Let's sit tight for one more day to make sure they aren't watching for us to come back."

"Back to the crack?"

"Yeah." Jessica shivered again. "It's cold out here."

They returned to their shelter and slept for a couple hours until sunrise, and then returned to the peak to keep watch.

As the sun began to warm them, Jessica struggled to keep her eyes open. Her eyes hurt, so she would close them for just a second, then startle awake as her head abruptly dropped.

She gazed over at Alyona, who was watching her with bloodshot eyes.

"If we keep this up, we will both be passed out in next couple hours, and nobody will be watching." Alyona rose to her feet. "You take nap, I'll walk perimeter to keep awake. I'll trade you in couple of hours."

Jessica was too tired to argue. She laid her head down and drifted off almost immediately.

"*Соня,* time to wake up." Jessica was awakened by Alyona's none too gentle nudging.

"How long did I sleep?" Jessica stretched groggily.

"How should I know? You're the human clock."

Jessica scanned the sky through bleary eyes. "Afternoon anyway," she said after checking the shadows.

"Whatever," Alyona groaned as she plopped to the ground, "Is your turn, I'm too tired to walk."

"Anything happen?"

"Squirrels and butterflies. Now go away."

Jessica smiled at the exhausted Alyona, then rose to her feet and began her vigil. The afternoon passed slowly. Jessica circled the hilltop, checked on her sleeping comrade, then circled the hilltop again. It was late afternoon when Jessica returned to find Alyona stirring.

"You didn't wake me," Alyona observed, "So I am guessing more nothing?"

"Yup." Jessica sat down cross-legged next to her.

It was frustrating, not knowing. Were men hiding out there somewhere, watching, waiting for the girls to come into the open? It seemed unlikely. The girls were at the best vantage point. If the men were hiding and watching, this would have been the place to do it. But there was still that uncertainty.

"How many days we going to do this?" Alyona seemed to sense Jessica's thoughts. Her tone expressed her own frustration.

Jessica studied the countryside. She began plotting a course of action in her mind. "Let's stay one more night. In the morning we will head northeast along that ridge." She pointed to an area north of the cave where the other girls were hiding. "We'll cross the river and follow it back down to the cave on the far side. We can scope things out from over there before we move in."

"Makes sense," Alyona said. "Come in from the other side, where they won't be looking for us."

They waited until dark and returned to the crevice for one final night. They were out of clean water now, and they ate the last of the dried venison. Jessica's lips were dry and cracked. She was sure the tiredness she had felt today wasn't just lack of sleep. They were both getting dehydrated. Possibly dangerously so. She had only urinated once today, and very little at that. She had a headache, and she had felt irritated several times throughout the day, for no reason. She was certain Alyona was feeling it as well. She recalled their interactions that evening. She felt they had both been trying to pretend they weren't annoyed with each other.

Jessica sighed. The dried meat diet wasn't helping either. The scant rations weren't giving them the energy they needed to hike these hills. One way or another, they needed to get food and water tomorrow, the day following at the latest.

They followed Jessica's chosen route and the river upstream until they found a shallow point to cross. They removed their shoes and socks to keep them dry and entered the water, shuffling, and probing with their toes. The impulse to dunk her head into the water and take several big gulps gripped Jessica, and Alyona let out a soft moan beside her.

"Don't do it," Jessica said.

"What?" Alyona asked.

"Don't drink the water. We don't need to be dealing with a case of Montezuma's revenge."

"Monte-what?"

"The runs? The trots? Diarrhea?"

Alyona stared at the water. "There is pretty good chance it will be okay." Her voice was filled with undisguised longing.

"But there is also a pretty good chance it won't," Jessica said, "No drinking."

Alyona moaned in frustration.

Jessica exited the river, dried her feet on her clothes and put her shoes and socks back on while Alyona did likewise. They continued down river, heading back toward the cave.

Taking up a position opposite the cave where they had a good view of the area below, they settled in and waited, surveying the landscape for any signs of activity. It was easy to tell where the men had camped, from the scattered litter and the charred remains of a fire. They watched quietly for several hours, seeing nothing apart from a few scurrying rodents.

"This is stupid." Alyona threw her hands up in frustration as she rose from her crouched position.

"Whoa!" Jessica grabbed Alyona's hand. Alyona whirled, cocking her free hand back. Jessica flinched, and Alyona froze, then lowered her fist.

"Sorry." Alyona relaxed, lowering her gaze. "I'm tired, and hot, and hungry, and thirsty."

"I know. Me too."

"So why are we still waiting then? Nothing is there but beer bottles."

"I know." Jessica expelled an exasperated breath, scanning the terrain.

"We can't wait here forever, what else can we do?"

"I don't know." Jessica sighed. "You're right, we've been as careful as we can. We need to make a move. Let's go."

They walked cautiously down the slope, and crossed the river, performing their usual ritual for keeping their footwear dry. They began a careful search of the area. Jessica's food baskets were still submerged and looked untouched since she had last checked them.

"Fire hasn't been used recently," Jessica said as she inspected the campfire remains. "Maybe not for a couple days."

"Maybe that day on the mountain was the last day," Alyona speculated, "and then they left."

"It certainly seems that way."

"So, where are they?" Alyona inclined her head toward the cave entrance.

The two girls climbed the slope. As Jessica entered the cave, her heart sank. It was empty apart from the cistern, and ashes from the fire. A few cigarette butts were evidence that others had been here. She took deep breaths to calm her worry. She didn't have to assume the worst. There could be any number of reasons the girls weren't there. However, as she looked around the cave for any sign of hope, it became hard to think of anything except the worst.

"They got them?" Alyona probed a cigarette butt with the tip of her shoe.

"I don't know." Jessica struggled to keep her tears at bay. "I don't see anything to suggest a struggle. No shell casings. I'm sure Meredith would've put up a fight."

"*Muy*?" Alyona's voice sounded puzzled.

"What?" Jessica asked, turning to face her. Alyona was looking at the ceiling.

Looking up, Jess could see the letters M-U-Y, scrawled on the rock in charcoal. The two stared silently at the letters for several moments.

"What does it mean?" Alyona asked.

"Spanish for 'very.'" Jessica puzzled it over in her mind. The M and the Y were very neatly written, crisp and straight, the U seemed out of place, the two sides curved in at the top, nearly coming together.

"Very what?"

"Wait," Jessica said, "Wasn't *moy* the Russian word for mine?"

"What, you think the 'U' is supposed to be an 'O'? But that still doesn't make sense."

"I think… Leticia... Remember, she mentioned the mine? Somewhere on that mountain?" Jessica pointed at the cave wall in a northerly direction.

"That's *shakhta*," Alyona corrected, shaking her head.

"Yeah, yeah," Jess waved a hand, "remember how we were talking about how '*moy*' and '*shakhta*' both translate to the word 'mine' in English? Or rather two different words with the exact same spelling?"

"Yes…"

"What if Leticia wrote this, to direct us to the mine?"

Alyona folded her arms. "It would have been easier to figure out if she wrote *shakhta*."

"Yes, but maybe Leticia was worried they might be able to translate it. I mean, kind of a long shot, but …"

"Okay…" Alyona tapped her arm with her finger, "but then wouldn't they be almost as likely as us to guess *moy* meant *shakhta*?"

“No, they wouldn’t,” Jessica smiled, cautious hope rising within her.

“They speak Spanish!” Alyona’s eyes lit up as the idea clicked.

“Right,” Jessica said. “Even if they guessed it wasn’t *muy*, which they probably wouldn’t because *muy* is a word in Spanish, they wouldn’t have a clue what language it was. How likely are they to guess it’s Russian? And be able to translate it?”

“No chance,” Alyona said, smiling, then her expression fell. “How are we going to find a mine on a mountain?”

“Don’t know,” Jess shrugged, “but it’s worth trying, right?”

Alyona’s eyes lowered and she chewed on her lip. “I don’t know. You really think Leticia would come up with something so… elaborate?”

“I know it’s a bit cloak and dagger, but…”

Alyona frowned and she took a deep breath. Then her face softened to a slight smile of encouragement. “Let’s go look.” She tilted her head back and groaned, “Across the water again! So annoying. I wish there was a bridge. And I’m still hungry…”

“And thirsty,” Jessica finished for her. “Fill up the cistern while I start a fire.”

Jessica got the fire ready and cut some venison from the baskets into thin strips, so it would cook quickly. Alyona collected water, and together the two cycled hot rocks in and out until the water was boiling. They waited impatiently for the meat to cool enough to be eaten, and filled their water bottles with the water, which was still too warm to drink, eager to be on their way.

The two girls made their way toward the mountain Leticia had pointed out. The only sounds were footfalls and measured breathing as the girls alternated between a fast walk and an easy lope.

Jessica found Alyona to be a perfect trekking partner. Aloyna's longer stride was matched by Jessica's greater endurance. They crossed miles of rugged climbing terrain in just a few hours. The excitement of a possibility giving them renewed energy. Jessica recognized the spot where she had climbed up to the road and stolen the van with the girls. Leticia's mine-mountain was just beyond that.

"What do you think?" Jessica asked. "We can move faster on the road."

"Plenty of trees to hide in if we hear anyone coming," Alyona agreed, "Is good plan."

Jessica frowned. "Even traveling on the road, we won't make the base of the mountain before nightfall."

Alyona placed a hand on her shoulder. "We'll go as far as we can, then search tomorrow."

Jessica did her best to ignore the questions playing over and over in the back of her mind. How would they find the mine? She didn't know how old the mine was. Would there be old rails? Would there be remnants of support buildings? Or would they be looking for a hole in the side of the hill, perhaps overgrown by trees?

Jessica again pushed the nagging doubts to the back of her mind. *Get there first.* Nothing could be done about finding the mine this evening. That was a problem for the morning.

As night fell, neither of the girls felt like sleeping, or stopping. The sky was clear, and a bright moon lit their way, so they pressed on in the darkness. It was slower going, as it was difficult to make out the fine details of the terrain. It was hard to be certain whether a dark patch was a rock, a pothole, or just a shadow. They pressed on, nonetheless.

"What now?" Alyona asked as they reached the mountain.

"Leticia knew where the mine was, right? Maybe she went there as a kid?"

Alyona shrugged.

"So, maybe there is a trail or road. Let's follow the road until it moves away from the mountain toward the town Leticia is from. Then we'll walk back from that direction as soon as it's light, look for any roads or trails leading up the mountain."

"Is a good plan," Alyona stated approvingly.

The girls trudged along the road slowly. Their rushed meal earlier had staved off, but not eliminated, their hunger. The water they collected was still barely survival rations, and they were exhausted. They were close to twenty-four hours now without sleep. They had been living on starvation rations for a few days. They really should have stayed at the cave longer and eaten more than one hasty meal. They should have rested and rehydrated.

Jessica shook her head and cast the thought aside. There was no point in second-guessing past decisions now. She needed to make a plan for what would come next.

"We aren't going to be much help to anyone if we overextend ourselves," Jessica said. "We've been short on food, water, and sleep long enough now, it's gonna affect our judgement. Let's agree now, if we haven't found the mine by noon, we'll head back, get some food and sleep, restock our water supply, and then try again."

"Agreed," Alyona nodded.

The two fell silent again. Talking was simply too much effort. They continued onward until the road veered away from mine-mountain, as the girls had taken to calling it. The road followed the path of the river into and through a winding valley. Jessica wondered if the town was close—perhaps in, or just beyond that valley. Probably not more than a mile or two from where they currently stood if that was the case.

They stopped to rest for a moment. Jessica gazed up at the sky, wondering what time it was. Probably a little after midnight. She yearned to begin the search for the mine, but it really would be impractical to start before the sun was up.

Chapter Fourteen

They started back along the road as soon as the sky began to lighten.

"Look there." Alyona pointed to a spot just ahead. Jessica could just make out the remains of a road—two partially overgrown tire ruts, really. But unmistakably an old road, which wound into the trees and up the mountain side.

"It's as good a place as any to start," Jessica said. They left the main road and followed the antiquated path. Jessica panted up the steep incline. Her muscles ached from the prolonged exertion. She raised her arm to wipe a few beads of sweat from her brow. She should probably be covered in sweat, but with as little water as she had been drinking the past few days, her body didn't have enough to spare on perspiration.

"Stop for a sec," Jessica puffed. "Need to catch my breath."

"What, you tired already?" Alyona gasped, bracing her body on her knees.

"We've got to be close," Jessica panted. Her heartbeat was beginning to return to normal when the rumble of an approaching vehicle drifted up the side of the mountain behind them.

Jessica bolted upright and glanced at Alyona, her eyes wide as her heart raced again, for a different reason. Fear shone in Alyona's gaze and her sunburnt skin paled.

They scurried for cover behind the trees near the roadside. In a few minutes, an old four-wheel-drive pickup came into view. There were three men in the cab, one of whom looked familiar.

"That's Marcos!" Jessica hissed, a ball of panic rising into her throat.

"Not good," Alyona muttered.

As soon as the vehicle was out of sight, the girls abandoned their hiding place and scampered up the road as quickly as they were able. After several minutes they came over a small rise onto a nearly level clearing. The pickup was parked next to a dark opening in the side of the mountain.

"That must be the mine," Alyona observed. The men were nowhere to be seen. The girls raced forward to the entrance and stepped into the blackness. As their eyes adjusted, they could see a flicker of light ahead.

"Lantern!" Jessica whispered. Somewhere in the back of her mind an alarm sounded, but her brain was too clouded by exhaustion and anxiety to process what it meant.

They scuttled forward into the dark, chasing the point of light in the distance. They advanced as rapidly as they dared, stepping lightly to avoid making noise, and feeling out the ground in the darkness. Fortunately, the pathway was firm and even. They were closing the distance.

"*Bleen*!" Alyona muttered as the point of light, which was growing larger as they raced toward it, suddenly winked out, leaving the girls in pitch blackness.

"They went round a corner," Jess hissed, "Hug the right wall and keep going."

Putting their right hands out, they felt for the wall. They both made contact and let it guide them forward.

A scream echoed through the tunnel. It was Meredith.

"Well, hello, *chicas*!" Marcos was speaking. "Right where Leticia said you would be. Where's the blond girl? Oh no you don't!"

There was a brief scrabbling sound, followed by a cry of pain from Meredith. Then a gasp, mingled with the thump of a body falling hard.

Then Marcos spoke again. "Ooh, *chica*, what are you doing with that? Don't you know guns are dangerous? You could hurt someone."

The light returned, and Jessica slowed as the wall bent away abruptly and the tunnel opened into a chamber. It looked as though the miners had dug into a natural chamber. The right wall was visible in the lantern light. The ceiling was lost in the darkness beyond the reach of the lantern light, as was the far side of the room. The left side wall was also lost in darkness, and the floor to the left ended abruptly, dropping into blackness.

"Don't run, *chica*, there's no place to go." Marcos waved the lantern in a broad arc. Between him and Jessica stood a man she did not recognize; he was also carrying a lantern. Ten feet beyond Marcos, a giant of a man stood next to Sarah, who lay prone on the cave floor. His right hand gripped a baseball bat. His left hand held the Colt pistol, which he was shoving into the waist of his pants.

Beyond them, at the edge of the lantern light, a trembling Meredith crawled backward slowly, eyes wide with terror.

Where was Leticia? What had Marcos meant about Leticia saying they would be here?

The giant finished depositing the pistol and reaching down, he gripped Sarah's clothing. She hung limply as he lifted her off the ground; her head flopped to one side. The giant inspected her, then cast her aside like an unwanted ragdoll.

"*Muerta*," he grunted.

"No!" Jessica cried, rushing forward, her fatigue-fogged mind failing to prevent her impulsive act. As she raced toward Sarah's crumpled form, her forward motion was arrested by an arm around her waist when the stranger closest grabbed her.

Marcos whipped his head around to focus on her, his eyes widening in recognition "You? Where did you come from?" His eyes narrowed as he clenched his fist at his side. "You stole the van from me."

"Thank goodness!" Alyona stepped into the light, a look of relief mingled with irritation on her face. "What took you so long?"

All three men turned to face Alyona, eyes wide and mouths agape.

Alyona's softened her expression as she spoke. "I tried to leave a trail for you, but this crazy American was always watching. She never left us alone." She sauntered toward Marcos with an exaggerated swing of her hips."

"Oh well," she continued, her voice taking on a syrupy, seductive tone. "You're here now…" She raised her arms slowly as she moved to stand directly front of Marcos who eyed her warily, his free hand balling into a fist.

Alyona placed her open palms against his chest and slid them up to wrap her arms around his neck. "I would do anything," she paused, licking her upper lip with the tip of her tongue, "for a warm bath and some food."

Marcos's hand unclenched as he leered at her. She leaned in, tilting her head to one side to kiss his neck. Then she moved to his throat. Marcos shifted his gaze to Jessica, and her captor, grinning at Jessica's bewildered stare.

What was Alyona doing?

Marcos stiffened as his eyes widened. He opened his mouth as if to scream, but only managed a strangled gasping cry. The lantern dropped from his hand with a *thunk*, landing upright on the ground at his feet. His hands shook as he reached up, trying to push Alyona away.

"Marcos? *Que pasa*?" asked the man holding Jessica.

Marcos twisted and wrenched desperately, allowing Jessica to see that Alyona had clamped her jaws around Marcos's windpipe.

The giant noticed this as well and lumbered toward them, brandishing his bat. He raised the bat over his head to make a slashing diagonal swing at Alyona's head. As he swung, Alyona deftly twisted, moving her head out of the path of the swing, and moving Marcos's head into it. The bat connected with a loud, solid *thud*. The force of the blow snapped Marcos's head to the side, knocking both Marcos and Alyona to the ground.

Jessica's peripheral vision narrowed as she watched Alyona fall. Everything else went out of focus. She struggled against her captor's grip, twisting and clawing. A scream ripped from her, but she couldn't hear it over the sound of her pulse throbbing in her skull. She registered the pressure, but not the pain of his fingers digging deeply into her arm as he fought to control her.

Alyona rolled away from Marcos and scrambled to her feet. The giant made a quick backhanded swing at her. Alyona tried to evade, but she was unable to move fast enough. She threw her right arm up to fend off the blow.

Jessica flinched as the bat connected, and the sound of bone cracking reverberated in her head. Alyona uttered a cry of pain as she staggered and dropped to her knees.

The man drew back and swung again, catching Alyona in the chest. She groaned in pain as the blow threw her to the ground. She didn't try to get up as the giant man loomed over her, sneering sadistically.

Jessica looked past them to where Meredith crouched, cradling Sarah's head. Meredith's chest expanded and deflated with her measured breaths, and their gazes met. Meredith looked down at Sarah's still form, her shoulders sagging as a look of defeat fell across her face. She closed her eyes and took another deep breath. When her eyes opened again and she looked up toward the behemoth towering over Alyona, the sadness and defeat were replaced by a look of grim determination.

Meredith jumped to her feet and launched forward in a low sprint. The big man was raising the bat high above his head, ready to deliver another blow to Alyona's still form when, with a fierce scream, Meredith drove her shoulder into the man's waist. Meredith was too small, too slight, to really affect the large man, yet it was enough to shift him off balance. He took a staggering step back in an effort to correct.

Meredith continued driving into the man with all the energy she could muster. It was just enough to keep him off balance. He took another staggering step back, a flicker of irritation on his face. He glanced downward at the bothersome little wisp of a girl like she was an annoying fly or gnat. He raised the bat again, preparing to swat her away like a pesky bug.

Another backward step.

The look of irritation shifted to one of surprise, then panic as he stepped backward onto nothingness. He released his grip on the bat and clawed futilely at the open air in front of him as he tumbled backward into the blackness.

Meredith could not slow her forward momentum. Jessica watched helplessly as Meredith disappeared over the edge with the big man, his own fearful scream drowning out Meredith's battle cry.

Jessica's own scream seemed soundless to her in that moment. She tried to run forward to the edge, but she couldn't seem to move, as though some invisible force was holding her back. The man's scream ended with a sickening, cracking, crunching *thud*.

An arm at her throat cut off her scream, and her captor's sinister voice broke into her mind, snapping her focus from the ledge. He was growling something in Spanish, but she couldn't translate it.

The sound of steel slicing through flesh cut whatever he was saying short. The choking grip on her throat released, and Jessica broke free, tumbling forward. She scrambled back to her feet and turned to face the man. He was staring down at his side in surprise. Alyona had crawled over to them and was holding the hilt of Marcos's knife which she'd driven into the man just below his ribs.

Alyona's eyes glazed over, and her hand slipped from the hilt as she collapsed in an unconscious heap at the man's feet.

The man looked up, staring blankly ahead, then turned toward the exit. He took one uncertain step forward, then another. Staggering to his knees, he released his grip on the lantern he was carrying and fell face forward on the ground, unmoving.

Jessica stood for a moment, awash in the devastation around her. The only sound now was her own breathing. Her gaze jumped from Marcos, to Sarah, to Alyona, then to the other man. Finally, she stared at the dark, gaping hole where Meredith and the giant had disappeared. A bombardment of thoughts and emotions threatened to overwhelm her.

She hurried to Sarah and felt for a pulse. Nothing. Tears welled up in her eyes and spilled onto her cheeks. She gently combed her fingers through Sarah's hair.

Shuffling to Marcos, she checked for and found no pulse either. She returned to where Alyona lay. She could faintly hear the sounds of breathing and, in the lamplight, she watched the slow, subtle rise and fall of Alyona's chest.

"Focus, Jess," she whispered, "Clear your head. What are the first steps?" She closed her eyes, piecing together memories from the first aid course. This wasn't exactly the car accident example they had used, but the same steps likely applied. Alyona was breathing, and there was no external bleeding.

"Okay, she's probably in shock. What did they say to do for that? Elevate the legs and feet, keep her warm." Jessica grabbed one of the two lanterns and raced out of the cave to inspect the pickup. It was a navy blue Ford F-150, probably mid to late 90s vintage—an extended cab model. A few minor scuffs and scratches were visible here and there, but the body appeared free of rust and dents. Haphazardly strewn in the bed were several pieces of camping gear, including a bundle of olive canvas which was most likely a tent, and several sleeping bags.

Grabbing two of the sleeping bags, Jessica returned to where Alyona lay. She unrolled one of the bags and folded it in half twice, creating a platform to place under Alyona's lower legs. The other bag she unrolled and unzipped into a blanket, which she used to cover Alyona.

"Okay, what's next?" Jessica looked around again. Her attention was drawn to the two dead men. "Seven men were searching for us, and there are only three here. Where are the others? Do they have another vehicle? Are they all still together or did they split up? Did they know where these three were going?"

Jessica paced around the chamber. The worst case she could imagine was the other four knew where these three had gone, had another vehicle, and would come looking for them in a couple hours if they didn't return. But what to do?

She returned to Alyona's side and moved the sleeping bag to inspect her arm. There was significant swelling near the middle of the forearm, where the bat had struck. She checked it gingerly. Nothing seemed to bend or move in the wrong place. Maybe it wasn't a total break, maybe just a crack.

Jessica pulled Alyona's shirt up to examine her chest. In the lantern light an angry red stripe marked her skin under her bra on the left half of her body. Jessica grimaced. It didn't look good, but there was nothing she could do except hope and pray there were no serious breaks or internal injuries.

She rose to her feet again, running both hands through and pulling her hair. If someone might come looking for them, it wouldn't be safe to just leave Alyona here. But where to take her? Grabbing the lantern, she began to explore deeper in the mine. Two tunnels had been created at the back of the natural cavern. The first one ran straight for thirty yards, with several small pockets along the sides, most less than five feet deep. The tunnel ended in a pile of rubble, suggesting a cave-in had occurred.

The other tunnel ran downward but followed no pattern before ending. Perhaps the miners had been following a vein of ore.

Jessica returned to the cave-in at the end of the first tunnel. Moving a few of the larger rocks revealed a small, low opening. She was able to crawl into it on her belly. The rock above her appeared solid—at least she hoped that was the case. A little farther back, and it opened enough for her to be able to crawl on her knees.

"Risky," Jessica said to herself, "but, better than the alternative, I think." She crawled back out and collected another sleeping bag from the pickup. Returning to Alyona, she uncovered her, unrolled the bag next to her, then she carefully slid Alyona onto the bag.

Grabbing the edge of the bag near Alyona's head, she dragged her into the tunnel. It was awkward trying to manage the bag and the lantern at the same time. Fortunately, the stone floor of the tunnel was quite smooth. Her thoughts wandered to Leticia as she worked. Where was she? What had she done? She shook her head, chasing the thought away. Nothing could be done about it.

Jessica placed the lantern to the side of the small opening then, struggling, she pulled the bag carrying Alyona into the confined space. She collected the open bag and re-covered her.

Returning to the cavern, she collected the second lantern and carried it back, placing it next to Alyona. She turned it off—Alyona had no use for it in her current condition, but if she happened to regain consciousness ... hopefully she would find it.

She returned once more to the cavern and paused to regard Sarah's body. Tears welled up again, as a gasping sob escaped her lips.

Jessica shook her head, clearing her thoughts. She wasn't sure if or how she could get Sarah's body home, but at least she could keep them from getting it. She pulled Sarah's body in next to Alyona, then she breathed a deep sigh as she stroked both girls' hair tenderly.

"I'll be back soon," she promised and crawled back out. She took a few minutes to move debris in front of the opening, concealing it from anyone who might come into the tunnel, then she returned to search the two dead men. She found keys for the truck in Marcos's pocket, and both men had wallets with cash and credit cards. The cards probably wouldn't be safe to use, but she kept them for now, just in case.

Jessica climbed into the driver's seat of the pickup, inserted the key in the ignition and gave it a turn. The engine turned over a few times, complaining like an arthritic old man, then roared to life. She turned the truck around and drove back down to the road.

Taking a chance, Jessica drove in the direction of the town, watching the sides of the road for a place she could safely pull off and hide the pickup. She spotted a small, grassy opening among the trees and drove into it. The opening curved to the left behind a thick cluster of trees which provided excellent cover from the road.

Jessica parked the truck, then walked back to the road. She walked back and forth along the road several times until she was satisfied the truck could not be seen.

Hearing a vehicle approaching from the town, she ran off the road into the trees to hide. An old Ford Bronco came into view. She couldn't make out any faces, but there were four men in the vehicle. Once it passed out of sight, she returned to the road and loped back toward the mine.

She slowed and moved into the cover beside the road as she approached the cave. She could see the Bronco parked near the entrance. So far, the worst case was on point. Quietly she circled the clearing, moving to a better vantage point where she could see the mouth of the cave. There was one man in the open pacing back and forth in front of the cave mouth, a shotgun cradled casually in his arms.

Jessica knelt and remained still while the man walked toward her, then she inched forward toward the hillside when he was walking away. She moved carefully and with patience, just like stalking a deer in the bow hunt. She was within fifteen yards of the mine and nearly parallel to opening when the man stopped pacing and faced the entrance. The other men came into sight, dragging the bodies of their comrades from the mine.

Jessica strained to hear the conversation.

"What happened?"

"Don't know."

"Bernardo?"

"Not here."

"And the girls?"

"No."

"You think Bernardo killed them and took the girls?"

"Why? Where?"

"Los Zetas? He was new blood, no? Maybe he was a spy."

"Maybe." The speaker sounded uncertain as he scratched at the back of his neck.

"The girls couldn't do this. They certainly couldn't take Bernardo prisoner. He's a monster."

"Maybe Leticia lied? Maybe they were rescued by militia? Or maybe Los Zetas got them?"

"Militia? The police don't bother us."

"So Los Zetas probably, and Bernardo's a prisoner. Or a spy."

"Spy, I think. Marcos was a coward, if they could take anyone alive, it would be him."

"We better tell Angel; have everybody start looking for Bernardo and the truck."

"What about Leticia?"

There was a pause. "Have someone watch her, see if anybody contacts her. Maybe she is working for Los Zetas too, no?"

The men loaded the bodies into the Bronco, then they drove away.

Chapter Fifteen

"Water," Jessica shook her head to clear her thoughts, "and food. And fast."

She stood up, moved onto the trail, then hesitated. She scrunched her face into a frown and bit her lower lip, staring pensively down the trail. She glanced back toward the mine entrance. Resolve filled her, and she started forward, first at a walk, then a jog.

She reached the truck before sundown. Digging through the back of the truck, she found a pair of dirty, well-worn jeans and an old black hoodie. She stuffed them into her pack, then continued toward the town, listening, ready to jump off the road at the first sound of a vehicle.

The town was closer than she expected, and she arrived before dark. It wasn't a particularly large town. The road on which she was jogging led right into the main street, where she could see a gas station and a small store close to her. She took cover in the trees and watched the few people who were about.

"The gray man isn't invisible," said the voice the father of one of her high school friends in her mind, "The gray man is uninteresting, forgettable." He was a bit off, in her mind, a doomsday prepper—the bomb shelter in the backyard kind. But he did know a lot; some of it fairly useful.

"Observe the people, how they walk, how they carry themselves. Watch where they go, what they do. The trick is to be so boringly ordinary that nobody gives you a first glance, much less a second one."

Jessica pulled the jeans and the hoodie out of the pack. She pulled the jeans on over her own. They were a little long on her and a bit baggy, but passable. The hoodie was also big on her. She experimented with the pack, wearing the straps backward and long, so the bulk of the pack was at her belly. With the hoodie pulled on, the pack looked like a pot belly, distorting her feminine features and giving her the appearance of a slightly overweight boy.

She scooped a handful of dust from the road and holding it her hands, began to spit—it was hard to work up much saliva, as dehydrated as she was. She finally managed enough to turn the handful of dust into mud. She rubbed the mixture on her face and her hands. She was reasonably tan from the past several days walking and working in the sun, so the dirt was mainly to roughen her complexion.

Jessica tucked her hair into the back of her shirt and out of sight in the hoodie. She wasn't sure if long hair was an in thing for guys here, and her brunette hair wasn't dark enough to pass as native. She scrutinized herself, looking for anything out of place—anything that might draw unwanted attention. She wished she had a mirror; it was hard to know exactly how she looked from a distance. Satisfied she had done everything possible with the resources available, she stepped onto the road.

She hunched her shoulders and tilted her head down. Putting her hands in the hoodie pocket, she adopted a slow, shuffling gait. She was careful not to look at anyone directly while keeping an eye on the people around her in her periphery, watching for any indication she was attracting undue attention. She grew more relaxed as she continued forward, drawing barely a glance from anyone.

Casually she strolled into the small corner-store. Looking at the food on the shelves made her acutely aware of how hungry she was. It was a struggle to resist grabbing everything in sight. She forced herself to act disinterested as she walked down the aisles. She grabbed several bottles of water, a couple cans of what appeared to be a beef stew, a bunch of bananas, a few oranges, and a head of lettuce. She found a bottle of Tylenol, and, thinking of Alyona, she picked it up as well.

She added up the price in her head, then making sure no one was looking, she pulled enough money out of the wallet and slipped it into a pocket, returning the wallet to another pocket.

As she walked to the checkout counter, she could see the clerk, engrossed in a book. Keeping her head down, she placed the items on the counter, then stuck her hands back into the hoodie pocket and feigned interest in a magazine on the rack behind her. When the clerk gave the total, she dug the loose bills from her pocket and handed them to the clerk, hoping she was close in her quick estimate. The clerk, a middle-aged woman with a weathered face, flicked through the bills, punched the keypad on the register, then opened the till. She deposited the bills and selected two small bills and a few coins, which she offered to Jessica. Jessica took them and stuffed them in her pocket.

"*Gracias*," she mumbled, deepening her voice, and grabbing the bag of groceries. As she exited the store, she glanced back and breathed a sigh of relief; the clerk had returned to reading her book.

Jessica continued her slow shuffling walk until she was sure she was out of sight of anyone in the town, then she slipped into the trees, looking back to see if there was any change in activity that might suggest someone had taken an interest in her. All appeared the same as before she had entered the town. Satisfied, she peeled off the cumbersome extra layer of clothing and stuffed the garments and groceries into the pack, keeping out a banana and one bottle of water.

After readjusting the straps for comfort, she struck out at a fast walk. She peeled the banana and ate as she went, taking sips of water between bites. Alternating a sip of water and a bite of banana helped control the urge to devour the banana or chug the bottle of water.

It was dark when she reached the pickup, and it was hard to decide if she was more hungry, thirsty, or tired. She ate one more banana, then curled up on the back seat and fell asleep.

"Don't leave me! Don't leave me!" Jessica snapped awake, her eyes already wet with tears. She'd had the Emily-Meredith dream again, and it brought the events of yesterday—what Meredith had done—into crisp detail in her mind. It was several minutes before she stopped crying.

Jessica had slept late despite the sunlight, and she felt rested as a result. She ate an orange and a third banana for breakfast, then she hiked back to the mine. It was nearly noon when she reached the entrance. She hesitated outside, reluctant to go back into that chamber, where memories were still too fresh, too tender. A twinge of guilt washed over her. Alyona was still back there, in who knows what condition. Had she left her there to die alone? Jessica exhaled sharply, shaking her head to clear the thought. No, Alyona was tough, resilient. She was still alive. She had to be.

Jessica breathed in deeply, and exhaled. She just needed a few more minutes to prepare herself. She gathered some wood and started a small fire. She used her knife to stab a hole in the top of one of the cans of stew, then dropped it into the fire.

There was something soothing about a campfire. The crackle and hiss of tiny bits of moisture in the wood escaping, the dancing flicker of the flame, the smell of wood smoke in her clothes. Jessica sighed, her dire circumstances momentarily set aside as she reveled in the memories of past campfires with family and friends.

Another scent caught her attention, drawing her back to the present. The aroma of the cooking stew wafted up from the can and into her nostrils. Her stomach gurgled in anticipation. She waited impatiently for the first bubbles to break on the surface of the thick gravy, her mouth watering in anticipation.

She let it boil for a few minutes, then kicked the embers away with her booted foot. Using the hoodie as a potholder, she enlarged the hole in the top of the can with the knife.

"Wonder if buying a spoon would've attracted too much attention?" she murmured after making a couple futile stabs into the gravy with the knife. The contents were too soft. She settled for tilting the can slightly and scooping some of the contents on the edge of the blade. She nibbled at the edges, checking the temperature, then took a bite.

The can was empty quicker than it should have been, but she was in much better spirits now, with a full belly. She took a deep breath, turned the lantern on, and entered the mine. She avoided looking at the drop-off, hustling past to the end of the tunnel. She moved the debris she had used to cover the entrance to the hideout and crawled in. Alyona was still breathing, which was a relief.

"Hey, Alyona," Jessica spoke softly, "How ya' feelin'?"

No response. Jessica furrowed her brow; she reached out and gently touched Alyona's forehead. She felt warm to the touch. Jessica folded the sleeping bag down to uncover Alyona's torso.

"You're running a touch hot there, girl." She pulled a water bottle out of the bag and opened it. Pouring some water on her hands, she gently wiped Alyona's forehead, eliciting a groan from her.

"Yeah," Jessica cupped her right hand and poured some

water in it, "you probably shoulda picked on someone your own size."

She held her hand just above Alyona's lips and let a few drops fall through.

"By way of good news, we have some money. Between them, those two were carrying a fair bit of cash. I managed to sneak into town last night and get some stuff from the store: food, water, and Tylenol for you, when you're conscious again. I imagine you're going to want something stronger but," Jessica shrugged her shoulders apologetically, "it's all I could do for now. I'll go back tonight and see if I can find anything better. Nice thing about Mexico, even some of the small stores are open late. Probably 'cause of the whole siesta thing, I guess. I'm going to buy as much water as I can carry, and a bit more food. I'll have to be careful not to draw attention, but I'll load up as much as I can."

Jessica let a few more droplets through. "We have a pickup too. They'll be looking for it, so we'd have to be real careful, but maybe I can change it up a bit, get a couple cans of spray paint, kick a few dents in it. Maybe we could get enough distance to get out of their search radius."

Jessica sat for a while longer, talking and administering water by droplets onto Alyona's lips. When her hand was empty, she grabbed the pack and began to unload it. "I'm going to leave all this stuff here, so I'll have more room to carry supplies. You're welcome to help yourself to the fruit or water, if you feel up to it before I get back.

"I'm going to turn the extra lantern on as dim as it'll go, so you aren't stuck in the dark. It's a nice LED lantern, so it should go for days, unless the batteries are already out. Maybe I'll pick up some extra batteries, just in case. I'll try to find a can opener too—might as well be comfortable and save the wear and tear on the knife."

Jessica sat for a while longer, hoping for some response from Alyona. There was nothing except irregular breathing.

"I better get going," Jessica said, the silence becoming uncomfortable, "Easy to lose track of time in here. I need to hit town right as it gets dark, so I have plenty of time to collect supplies. See ya soon."

Jessica crawled back out, covered the crack again and exited the mine. It was early afternoon, giving her plenty of time to get back to the truck, dig around for some sacks or anything to carry more supplies, and still get to the town around sunset.

She found a couple of burlap sacks in the pickup which would work great for lugging groceries. She could probably fill the sacks with more than she could carry, which the large quantity of supplies would be great, but dragging a couple of burlap sacks through town would probably be memorable for people. She also wanted to avoid making too many trips to town, as that would also increase the chances of getting caught. Maybe she would fill one bag, take it to the edge of town and hide it, then go fill the other bag. From there she could drag them if need be.

She took a moment to appraise the truck. Could she disguise it enough to drive it? A couple cans of spray paint would change the color, but it would be pretty obvious it had been painted. She could probably put some pretty good dents in it. Could she use an ugly brown spray paint and get it close enough to rust-colored to pass a casual inspection? What about removing the bed? She'd taken a bed off a truck with her brothers once—on the farm. That might change the profile enough to be overlooked. She'd need tools for that though. Could she buy them in this town? And how would she lift it off? She might get away with tying a rope from the bed to a tree and driving out from under it. She might also damage a tire trying that. She sighed, shaking her head. No, better stick with paint and dents. She stuffed the sacks into the backpack and started for town.

Jessica donned her disguise and entered the town as the sun was setting. Deciding to save the grocery store for last in case the clerk recognized her, she found a pharmacy which had over-the-counter Tramadol and purchased a bottle. She also picked up a shoulder sling, compression bandages and some tape.

She found another grocery store a bit farther into town, and she took advantage of it to buy the first load of supplies before returning to the other store for the second load. The clerk from the previous night was there, but she didn't give any indication she recognized Jessica.

The combined sacks were quite heavy. Jessica found a sturdy branch of reasonable length with a spot near the middle that was comfortable resting across her shoulders. She used a bit of rope to tie one of the sacks to each end of the branch, then positioned the branch across her neck and shoulders. She stood up slowly, checking the balance of the bags as they lifted off the ground. After a few adjustments she made the trek back to the pickup.

She had to stop and rest several times, and she chided herself for biting off more than she could chew, but she finally made it back to the truck, exhausted and aching. She loaded the supplies onto the floor in front of the back seat, then collapsed on the back seat.

Jessica lay still for a moment, then sighed, "Hey God, I really don't feel like praying tonight, which Momma says means I probably really need to. Plus, I haven't missed since that one night.

"I really hope you can help me understand all this. I mean …I felt like I was guided to rescue my friends and the other two but …if they all wind up dead, what was the point?"

She paused, blinking away fresh tears. "Please help me understand."

She lay still again, waiting, hoping for some response, until she drifted off to sleep.

The next morning Jessica packed several bottles of water, a loaf of bread, some fruit, and a couple cans of food into the backpack. When she returned to the mine, she stopped briefly at the entrance and prepared herself for the worst. She took a deep breath and steeled herself, then entered.

"I'm back," she announced as she crawled into the hidden chamber. As she sat upright, she widened her eyes and gasped. Tears flooded her eyes.

Sarah sat next to Alyona, dabbing at her forehead with a moist piece of cloth torn from the bottom of her skirt.

"Y-you? H-how?" Jessica stammered. "I thought you were dead!"

"I..." Sarah looked down, her voice so soft Jessica could barely hear her. "I think I was."

Jessica rushed to Sarah, catching her in a fierce embrace. Tears flowed freely as she buried her face in Sarah's neck and squeezed her waist, inhaling the scent of her, feeling her warmth—feeling the rise and fall of her chest with each breath, drinking in the evidences that Sarah truly was alive.

Jessica didn't want to be the first to pull away, but she needed to know. Lifting her head, she looked her friend in the eyes and asked, "what happened?"

Sarah released Jessica and turned her attention back to Alyona, placing the bit of cloth on her forehead again. "Leticia was worried the men were camping right outside the cave. She suggested we leave a code for you to find us, and then we'd go to the mine to hide. They had to carry me a lot."

Sarah winced, touching her hand to her temple. "I was getting worse, and we didn't have any food or water, so Leticia said she would go to the town—to her home—and get some food for us. After that I was kind of... in and out... I guess. I remember hearing some crying or screaming, and I remember feeling someone pick me up, but I couldn't open my eyes or move. I heard a man's voice say something and then I remember falling ...or flying, and a strange feeling. I don't know, maybe it was a dream..."

"Go on," Jessica urged.

"The pain stopped, and I was standing up, looking at Alyona, and... me. Then this old lady appeared—like ...an old-timer lady. She had a pioneer dress or something. She told me I had to choose. She said if I wanted, she would take me home..." Sarah stared at her lap and twisted her fingers together, "or, I could stay here, and help Alyona and you. Then the pain was back, and I heard you saying something to Alyona before you left."

"How's she doin'?" Jessica asked.

"She's woken up a couple times. I gave her some Tylenol, and she drank almost a whole bottle of water. We split an orange, and she had a bite of a banana."

Sarah lay back to rest while Jessica related her adventures. Then Jessica went out and heated a can of stew over a small fire. She brought it in and watched as Sarah devoured it, along with half a loaf of bread. The color returned to her cheeks and her eyes brightened with every bite. Jessica settled for a few bites of the bread and some fruit.

"Can I ...have some food, or are you two planning to...to watch me starve to death?" Alyona panted. Her attempt at levity only partly covered her struggle to breathe and the inflection of pain in her voice.

"You mean you want us to fan you and drop grapes in your mouth or something? Slacker!" Jessica quipped.

Alyona's gasping chuckle was cut off abruptly by a groan. "Please don't make me laugh, I really can't handle that much pain just now."

"Sorry." Jessica winced. "I'll go heat up another can of stew."

Once the stew was heated and consumed, Jessica checked the state of Alyona's side and arm. She created a splint from the materials she'd purchased, and she put the shoulder sling on and adjusted it to hold and immobilize Alyona's arm. Alyona grumbled about it, yet in the end acknowledged it did alleviate some of the pain.

"All right," Jessica said as she tucked the now emptied burlap sacks into the backpack, "you two gonna be okay for a while now? I need to go see about disfiguring a truck. I'll leave the food and supplies, and I'll bring some more tomorrow."

"Are you going back to the town?" Sarah asked.

"Not tonight." Jessica shook her head. "Maybe in a couple days, I'll make one more supply run before we make a run for it."

"Be careful." Sarah reached out to gently touch Jessica's leg.

"You too, Sare-Bear." Jessica smiled. She picked up her lantern and turned to go, then paused. "Oh yeah, I have spare batteries for the lantern too."

She pulled off the pack and dug to the bottom of it, "Here you go," she said, handing the batteries to Sarah, "See ya later."

Chapter Sixteen

Jessica examined the truck critically. She had used the back of the hatchet to break off all the chrome trim, and to hammer several dents in the sides. It was a start, but not enough. She chewed on her lower lip, considering. There was still time to make a quick trip to the town again, but would one more trip be pushing her luck? She inhaled deeply, held her breath for a few seconds, then exhaled.

"Quick trip," Jess muttered, "In and out."

She grabbed the backpack and her disguise and took off at a quick lope.

When she arrived at the town and transformed once more into her alter ego, she had to wait for nearly an hour in her hiding place. Three teenage boys were milling about, laughing, harassing teenage girls, and pushing and hitting each other. She was fairly certain her disguise fell into the category of their natural prey, and if she happened to be seen by them, she would end up attracting all kinds of unwanted attention.

They finally grew bored of their entertainments and moved on to find new hunting grounds. Jessica heaved a sigh of relief and hurried into the town. She walked down the street until she found the small hardware store that she had seen the night before. Entering it, she went straight to the paint aisle and selected a few cans of primer gray spray paint, and a couple in forest green.

She glanced at the other colors available to her. With some brown, red and orange paint, it might be possible to make simulated rust spots. How artistic was she feeling? Would it be worth trying? If it didn't work out, would the resulting mess attract attention?

"*Puedo ayudarle?*"

Jessica froze as she realized the question was directed at her. A middle-aged man was standing to her left, staring suspiciously. She hadn't been paying attention, what did he say?

"*Puedo ayudarle?*" the man repeated with some irritation.

"*No, gracias.*" Jessica inclined her head slightly to acknowledge the man, but not so much as to give him a clear view of her face.

As she glanced back to the shelves, she noticed a can of paint stripper. A new idea forming, she grabbed it and some brushes. She wandered down the aisle in search of a scraper. The man was following her, watching her closely. She located a scraper with a three-inch blade and a wire brush next to each other. Grabbing both with a trembling hand, she turned and made a beeline for the register. As she paid for the supplies, the man watched from a distance. Once the clerk reached out with change, he lost interest and wandered away. Jessica breathed a sigh of relief as she exited the store.

She stopped at the pharmacy to purchase a bottle of hydrogen peroxide, and then back to the grocery store once more to get vinegar and salt.

As she walked out of the store, she met the gaze of a familiar young woman and froze. Leticia was shuffling toward the store. Before Jessica could react, her eyes widened in recognition, then panic. Thinking quickly, Jessica smiled, opened her arms, and took Leticia in a warm embrace. Leticia went statue rigid.

"I'm so glad you're okay!" Jessica spoke softly into Leticia's ear. "I was so worried."

Leticia trembled in her arms as Jessica scanned the area for anyone who might be taking an interest. Half a block back, skulking behind a display of clothing, she saw a man staring intently at them. His left arm was in a sling, and he seemed to be favoring his right leg as he shuffled. Was he the victim of her spike trap? For the moment he remained where he was.

Jessica turned her head slightly so the hood would better conceal her face. "Do you know you're being followed?"

She felt Leticia start, and she gripped her tighter, preventing her from turning. "Don't look. You'll give us away if you do."

Leticia's trembling grew more violent. "*Lo siento,*" she whispered. "*Lo siento. Lo siento.*" She was sobbing now.

"Hey, hey, hey!" Jessica spoke reassuringly, "It's gonna be okay."

"Sarah was so sick. I went to my home to get food and medicine, and then they broke our door! They said they would hurt my little sister and ..."

"Leticia." Jessica drew back, placing her hand on Leticia's shoulders. She stared directly into Leticia's eyes. "It's okay. You had to protect your family. I understand. It's okay."

"*Y tus amigas*?" Leticia asked hopefully.

"Sarah's still alive. Doing better in fact. Alyona's in pretty bad shape." Jessica stopped, her throat catching, and she fought back the tears threating to spill over her lower lids; she needed to keep a clear head. Leticia's eyes widened, then filled with tears.

"It's not your fault," Jessica insisted. "They did this. Not you."

Jessica glanced over Leticia's shoulder, where the man was limping toward them, his hand fumbling with his waistband.

"Look," Jessica spoke quickly, "I gotta go, are you gonna be okay?"

Leticia gazed at her with wide, pleading eyes, and Jessica knew the answer to the question. Sweet, timid, little Leticia would not be capable of subterfuge.

"That guy is gonna wanna know who I am," Jessica sighed, "If you slap my face then walk away, you can say I was some stranger that was trying to flirt with you. Can you do that?"

"I-I think so," Leticia said.

"Okay, you only get one chance so make it look good! Do it now!"

The slap stung more than Jessica had anticipated. Leticia turned on her heel and stormed away as Jessica shook her head to try clear the ringing. She looked around, not focusing on anyone, but keeping an eye on the man tailing Leticia. He was moving rapidly to intercept her.

"Who was that?" the man demanded as he grabbed Leticia's wrist.

"I don't know," she replied timidly.

Jessica slipped around the corner of the store where she was out of sight, but where she could still hear the conversation. She reached into her bag, fumbling around until her hand closed on a can of spray paint. Gripping the can, she let the bag drop to the ground.

"What did he want?" the man persisted.

"H-he was f-flirting with me."

Jessica popped the cap off the can and gave an experimental press of the button to ensure paint was flowing. Can at the ready, she peered around the corner.

"You're lying!"

Leticia recoiled from the man, shaking her head with wide eyes. "No."

"Tell me the truth or your little sister is coming back with you!"

"I swear I never saw that boy before!" Leticia wailed.

Jessica crept from behind the corner and slunk toward the two.

"You stupid little..." The man raised his hand, preparing to strike Leticia across the face.

"Hey!" Jessica marched up to the man. He turned his face toward her, and she raised the paint can, pressing the button and firing a stream of paint into his eyes from mere inches away. He let out a strangled cry, lifting his hand instinctively to cover his face.

In one smooth motion, Jessica dropped the paint, placed her right hand on his shoulder, and drove her knee into his groin. She reached to his waistband with her left hand, finding and gripping the hilt of the pistol he had been fumbling for earlier. She drew it out as he dropped to the ground.

Not wanting to take chances, she kicked out hard at his face, connecting with his nose. His eyes rolled back, and he went limp.

There were only a few people nearby, but they were all screaming and running for the nearest shop door now.

"Sorry," Jessica said to Leticia through gritted teeth as she picked up the paint can, grabbed her by the wrist and towed her into the darkness back to where she had dropped the bag of supplies.. She checked the safety on the pistol and shoved it into her own waistband, then she retrieved the bag from the ground

"So much for a quick trip," Jess muttered. Things were spiraling out of control, "Leticia, we need to get to your house. Fast."

"What?"

"Mr. Limpy is gonna call his buddies and go there to make trouble for your family. We need to warn them. Which way do we go?"

Leticia led the way through back streets, moving at a fast jog. They were just rounding the final corner when a vehicle raced down the street and skidded to a halt in front of Leticia's home. The man stepped out of the vehicle and limped toward the house. Jessica grabbed Leticia's hand and gave it a squeeze, in part to offer reassurance, and also to keep Leticia from panicking and drawing attention to the two of them.

Jessica let out a small snort of frustration. "Can't catch a break today."

They slowed to a brisk walk, eyes alert as they approached the house. A woman yelled and a door slammed. They ran up to the house until they were close enough to make out the conversation.

Jessica didn't catch all the conversation, and Leticia was too absorbed to be helpful. She identified three distinct voices; two men and a woman, she assumed it was Limpy and Leticia's parents.

She caught bits of the woman's pleading. It sounded like she was invoking a promise that had been made—that the men would leave the family alone if they helped them find the girls.

Limpy was yelling back. Jessica only caught a few words: "traitor", and "Los Zetas" and something about butchering a pig. No, butchering like a pig. Jessica gripped Leticia's hand tighter to prevent her from running into the house. She looked around quickly, trying to put together a plan.

"Does your dad have tools?" Jessica asked, pointing to a small shed on the side of the house. Leticia nodded, her eyes still riveted to the small window. Jessica grabbed Leticia's head in both hands and forced her to make eye contact.

"Hammer, screwdriver, a bat or shovel or heavy stick, and some rope, and something to make fire!" Jessica said slowly and clearly, giving time for Leticia to register each item.

Leticia nodded and raced away.

Jessica crept to the man's car. It was parked on the sloped dirt road in front of the house, the front facing downhill. It was unlocked, but the key was not in it.

In less than a minute Leticia returned, her small arms overflowing with all the items Jessica had asked for. However, the request for something to make fire was met with a bag of charcoal and a bottle of lighter fluid. Not quite what Jess had asked for, but combined with the fire steel still tucked in the backpack she was carrying, it would do.

"*Gracias,*" Jess said as she grabbed the hammer and screwdriver. Crawling under the vehicle, she located the gas tank and placed the tip of the screwdriver against it. Jessica smacked the back of the screwdriver with the hammer. Several times, she worried the man might hear it and come to investigate before she was ready, but the yelling seemed to drown out her noise.

A solid hit caused the screwdriver to puncture the tank. Jessica yanked it free and scooted back as gasoline gurgled out onto the ground.

Standing up again, she removed the gas cap, and the gasoline began to flow more freely from the hole.

Jessica grabbed the bottle of lighter fluid and strode to the front of the car. Looking underneath she could see the puddle of gasoline growing and moving forward, following the slope of the ground. Jessica aimed the lighter fluid under the car and sprayed, creating a line of fluid out from under the car and several feet away. Tossing the bottle aside, she pulled the fire steel from the pack and struck a spark to the lighter fluid. The flame raced along the line toward the car.

"Shovel!" Jessica barked as she jogged toward Leticia. A bewildered Leticia held out the shovel in trembling hands. Jessica grabbed it and raced up to the house, positioning herself to the left of the door, just as the flame reached the pool of gasoline. There was a loud *whoomph!*—not quite an explosion, and a bright flash of light as the flames leaped up, surrounding the car. Jessica took a batting stance and brought the shovel to the ready.

A strangled cry came from the house, and the door opened. Limpy barreled out of the house at a surprisingly fast pace. Jessica stepped in and swung with all the force she could muster. The flat back of the shovel blade connected with a resounding clang on Limpy's nose, arresting the forward momentum of the upper half of his body. His head snapped back, and his feet went out from under him, rising above his head as it struck the cinderblock porch with a *thud*.

"Rope!" Jessica yelled, holding her hand out. Leticia ran to Jessica's side holding the rope in front of her. Jessica took the coil, then grabbing one of Mr. Limpy's arms, she gave a rough tug and flipped him onto his stomach.

She deftly tied a slip knot in the rope, around the wrist of the arm she was holding, then she grabbed the other arm and slipped it into the loop as well. Shifting the knot to sit between the man's wrists, she fed the rope through his arms, then between his hands, creating loops which covered the knot, and at the same time removing any free space in the loop which might allow him to work his hands free.

Once satisfied the arms were contained, she reached back and grabbed a booted foot, pulling it to the tightly bound arms. She wrapped the rope around his leg several times—just above the boot. The process of trussing him up conjured a memory of calf roping. Grabbing the other leg, she repeated the process, finishing up with a couple loops around both legs, and a knot that he couldn't hope to reach.

As she stepped back to appraise her work, Leticia's father came through the doorway.

"Leticia, what have you done?" His whole body was trembling, and his face displayed equal measures of fear and anger. "You've killed us all!"

"I'm sorry," Jessica interjected, interposing herself between father and daughter, her arms spread wide in a placating gesture. "It's my fault. I wasn't going to come into town today, I shouldn't have—but I did. If I hadn't been in town, Leticia wouldn't have seen me, and Limpy wouldn't have thought I was a rival gang member meeting up with Leticia. I am so sorry."

Leticia's father was brought up short. Jessica's intercession took the fire out of him. He held his trembling hands out with his palms up. "They said they'd leave our family alone if we helped them get the other girls back. They said Leticia wouldn't have to go back."

"Forgive my skepticism," Jessica said as she laid her hand on his shoulder," but I seriously doubt they intended to keep their word."

Leticia's father looked at Jessica, as if only just seeing her. His eyes widened, and his face went pale. "I d-didn't mean…"

"It's okay," Jessica said, "You're trying to protect your family. You'd do almost anything to protect your kids." Jessica thought of her father, and she was abruptly awash in a dozen different emotions. She had called home nearly every night since they'd been in Mexico. Her dad must be worried sick by now. She missed him. She swallowed hard against the lump forming in her throat and blinked away the burgeoning tears.

Leticia's father shuffled his feet, looking about apprehensively, then his indignation returned. "What am I supposed to do? Huh? What do I do about this?" He gestured toward the bound man and the burning car.

"We take a few things," Leticia's mother said from the doorway, "we take our girls, we get in our car, and we leave."

Her husband looked at her uncertainly, his mouth agape as he searched for a response. "What about our son?"

She raised her hand as if warding off evil, and she clicked her tongue. "Our son is one of *them.*" She spat the last word, gesturing at the bound man the ground. "Our son is the reason Leticia was taken."

"Where will we go?" He slumped his shoulders in resignation.

"Hermosillo. I have a cousin there. He can help us find work, and maybe he will take us in for a while. Also,

Los Templarios don't work there, and they don't have influence there."

"You should probably hurry," Jessica said, looking at the flaming car. "I'm afraid I attracted some attention. Again, sorry."

Leticia's mother waved her hand. "It couldn't be helped. Are you coming with us?"

"Thank you, but I need to get back to the others. Are you okay? Do you need help getting ready?"

"No. Do you need something? Food? Clothes? Blankets?" Leticia's mother was in full matronly swing. "Aye, you two," She directed a stern commanding look at Leticia and her father, "why are you standing there still? Get your things, get Rosa, and get in the car!" She turned back to Jessica, asking, "what do you need?"

Jessica thought for a moment. "Do you have a map? Or could you tell me how to get to Mexico City? It's not very far from here, is it? Are there roads people don't use much so I am less likely to run into police or anybody, really?"

Leticia's mother gave her a shrewd look. "Come inside a moment, I think I can help you."

Jessica helped Leticia and her little sister gather their clothes and a few trinkets and carry them out to the car, while Leticia's mother scrawled directions on a piece of paper. She would occasionally pause to direct the girls as their packing efforts progressed to the kitchen and living room.

After several minutes, Leticia's mother finished her rudimentary map and directions, and she called Jessica over to review them. Jessica thanked her profusely, hugged each of the family members goodbye, then stepped out the door. The fire had died down. Jessica was a little surprised there were no emergency vehicles outside, but it was probably for the best. Less attention just now would make it easier for the family to slip away.

Limpy had been moved behind the house, out of sight of any curious onlookers. The street, however, was empty. Evidently the neighbors preferred not to be involved. Jessica paused for a moment. How long before reinforcements arrived and found Limpy? What would he tell them?

What might she be able to learn from him? She should get going, get as much of a head start as possible. Maybe she could buy a little more time though.

She walked to the back of the house where Limpy lay. He was conscious again, struggling to move. His efforts yielded no results, however. Jess had trussed him up effectively, and Leticia's father had added a piece of duct tape over his mouth to keep him from yelling for help.

Jessica crouched in front of him. He looked up, glaring, but his eyes widened with surprise when she removed the hood, exposing her face.

"No," she said smiling, "No Los Zetas were here. Leticia wasn't working with or for anyone. This," Jessica gestured expansively with her hands, "was me." Then she pointed to the house. "She was just in the wrong place at the wrong time."

She inched closer. "Do you mind if I ask you a few questions? I'll take the tape off. Of course, if you make a noise, I'll have to shut you up."

He stopped moving and stared at her. Jessica reached down and peeled the duct tape off.

"You don't by chance have my wallet, do you?" she asked.

He stared at her incredulously for a moment, then shook his head. "We take the money, and throw the rest away."

Jess raised an eyebrow. "Credit cards?"

"We have a group in Acapulco, they take them, harvest them, and dump them."

"What about my phone?"

"Gone."

"So, you don't know who I am?" Jessica looked up. She glanced back down to see him staring at the house darkly.

"Oh," Jessica chuckled softly, "she doesn't know who I am. Like I said, wrong place, wrong time. Poor girl, her family has to run and hide, 'cause you jumped to the wrong conclusion."

"You're hiding with them?"

"Oh no. I'm going home. Speaking of which," she fixed the tape back over his mouth, cutting off his startled protest, "I have a plane to catch, in Acapulco. Day after tomorrow. Thanks for the talk."

Jessica stood up. Pulling the hood over her head, she ran into the darkness.

Chapter Seventeen

Jessica was exhausted when the sun intruded on her sleep. No more than four hours had passed since she reached the pickup. She had fallen asleep before even settling into the back seat. Groaning, she ducked her head into the hoodie to block the sun.

"Get up, Jess," she berated herself, "gotta get moving." She dragged herself out of the truck and set to work pouring paint stripper on the hood and sides of it.

As the paint stripper worked its magic, she pulled the tailgate from the back of the truck. She set it on the ground and spray-painted on three coats of forest green, letting it dry between coats. The finished product was rather too matte to pass any but the most cursory inspection at a distance, yet since this was just one component of the larger illusion of an old beat-up truck with mismatched parts, with any luck anyone looking at it would simply ignore that small detail in favor of keeping with the overall theme.

And hopefully they wouldn't ever be close enough to anyone long enough for them to give such minor details a second thought.

Satisfied with the tailgate, she set about the arduous task of scrubbing the paint and paint stripper off the truck with the wire brush and paint scraper.

It was nearing noon and the hot sun beat down on her, even with the partial shade provided by the trees. Jessica lifted an aching arm to swipe the beads of sweat off her forehead. The acrid fumes of the paint stripper burned in her nostrils, in spite of working in the open air. She tried recalling if she had seen face masks or respirators in the store. Not that it mattered now. She couldn't go back.

"Don't try this at home, kids," she mumbled, stopping to pull her shirt off and tie it around her head, covering her mouth and nose as a sort of makeshift filter.

I doubt this will help at all. Now instead of dying from the fumes, I'll die from sunburn, and fumes.

Sometime late in the afternoon, Jessica stepped back to rest her aching muscles and critique her handiwork. She smiled as she studied the hood which was cleared to the bare metal. The sides were a less impressive patchwork of stubborn paint and exposed metal. However, she had used all the paint stripper, and she had invested more time than was wise as well. The sooner they got underway, the better.

Jessica opened the jug of vinegar and poured some onto the hood and sides of the vehicle. She decanted the hydrogen peroxide and salt into the jug with the remaining vinegar, capped the bottle, and shook it vigorously to mix it. She then proceeded to pour and splash it on the exposed metal, taking care to avoid splashing any on herself. By the time she had finished working her way along the sides of the truck, the hood was already beginning to form several rust spots.

Jessica briefly surveyed her work, then looked up at the sky. Only a couple hours 'til sundown. She quickly replaced the tailgate, threw the stray materials into the pickup bed, and climbed into the driver's seat. She started the engine and drove to the mine, backing the pickup to the entrance.

She turned on the lantern and walked swiftly back to where her friends were concealed. "Good evening, ladies!" she called out as she approached so as not to startle them.

"Is it evening?" Sarah asked, "how many days? Kinda lost track of time sitting here in the pitch black."

"Just one day," Jessica replied, dropping to her hands and knees, "and you do have a lantern, you know."

"Saving batteries," Sarah answered. There was a click and light appeared from the hole.

"Fair enough. How's everybody feeling?" Jessica pushed her own lantern forward and crawled into the chamber.

"Hungry. Thirsty."

"Yeah, sorry." Jessica massaged the back of her neck. "Things went a bit sideways last night, kinda threw me off."

"What happened?" Concern filled Sarah's voice.

"I went to town after I said I wasn't going. Decided I would get some stuff to try and camouflage the truck. I ran into Leticia."

"Did you execute the little traitor?" Alyona said, her voice dripping with bitterness.

"No, but I did get in a bit of a tussle with the guy who was spying on her for the Templarios."

"Spying on her?! She led them to us!"

"She was forced to, she was given a choice to give you up, or watch her family get killed."

There was a pause. "So," Alyona continued slowly, "What did you do to the spy?"

"Lit his car on fire and broke his nose. Twice."

Alyona let out a sound somewhere between a chuckle and a snort. "Where is he now?"

"Tied up in Leticia's back yard." Jessica sighed, "Well, it was their back yard. They are on the run now."

"You think he will come looking for us here? He knows you're alive, yes?"

"He knows it was me, and he might check here. I told him we were headed back to Acapulco to catch a plane. If we're lucky his gang mates will find him and believe him. But, even then, they might check here first. That's why I have the truck out front. You up for a short walk, and a long drive?"

"Sounds like I better be."

"Where are we going?" Sarah asked.

"The American Embassy in Mexico City," Jessica said, "I've got directions to get there taking back roads. Do you think you are okay to move, Alyona?"

"Sure." Alyona shifted, attempting to lean forward. She managed a couple inches before she hissed and winced. "I think ...you'll need to give me a hand."

"How about you lay still, and Sarah and I will drag you out of here and into the main cave? Then maybe you can give walking a try."

Sarah and Jessica grabbed hold of Alyona's sleeping bag and pulled, dragging it along the cave floor with a soft hissing sound. Once they were back in the main area, they gingerly helped Alyona to her feet, mindful of her arm and ribs. It was tricky and involved considerable grimacing and groaning. Once Alyona was upright, Jessica picked up the lantern, and Sarah supported Alyona as they made their way out of the cave.

It was dark outside. There was a heavy cloud cover blocking out the moon and starlight. Still, it was not as dark as inside the cave. Sarah emitted an audible sigh of relief.

"Okay?" Jessica asked.

"Fine," Sarah replied, "Just glad to be above ground again. Looking forward to seeing the sun."

They reached the pickup, and Jessica opened the back door on the passenger's side for Alyona.

"You might be best off laying on the back seat," Jessica suggested. With great care, Jessica and Sarah managed to maneuver Alyona into the back of the pickup and onto the seat. They rigged a harness as best they could with the seat belts to hold Alyona in place in case of bumpy roads or sudden stops.

Jessica took a moment to move the supplies from the back of the pickup to the floor in the back. "Looks like more rain," she explained as she did so. Sarah helped her with the last few items, then buckled herself into the passenger seat.

Jessica looked sadly back into the cave mouth one last time, thinking of Meredith. She inhaled deeply, then exhaled, climbed into the driver's seat, and started the engine. "On our way, then."

Following the directions she had received from Leticia's mother, she drove along empty back roads, eager to put miles between them and the town before daylight. It was slow going. Some of the roads looked more like abandoned walking trails, and at times, Jessica had to crawl in low gear to avoid jostling Alyona for fear of exacerbating her injuries.

Before long, black clouds rolled in, dumping a torrent of vision-reducing rain and turning sections of the rutted roadway into slippery, muddy puddles. Jessica shook her head in an effort to clear the brain fog. She forced her bleary eyes wider as she fought to keep the pickup on the nearly non-existent road in the darkness, and to keep the ride reasonably smooth for Alyona's sake. Her concentration was waning as the hard day's labor and minimal sleep caught up with her. Perhaps it was time to consider pulling off and resting, rather than falling asleep and crashing.

"How am I even going to find a safe place to pull off in—"

She slammed on the brakes as the ground disappeared in the headlights. She exhaled sharply, her hands shaking from the sudden surge of adrenaline. Had she missed a turn in the road? She threw the pickup into reverse and backed up slowly. There was the ground again, and the barely-there road went straight into the nothing.

"What's wrong?" Sarah asked.

"Not sure," Jessica said, "Can't see well enough to tell. I'm gonna get out and check something real quick."

"Be careful."

Jessica put the pickup in neutral and set the parking brake. She opened the door and slipped out into the downpour. Shuffling over the wet, treacherous ground, she made her way to the front corner of the pickup. Bending down, she could just make out the abrupt drop in the terrain in front of her. The road went over the edge of the hill they were on and straight down a steep slope. She couldn't see how far down it went, or if it grew steeper.

"That'd be a tough drop in daylight on dry ground," Jessica murmured. She went back to the cab and climbed in, soaking wet from the downpour.

"What is it?" Sarah asked.

"Well..." Jessica paused, trying to think of a way to put a positive spin on it. "The road gets a bit steep up ahead. A little hard to make out the lay of the terrain in this weather."

"Will we have to turn around?" Sarah's voice carried a note of fear.

"Nah." Jessica gripped the steering wheel, surprised by her sudden confidence. "Just might get a bit intense for a while." She looked back where Alyona lay, double-checking the harness.

"Guess we'll see how well it works," Jessica murmured.

She worked the clutch and put the pickup in gear. Taking a deep breath and a firm but relaxed hold on the wheel, she pressed the gas and popped the clutch. The truck lurched forward. She applied more pressure to the pedal, giving as much gas as she could without breaking the tires loose. The front of the truck dropped abruptly as the tires went over the edge.

Jessica heard and felt the bottom of the pickup hit ground, the grating of rock and dirt on metal sending shuddering vibrations through the cab. She gave it a little more gas, trying to urge another few ounces of momentum before the truck high-centered. The rear tires began to slip, and the forward momentum slowed.

Jessica held her breath as the pickup teetered forward. Then the grating sounds intensified as the vehicle began to pick up speed again, pulled by gravity. The front tires came in contact with the ground, and she pressed the gas pedal, coaxing the truck forward. The back of the truck bounced as the rear wheels found purchase at the precipice. She gave it a little more gas, trying to accelerate the front of the pickup to keep it from flipping over, then let off as the bed settled back to the ground.

Jessica shifted the pickup to low gear, which helped to slow the descent somewhat, but the tires slipped frequently on the wet, muddy ground. Sarah whimpered as the truck was roughly jostled when the tires dropped into a section of deeply rutted tracks. Jessica held the steering wheel straight as she could, though she had no real ability to direct the vehicle, the ruts holding the truck's course much like rails to a train. She finally relented and shifted up a gear, realizing the tires were just slipping uncontrollably in low gear. At least in a higher gear, they would roll rather than slide.

With an abrupt bump, the vehicle was ejected from the ruts. The pickup fishtailed, the back of the vehicle nearly catching up to the front at times. Jessica spun the wheel left, then right, keeping the front tires pointed down the slope.

"You're going to want to go to the left up ahead."

Jess looked around. Had she heard that voice, or was it just in her head? It was the same voice as Grandma Dalton in her dream.

Peering through the rain, she could make out the primitive road, which continued straight down with a slight veer to the right. To the left was a drop into a gulley. Going left would take her off the course plotted out for her by Leticia's mother.

"Now, dear."

Jessica steered left. The pickup drifted, protesting the new choice of direction. It continued the angled slide as the vehicle hit a more level section of ground, then was snapped into the new direction of travel as it dropped over the edge and into the gully. The ground here was miraculously and mercifully smooth, with only the occasional scrub brush, which they barreled over.

Jessica kept a close watch on the rushing terrain ahead. At some point they would likely hit the bottom of the gully. How abrupt would that be? Too abrupt and they would end up in a head-on collision with the other side of the gulley. She edged right, trying to close in on as close to parallel with the valley floor as she could, without risking a rollover on the steep side.

"It'd sure be nice to have a little light," she complained out loud.

A moment later a bolt of lightning flashed directly in front of them. She could just make out the bottom of the gulley another fifty yards below. She was running just above a rise which angled down to the bottom of the gulley in a smooth finger. She turned left, then right as the truck leveled out on the rise, then the little finger of ground ran her down into the valley floor.

The ground was a mixture of sagebrush and loose rock. It made the ride a bit bumpy, but also gave the tires some purchase. Jessica took advantage of this to tap the brakes. Ever so slowly she regained control of the vehicle's speed. By the time they reached the bottom of the gulley, she was in control of the vehicle.

A small stream flowed down the gulley, most likely the product of the rain. The small area lit up in the headlights looked much like the high desert she had grown up around. Rain was a rare occasion. And a hard rain like this, in terrain like this, was known to cause gulley washers. A normally dry gulch could go from a trickle to a torrential flood in less than a minute. A wall of water could tear out full-grown trees and displace massive boulders. It could toss a pickup truck around like an empty soda can.

"I sure hope you know what you're doing," she murmured, watching the water behind her for any indication of an increase in volume.

The ground was rough and uneven, limiting the speed at which she could safely drive. How far did this gully go?

And what did the end look like? Did it drop out on a flat, or end at the intersection of other mountains?

She debated between going faster to avoid being overrun by a potential flash flood, and going slower to avoid accidentally driving headlong into a mud wallow or impromptu pond. She listened for any guidance, inspiration, feeling. Nothing materialized to tip the balance one way or another.

"Sarah, quick, pick a number between one and five!"

"Two?" Sarah responded.

"Slower, then."

"What?"

"I couldn't decide whether to go faster or slower, so I flipped a coin, so to speak. One or two was go slower, three was same speed, four and five were go faster."

"Okay," Sarah said, drawing out the word. "What danger are we trying to decide between?"

Jessica kept her gaze on the road. "Both pretty much boil down to crashing, drowning, or crashing and drowning—just different ways for it to happen."

"Oh," Sarah mumbled, "I think I'm sorry I asked."

"Not to worry," Jessica said brightly, "I have complete confidence in your decision!"

Sarah shot Jessica a considerably less bright and less confident look as she gripped the grab-handle on the door frame.

"Whoa!" Jessica braked hard and swerved right to dodge a large boulder. "Good call on going slower, Sarah."

Sarah grunted, flashing a fake smile as she did so. Jessica chuckled, then returned her focus to the rain-obscured terrain ahead. The stream was increasing in size, though not so rapidly as to portend imminent disaster.

Another well-timed flash of lightning revealed another ramp-like finger ahead to the right, climbing upwards, out of the gulley onto a modest sized bench. A dark patch on the ledge suggested a cluster of trees.

"That might be a good place to stop for the night." Jessica pointed in the direction of the ledge once more obscured by the rain and darkness. "Let's take a look."

The ramp-like finger became a ledge, just a bit wider than the pickup with an increasingly precipitous drop-off the farther they climbed. "Hope there's a spot to turn around up there," Jessica murmured, "it'd be a serious pain in the butt to have to back down this."

She glanced over at a wide-eyed and white-knuckled Sarah. She had scooted as far to the right as she could as though doing so would keep the pickup—or at least her—from tumbling over the edge.

The ledge stopped climbing, and then widened out onto a small landing, which was home to a small but thick cluster of trees, now visible in the headlights. They were a mix of ancient and young, deciduous and evergreen, an impenetrable wall of foliage. She stopped just a few feet from them.

"Well, I suppose this is as good a place as any to stop for the night," Jessica said, "Alyona's hogging the back seat, so I guess we'll have to make do where we are." She laid the seat back slightly and let out a mock sigh of comfort. "Sweet dreams y'all."

"Is there enough room?" Sarah asked quietly.

"What?"

"Is there enough room to turn around?"

Jessica sat up and peered outside, examining what little of the terrain to the back and sides of the pickup could be seen. "Yeah, piece of cake."

Chapter Eighteen

Jessica was awake with the sun's first light. She got out of the pickup to stretch her stiff, aching joints, and to work the knots out of her muscles. She collected some leaves to use for her morning bathroom break—toilet paper was something she definitely had a profound appreciation for now. Once that unpleasantness was completed and the evidence properly buried, she walked over to the edge and around the cluster of trees to study the area below.

The entrance to the draw was a mess of brush and debris, indicating there may have been a little flooding at some point during the night. The ground could probably stand to dry out for another hour or two before driving. In the distance she could see a narrow, paved road. The area looked quite desolate, at least at this hour, but the road appeared smooth, and well cared for.

Pulling out the crude map she had been given, she

studied it. Estimating the path they had taken with the detour, she concluded the road was part of their intended course. It was a stretch Leticia's mother had noted was more traveled than the other sections in their journey. She had warned her to take extra care driving that section, so as not to draw attention, particularly from *policía*, who would make things difficult for a foreigner at best.

If her guess as to their present location was correct, the detour had allowed them to bypass a little over half that section. A few miles more and they would again slip onto primitive roads until they reached the outskirts of Mexico City. From there it would be a quick dash to the embassy and safety.

At least, that's how she hoped it would go. She realized she was basing her plan mostly on things she had seen in movies. Would real life actually work like that?

"Actors lie for a living," her father had said once, after hearing a celebrity make a wildly uninformed declaration about some current political matter, "They get paid to play make-believe. You shouldn't use them as your source for truth and wisdom."

She hoped in this instance that they were close enough to the truth. The alternative would be to drive all the way to the US—around a thousand miles, Jessica guessed. That would take a day or two on good roads, and she doubted they had that much gas money left. Jessica wondered for a moment if they would already be in Mexico City, had they driven the main roads. Possibly. Of course, that assumed they didn't run into any trouble on the main roads.

No, she thought. *Better to take a little longer and reduce that risk.*

Just then a flash of reflected sunlight to the south caught her eye. Squinting, she could make out what appeared to be blockade on the road. A pickup maybe, and two figures moving about nearby. Was it meant for her, or for some other reason? It probably didn't matter; either way it would have been trouble, and she was grateful of the impromptu detour which took them around behind it.

Jessica returned to the pickup and, opening the back door, she reached behind the seat and dug in among the piled supplies while the others still slept. She fished out a loaf of bread and a banana to eat for breakfast. She climbed back into the driver's seat and tore off a hunk of bread. As she ate, she debated how long to wait before moving on.

Alyona moaned in the back seat, reminding her the downside of the slower route was that Alyona went longer without receiving medical attention. Maybe leaving sooner would be better. It would also allow them to get away from the roadblock before it had a chance to move.

Jessica finished her meager breakfast, grabbed another banana, and started the engine, rousing Sarah from her slumber.

"Good morning," Jessica said, handing the banana and the rest of the loaf of bread to Sarah. "I made you breakfast."

She put the pickup in reverse and turned it around on the level area, then made her way down the narrow ledge. Sarah shifted to the left on the bench seat until she was nearly in Jessica's lap. "Not a fan of heights, are you?" Jessica quipped. Sarah didn't reply. She continued to stare out the window while she chewed nervously on the end of the bread.

"You should really put your seatbelt on." Jessica glanced at her from the corner of her eye. Sarah scowled at her, then slid over and fastened her seatbelt.

Jessica made a hard right as they reached the bottom of the ledge, to make the sharp 180 degree turn into the gulley. There was a bit of mud in the bottom, and the tires slid as they went through, Jessica manipulated the gas pedal and the steering wheel to compensate and maintain control of their direction of travel. Once positioned, the wheels straddled the muddy area for the most part, keeping the ride relatively under control.

She glanced back over her shoulder at the sound of a groan from the back seat. Alyona was pale, her eyes screwed shut with pain. Jessica winced as another bump jostled the pickup. "Sorry."

"S'okay," Alyona mumbled, though her grimace and her panting belied her words.

As they reached the bottom where the gulley opened onto flat terrain, Jessica veered to the left, aiming for drier ground. There was small area of muddy silt right at the bottom, which threw up dark rooster tails as the pickup plowed through it, then the vehicle accelerated as its tires found purchase on drier ground.

Jessica glanced to the right. She couldn't see the roadblock; hopefully they were far enough away to avoid attracting the attention of the people manning it. For the first time, she was grateful for the torrents of rain last night. It left the ground slightly damp and prevented an attention-drawing dust cloud from forming behind her as she drove across the open area and intercepted the road she'd seen in the distance.

As she had determined, it was a narrow, paved country road—a smooth ride. It was a pleasant change from the off-roading.

"This is much better," Alyona said from the back.

"What's that?" Jessica relaxed her grip on the wheel and accelerated.

"Smooth ground. Is much less painful to drive on."

"Sorry," Jessica responded sympathetically."

"Sorry for what," Alyona said, "for running over every rock in Mexico?"

Jessica looked back and smirked. "Sarah, can you try and find something for Alyona to eat? She's naturally grumpy in the morning, but it's worse when she's hungry."

"*Ungh!*" Alyona grunted, "I'm beat nearly to death by an ogre with a club, then dumped in the back of a truck while you drive around looking for the biggest bumps you can find to run over, and you blame my mood on my stomach?"

"Maybe a piece of fruit," Jessica ignored Alyona, "a little sugar might sweeten her disposition."

She settled back in the driver's seat and slowed as a small town came into view ahead. She checked the gas gauge, having ignored that detail thus far. They would need more gas to make it all the way to Mexico City, but she wasn't sure how they were going to go about getting it. She didn't want to interact with anyone who would identify her as a white girl out of her natural habitat, and she wasn't sure how much money it would take to fill up or how much money she had left. Even if she did know, she would still have to interact with a clerk to pay cash, and not knowing how much would certainly cause the clerk to take notice. They were probably out of the range of the Templarios, but at the moment, she considered all of Mexico enemy territory.

"Sarah." Jessica glanced at the side mirrors, checking for following cars. "I've got a hoodie back there, maybe you should put it on and make sure all your hair is tucked into it."

"Why?" Sarah asked.

"Just trying to be cautious." Jessica checked the mirrors. "Not sure a couple of white girls should be traveling alone out here, so..."

Sarah located the hoodie and pulled it on. She tugged the top of the hood forward and down, obscuring her face. "How's this?"

Jessica scrutinized her. "Good."

Slowing more as they began passing buildings, she spied a gas pump and pulled up to it. Turning off the engine, she looked around for a sign with identifiable gas prices—sixteen something, maybe. Did they use liters or gallons in Mexico? Liters probably. How many would she need? The pickup was reading a little over a quarter of a tank.

She bit her lower lip and twirled a few strands of hair around her finger as she tried to puzzle through how much gas she would need to ask for. She pulled out the wallet and counted the bills. She had a little over two hundred pesos left. All of it probably wouldn't fill the tank. Should she spend it all or should she keep some money, just in case?

A knock on the window startled her from her musing. She turned to see a young man, probably close to her age, smiling at her. He was of medium height and build, with a thick head of wavy dark hair. He had brown eyes which shifted nervously, contradicting the easy smile on his lips. She rolled the window down, keeping her face emotionless.

"Good morning, *señorita*. I am guessing you need gas, yes? If you'd like to give me your card, I will take care of it for you, so you can stay in your car."

"No, *gracias*," she responded coldly, and began rolling up the window.

"Wait," he hissed. "Look, some men came through here late last night. I heard them talking to the old men who sit outside here during the day—they will be here soon." He glanced around nervously, as if confirming they hadn't already arrived. "They told them to watch for a pickup with white girls in it and to call him and tell him if they saw you. They said there was a reward."

"Which way did they go?" Jessica asked, her voice tight. Could they have been the men at the roadblock?

"South," he responded. "Please, stay in your car, so nobody sees you. Let me get your gas. I promise I will give your card back."

"I don't have a card. Only cash."

The young man's jaw clenched as he glanced around. "Okay, stay in the car, I'll take care of it." He turned, pulled out a credit card, and jammed it into the slot on the pump.

Jessica watched him closely as he grabbed the hose,

opened the fuel door on the truck and inserted the nozzle. "Why are you helping us?"

He squeezed the trigger, locking it in place, then turned to stare at the changing numbers on the pump display.

"They're bad men," he said, not taking his eyes from the pump. "What they do is wrong." He paused, then opened his mouth as if to say more, then closed it again. His turned his gaze to the interior of the pickup, jumping from one girl to the next, then he scanned the surrounding neighborhood.

"The hoodie," he gestured to Sarah, "that's a good idea. You look more like a boy than a girl in that, and you can't really tell you're a *gringo*." He focused on Jessica, "Do you have another one?"

"No." She shook her head.

"Wait a moment." He ran over to a scooter. Digging in a backpack sitting on the seat, he pulled out a hoodie and brought it back to the pickup.

"Here," he offered it to Jessica, "put this on."

"Oh, I don't want to take your stuff—"

"Take it." He pushed it through the window. Jessica complied, pulling it over her head and into place. He examined her critically. "Good, better."

"Thanks," Jessica said.

He waved a hand dismissively and turned back to the pump.

"Gotta admit, I'm surprised they spent so much chasing us," Jessica said to break the silence. "Lotta man hours, and distance. I mean, I've been driving back roads—going the long way round—but even taking the straightest route, we gotta be close to two hundred miles from where they took us. Doesn't seem like good business sense."

The young man looked at her curiously for a moment, then returned his gaze to the pump. "They'll make about a hundred thousand American dollars a year for you. They can make as much as a million dollars from each girl in the end. They can spend quite a bit and still do okay."

Jessica whistled. "A million dollars? In Mexico?"

"Not here." He shook his head. "They will take you somewhere near or across the border, or near one of the expensive resorts, where the rich Americans go." His lips curled into a snarl as he finished. Then looking over at her, his expression softened, and his eyes fell. "They come from other places also..."

"But mostly from America," Jessica responded. He nodded. "Don't worry, I'm not offended. There's plenty of good people in the US, plenty of bad ones too."

His returned his gaze to her, this time with an expression of curiosity. She flashed a smile. This seemed to rattle him a bit. His gaze snapped away and he stuffed his hands into his pockets.

"It's not just the money though," he hurried to continue. "It's a matter of reputation." He leaned against the truck and lowered his voice. "There are stories going around about girls who got away. About men—soldiers—disappearing, maybe even dying. There's even talk of a man getting beaten nearly to death in a public place by a little *gringa*."

Jessica felt her face grow hot at the mention of this.

"That's bad for a man's reputation," he continued, his

voice tightening with a feverish excitement, "If he doesn't catch the girl—doesn't make an example of her—maybe people will start to fear him less, maybe they will start to stand up to him, maybe…"

"I'll try my best not to disappoint you." She flashed another warm smile in his direction. This time he returned it. She extended her hand out the window. "My name's Jessica, by the way."

He glanced around then took her hand. "Nicolas."

"Pleased to meet you, Nicolas." She drew her hand back into the pickup and grew serious. "Just something to consider, heroes have a way of disappointing people—they're human, after all. They'll never live up to the image people create. Best not to wait for a hero to solve your problems."

Nicolas regarded her for a moment, as if preparing to protest, then his shoulders slumped. "How can anyone hope to stand up to something as powerful as the Templarios?"

"You know, a few years back, I was running in a state cross-country championship. There was this girl a year older than me. She was the defending state champion and always finished a good minute ahead of second place.

"I was watching her practice and getting more intimidated every second. She didn't just run up the hills, she sprinted up! And going down …It was like she was gliding. She was an absolute machine!

"Well, I was standing there with my jaw down to my knees, already defeated, when my dad walks up and says I should go over, shake her hand, and wish her luck. Can you imagine?

"Anyway, I do like he says, and she's super nice! She smiles and hugs me and thanks me, and she wishes me good luck too. She tells me she knows I'll do amazing!

"I go back over to my dad, and he says, 'could you touch her?' Well, yeah, obviously!

"'So, she's not a ghost or a unicorn or a winged fairy or something?' he asks me. 'She's a human being?' Yeah, I reply, and then he says, 'If you can touch her, you can beat her.'"

"So, you beat her?" Nicolas asked.

"Oh no, she was crazy fast. But I was only twenty seconds behind her.' Jessica chuckled. "Thing is you don't know if you don't try, and you can't really try if you already think you're beat."

Jessica reached out and touched Nicolas's arm, making sure she had his full attention. "If they aren't untouchable, they aren't unbeatable."

Nicolas met her gaze for a moment, then glanced toward the pump. "Oh, I didn't hear it click." He withdrew his arm, replaced the nozzle, and closed the cap. "Please hurry, before someone sees you. Do you know where you're going?"

"Yes, Thank you." She extended a handful of cash. "Here, for the gas."

"No, you keep it, you might need it."

"I still have some."

"No."

"I will be on my way a lot quicker if you stop arguing with me and take this."

"Okay." Flustered, he took the handful of pesos.

"Take care, Nicolas." She smiled, started the engine, and rolled up the window.

Nicolas stepped back and waved, his expression thoughtful—as if he was trying to commit her face to memory. Jessica put the pickup in gear and drove away from the pump.

Jessica looked at the road ahead, considering her options. Staying on the main road would probably get them to Mexico City in just under two hours. Taking the route Leticia's mother gave her would likely double that time. There weren't that many vehicles on the road, though she was sure traffic would increase as they drew closer to the capital. She was anxious to be done with this journey, but would she be able to work out the route to the embassy going the short route? She was pretty sure she could fill in the gaps; the park Leticia's mother had detailed was likely an easy landmark to find from any direction, and there would probably be signs. If all else failed, Mexico City should be safe for them to ask someone directions without connecting with Templarios.

"Yeah, let's take a shortcut," Jessica said, giving a little more gas as they passed the turnoff identified in the directions she had been given.

"What did you say?" Sarah asked.

"Just a couple more hours."

Sarah's face brightened. "Home."

Chapter Nineteen

A short distance from their stop, they merged onto a large highway with three lanes in each direction, and concrete barriers in the middle. The traffic wasn't heavy though, not at this time of day at least—mid-morning by Jessica's estimation. She counted maybe five cars in front of them, and another six or seven behind them.

The road veered left around a bend, and the scattered buildings gave way to thick vegetation. Tall trees lined the road to the right, and beneath the trees was an impenetrable mass of green growth. The left side looked identical, with the exception of a few areas where the road had been cut through a hill, exposing a near vertical surface of rock, soil and dried pine needles, climbing as high as twenty feet, with trees running right up to and occasionally just over the edge of the precipice, their exposed roots protruding into empty space.

Jessica noted with some curiosity that, although the forest was a mix of deciduous and coniferous trees, the trees on the right side of the road—at least near the road—were predominately deciduous trees of varying sizes, shapes and shades of green, while to her left the trees were primarily tall coniferous trees, with thick clusters of long needles. The base of the trunks of many of the trees on the left had been painted.

"This is pretty," Jessica commented, "Do you suppose this is like a national forest, or a park, or preserve or something?"

Sarah gave a noncommittal grunt and a shrug of her shoulders.

Farther on, the road began to ascend. They rounded a horseshoe bend, and the climb became more pronounced as they traversed back the way they came and up the side of a… mountain? Would it be fair to call it a mountain? Not as rugged or elevated as the Rockies back home. Her friends would likely consider this a hill, but around here, it was probably a mountain. The ground climbed steeply to her right, and to her left, it gave way to a grand view of a broad expanse dotted with craggy little peaks, and clusters of civilization. Jessica sighed as she took in the beautiful vista.

Slowly then civilization began to make itself known again, as the natural scenery was interrupted by the occasional billboard or rundown building. The closer they got to Mexico City, the more cars they saw, yet nobody seemed to take any real interest in the beat-up pickup which appeared to be carrying two teenage boys wearing hoodies. Jessica was driving with her hands low on the wheel, keeping them out of sight, and both girls had pulled their hoods forward and down as much as they could without blocking their vision.

The cars in front began to slow, and bunch up, then fanned out into additional lanes. As they got closer, Jessica could see a structure that reminded her of the pay gates at the exit of long-term airport parking. Was this a toll road? She had heard of them before but had never seen one. She dug into her pocket anxiously. She had given most of the money to Nicolas, keeping just a few bills. Would it be enough?

She glanced to her right and her heart sank. Next to them was a blue four-door pickup. Across the doors in white were the words *Policía Federal*. Jessica gripped the steering wheel and stared at the rear fender of the car directly in front of her.

"Jess?" Sarah's voice telegraphed alarm.

"I see it, Sare," Jessica said without moving her head.

"See what?" Alyona asked. Jessica heard rustling followed by a groan.

"Nothing to worry about," Jessica spoke quickly, "You just stay still and out of sight."

"Take it easy, Jess," she murmured, "don't jump to conclusions, not every cop in Mexico is corrupt." But how many? And which ones? She focused on keeping her behavior as natural as possible.

Jessica stopped the truck at the booth, and a man opened the window to say something. She was too nervous to make sense of it, but she assumed he told her the toll price. Robotically she extended her hand, offering him all the money she had left. He frowned, arching one brow. He removed one of the bills and handed her a couple of coins.

"*Gracias*," she said, heat creeping into her cheeks. She pulled forward slowly, watching for another exiting vehicle to match her acceleration to.

Ahead she could see signs of construction work, and a series of orange and white temporary barriers funneled the many lanes into one. Before that, parked in a gap in the barrier blocks on the left, was a second police pickup. On the right side, parked in a closed off-ramp, were two police cars with similar markings. Three uniformed officers were standing together, talking with another man dressed in a black shirt and camouflage pants. He leaned against another official-looking car. It was white, with a colorful stripe like a rainbow, down low between the front and rear wheels. The top of the vehicle was purple, and it had the word *Metropolitano* printed on the side. There were no lights visible on the top, so maybe some sort of government worker?

Jessica kept her eyes forward as she passed through the gauntlet. She breathed a sigh of relief as she passed the vehicles without garnering a glance from the uniformed individuals. Peeking in the rear-view mirror, she saw that the police truck that had been driving beside them pulled off next to the cars. Jessica began to relax as she continued along the single lane. It was comforting knowing that nobody could pull up next to them and inspect the interior of the pickup.

She stayed back a few car lengths from the vehicle in front of her, making it harder for them to make out details. It wouldn't be for long, and it probably wouldn't matter, but after passing all those police she felt like being extra cautious.

The construction lasted for a little over a mile, then the road returned to two open lanes in each direction, and the traffic picked up speed.

Jessica began to consider how far off course they were from the directions she had been given. They were still heading toward Mexico City, but how would they go about intercepting the route, so she could find her way to the embassy? The closer to Mexico City they got, the more roads and intersections there would be. Which of the roads from Leticia's mother's directions would they intercept?

As she pondered the challenge of getting back on course, she glanced in the rear-view mirror. A police truck was right behind her. Was it one of the pickups she saw at the toll booths?

There still wasn't very much traffic; nine or ten cars spread out ahead of her, and there were maybe half that many behind her. She slowed down a bit and glanced to the side of the road. A car passed her, but the police vehicle remained behind, matching her speed. A little farther ahead there was an exit onto a road which ran parallel to the freeway. She considered her options for a moment, not wanting to get farther off course and into the weeds, so to speak. If there was a way off, there had to be a way on nearby as well, right? Her mind raced, evaluating and discarding argument after argument as the exit drew closer. With only seconds to spare, she flipped on the turn signal and took the exit. The police truck followed.

She drove along a narrow, poorly kept road lined with dirty buildings constructed of cinder block. They were painted in drab, dirty whites and pinks, splashed with the occasional colorful graffiti. Here and there an old car or pickup was parked in front of the one of the buildings, narrowing the road to a single lane of traffic. The pickup and the police vehicle were the only cars driving.

Occasionally a narrow road would appear between buildings on her right. To her left, a crumbling concrete curb and a six-foot-high steel fence separated her from the freeway. Glancing in the rear-view mirror, she saw that a lone policeman in the pickup was holding a cell phone to his ear. She tightened her grip on the steering wheel.

As she moved right after passing a parked sedan, the police truck accelerated to draw level with her on the left. Instinctively, she braked and pulled to the right. The police truck flew past, overshooting her, then braked hard and turned to the right, stopping diagonally across the road. She assumed the policeman was attempting to block her, but whether he was thrown off by her sudden deceleration, or he just wasn't particularly skilled, he had left a large enough gap on the left side for her to drive past.

She considered gunning it, or throwing the pickup in reverse and backing to the freeway, but what then? A high-speed chase would further complicate her efforts to get back on course. Sarah whimpered.

"Easy," Jessica said in the same soft tone she used when speaking to a spooked horse, "Might be a routine stop."

It was an unconvincing lie. She doubted abruptly pulling in front of a vehicle without turning on the lights was likely to be any more routine in Mexico than it was in Utah. Nor was it likely to be routine for the officer to jump out of his vehicle and approach with his weapon drawn.

The officer was on the short side, with a rather large girth, making his abrupt exit and combat-ready stance even more impressive. His face had a roundness to match his midsection, with a long dark mustache that drew attention to his diminutive nose. His hair was short and greasy, and his face glistened with sweat.

Even with the windows up, the engine noise, and the noise of passing cars, she could hear his bellowing voice ordering her out of the truck.

"Sarah, I'm going to leave the truck running and get out." Jessica slowly unbuckled her seatbelt. "As soon as you are able, slide over to the driver's seat. If things go sideways, I want you to drive around him on the left, get back on the freeway and get into the city. Stay away from cops. Look for old ladies, stop and say 'American Embassy'. Then go in the direction they point."

Jessica opened the door and began to slide out of the seat. "Keep doing that until you see an American flag, or American soldiers. Let them know you're American and kidnappers are chasing you."

"Jess, no! You can't—you don't know what it's like—" Sarah's panic was palpable.

"It'll be okay." Jessica reached over to touch Sarah's knee. "You're gonna be okay."

Jessica slipped out of the truck and closed the door. She raised her hands above her head.

"Is something wrong?" Jessica modulated her voice, trying to pass as a native teenage boy.

"Step away from the pickup!" the policeman said in heavily accented English.

"There must be some mistake—"

"You shut up!" the policeman yelled. "Move away from the pickup and get on your knees!"

A siren sounded once behind Jessica. The portly officer looked up, his face shifting to surprise and then irritation. Jessica heard a car door open, and she turned and glanced. A younger officer, gun drawn, stood behind his open car door. She returned her attention to the man in front of her.

"It's okay." The bigger policemen spoke to the new arrival. "It's under control, carry on." He waved a pudgy hand in a gesture as if shooing the officer away.

"Comisario Perez?" The other officer's voice sounded puzzled.

"I said I have this!"

Thinking quickly, Jessica pulled her hood down, revealing her long hair. She twisted again to look at the younger officer; his eyes went wide.

"We were kidnapped," she said, inclining her head toward the pickup. "We're trying to escape, to go home."

"I said shut up!" the pudgy officer barked.

"He's working for them," Jessica inclined her head, indicating the pudgy officer, "He's going to take us back to them—to the Templarios."

The officer frowned, his gaze darting between the pickup and Jessica.

"Sir?" He turned to the pudgy officer for confirmation.

The rotund man wiped the sweat from his forehead. "Do you like being a policeman?"

The officer's eyes shifted from the captain, to Jessica, and back again. Slowly, he lowered his gun.

"Please!" Jessica fixed a pleading gaze on the young officer. He looked at the ground.

Jessica turned back to the captain.

"Employee or relative?" she asked, trying to buy more time to find a way out of the situation.

"Why?" Perez smirked, "You see a family resemblance? Or were you hoping to bribe me?"

"You don't much look like any of the guys I met," Jessica remarked, "but I really didn't meet very many."

"You killed quite a few." Perez's smile changed to a glare.

"I didn't kill anyone. Did your relative die?"

"No." The smile returned. "The boss is my cousin."

"How'd you end up a cop instead of working for him then?"

The man shrugged. "I was a policeman before he took over for his father. I became a cop because I like the uniform, and the gun."

"So, you were never really a policeman then," Jessica observed sadly.

Perez scowled. "What do you mean?"

"You don't protect and serve. That's what policemen do."

"Oh, so it's because I don't march around doing good deeds? I'm police, not a boy scout! I keep order, and I protect my own! You think your papa's any different? Stupid, spoiled, naïve *gringa*."

She turned back to the young officer, who was holstering his gun. "You're really gonna just let this happen?"

"Sorry," he mumbled, shuffling his feet, "I have a family."

"So do I."

"And you should get back to work, so you can feed your family," the comisario barked at the junior officer.

The young man slipped into his car, closed the door, and started the motor. Before he could drive away, a scooter shot past, with two people wearing bandanas over their faces. As the scooter passed Jessica, the passenger raised a baseball bat and cocked it back, ready to swing.

"Run!" the driver yelled back at her. The scooter veered closer to the startled policeman, and the passenger swung the bat, catching the fat man in the gut.

Perez folded in half and fell backward. The scooter slowed and turned sharply. The passenger jumped from the back before it began to accelerate again. He turned to face Perez and brought the bat down hard between the pudgy man's shoulder blades as he tried to rise to his knees.

"Stay down or I'll break your skull!" the young man yelled.

Jessica turned to follow the scooter, which raced toward the young officer, who was opening his door again and climbing out. He was halfway out when the scooter driver collided with the door. There was a grunt of pain, and the clatter of a gun falling to the pavement. The scooter driver looked down, and kicked wildly, connecting with the gun and sending it spinning under the car and out of reach.

Jessica turned back to the passenger and Perez. The comisario rolled to his side, holding his hands above his head.

"Please, don't hurt me!" he begged.

The masked youth stepped forward, brandishing the bat threateningly. He glanced back toward Jessica. "I thought we told you to run!"

With surprising speed, Perez kicked out, catching the young man in the side of his knee. The boy cried out in pain as his leg buckled, and the policeman rolled to his hands and knees, reaching for his gun.

A shot rang out, and fragments of the ground exploded in the space between Perez's hand and his gun. Everyone froze.

Sarah stood just in front of the passenger-side headlight, staring grimly down the barrel of the gun she must have dug from the rucksack while Jessica had been stalling. Everyone stared at her in stunned silence.

The young man with the bat struggled to his feet, limping.

"You," Sarah said, barely inclining her head toward the limping youth, "the keys to the cop cars."

"Come on, young lady," Perez spoke soothingly, "You don't want to shoot anyone. You're not a murderer."

"I've met your cousin," Sarah said, her voice dangerous and her gaze darkening "He got very close to me. I can see the resemblance." She took a step forward. "I promise you; I very much want to shoot you."

Perez opened his mouth to speak again, then paused.

"Please," he said finally.

"I said please to him too." Sarah's voice trembled—almost a growl. "Didn't stop him. Why do you think it'll stop me?"

"Sarah," Jessica spoke softly to her friend. The muscles in Sarah's jaw clenched and her nostrils flared. The young man limped over to her, holding the keys from the captain's car at arm's length.

"Give 'em to her." Sarah gestured toward Jessica.

The lad hobbled to her, offering the keys. At the same moment, the scooter driver walked past, pushing the young officer ahead of him.

"On the ground next to your friend," he said, pushing him roughly. He then turned to Jessica, holding the second set of keys. Jessica looked at the eyes visible above the bandana, and gasped.

"What are you doing here?" she whispered.

"Not waiting for a hero," Nicolas replied.

"Please be careful," Jessica said, "this guy is cousins with the Templar leader!"

Nicolas's eyes widened, then narrowed as he studied the policeman. "So that's how..."

"What?" Jessica asked.

"Long story," Nicolas responded tersely, "No time. My sister's dead because of him, my family good as dead."

"Get their guns too," Sarah said, "Unload 'em and throw 'em in the back of the truck."

Nicolas gathered the two weapons. He removed the magazines and cleared the chambers, tossing everything into the pickup bed.

"What now?" he asked.

"Get your scooter and get out of here."

"What about you?"

"We're gonna go too. Right after you."

"Where?"

Sarah turned her head and gave Nicolas a scathing glare, then gave a barely perceptible nod in the direction of the two prone policemen, causing a flush of red to creep up onto Nicolas's face.

"The airport," Jessica interrupted, hoping the police would buy into the misdirection.

"*Shh*," Sarah hissed. "Get outta here!" Her face and voice both convincingly portrayed irritation.

"Be safe!" Nicolas called back as the two boys climbed on the scooter. He started the motor and zoomed away.

"Let's go," Sarah ordered.

Jessica moved to the driver's side door. "You too?"

"Soon as you are in and ready to drive," Sarah replied.

"You're not gonna shoot anybody, are you?"

"Depends."

"On what?"

"On whether the skinny one moves, or the fat one continues breathing."

"Okay." Jessica dragged out the word. She couldn't tell if Sarah was serious or not. She stepped back toward the door of the pickup, her mind racing as she tried to think of something to say to Sarah, to talk her down.

Sarah began walking backward slowly, bumped into the pickup, slid along the bumper, then backed up while keeping her hip against the side of the vehicle until she connected with the passenger-side mirror. Relieved, Jessica relaxed.

She opened the driver door and slid into the seat, then watched Sarah do the same.

"Go!" Sarah hissed.

Chapter Twenty

Jessica threw her seatbelt on in one smooth motion and grabbed the steering wheel and gear shift simultaneously.

Throwing the pickup in gear, she stepped hard on the gas, causing the tires to squeal as the truck lurched forward. She kept the pedal to the floor, only bringing it up briefly to press the clutch and shift. Glancing in the rear-view mirror, Jessica watched as the two policemen rose to their feet, Perez's arms waving wildly as he berated the junior officer. Returning her attention to the road ahead, Jessica noticed a break in the fence.

"Seat belt!" Jessica prompted Sarah as they approached the break.

Sarah buckled her belt moments before Jessica swerved hard to the left. The pickup bounced onto the weathered curb, fishtailing through the gap in the fence. The tires squealed in protest as they crossed from the small strip of dirt and grass back onto the highway. Fortunately traffic was still sparse, giving her plenty of space to maneuver. Once the vehicle was under control, Jessica let off the gas, matching speed with the other cars.

"Why are you slowing down?!" Sarah demanded.

"They can't chase us," Jessica responded. "We have their keys. I don't know how likely he is to call this in, but I am positive any police that see us racing down the road will give chase. We'll take our time to draw less attention, and then we'll run again if we see anything that looks like trouble."

The highway split ahead, and Jessica stayed to the left. Jessica tried to remember the directions Leticia's mother had written down, trying to recall street names. Traffic was beginning to grow heavier. She saw a Honda dealership on the right. A while later they passed a McDonalds. There was something strangely comforting about the familiar names.

"Keep your eye out for a sign that says 'Constituyentes'... "She paused, thinking, "It might say Avenida or Avenido before that, or maybe just the letters A-V."

"What's that?" Sarah asked.

"It's the street we are most likely to run into from our directions to get us back on course."

"What if we miss it?" Sarah worried.

Jessica squinted, trying to visualize the written instructions in her mind, "watch for Anillo too."

"*Anillo?*"

"Means 'ring'. It's a sort of highway that more or less

circles the city. Leticia's mom mentioned it as a sort of landmark we'd pass. Constituyentes goes through it. Or under or over it." Jessica glanced at Sarah. "I think she said the signs to it might say 'Periferico' or something like that.

To the left, Jessica glimpsed a building with a large billboard of a female silhouette in lingerie. Before she could read the text, it was blocked from her view by a long hinged bus. She wondered if the sign was for a women's clothing store or a club for men—like the kind she had seen signs for once when her family drove through Nevada when she was thirteen. She remembered asking her mom what it was, and she remembered being surprised and bewildered about why a woman would do such a thing when her mother had explained.

Now, she found herself wondering if the girls there actually wanted to be there, or if they had been compelled to be there? Did the customers know? Could they tell the difference? Did they care? She shook her head, chasing that uncomfortable thought away.

"Is that the ring street?" Sarah pointed up at a sign.

Jessica looked and saw it indicated they were traveling on Av. Insurgentes Sur. An arrow pointing in their current direction of travel was labeled 'Periferico'.

"I believe so," Jessica replied, hope bubbling within her.

"So we'll get on the ring and watch for the Constitution Avenue?"

"Yes," Jessica smiled, "more or less."

The road curved to the right and continued past a variety of shops—a mix of old and new, clean and graffiti-covered. Another bend slightly to the right, then a hard left, and another sign reassuring them that the Periferico was somewhere ahead.

Jessica began to consider which direction they should enter the road. She was confident they were to the east of where they would be if they had followed the directions—a decision she regretted after the run-in with the police captain—so west made the most sense.

They passed under a road, with another raised road above that.

That must be the ring, she thought.

She took the exit onto a clover-ramp, which curled around, finally heading west. Jessica was pretty sure it was west, anyway. She really missed her mountains. They merged into the heavy traffic on the lower level of the double-decker roadway, and Jessica did her best to keep from getting boxed in by the many commuters, moving to the middle of three lanes.

Her heart sank as a car with a light bar on top entered the ring beside them on the left from another merge lane. On the side of the car, she could see the words "*Vigilancia Auxiliar*" and below that "*Estado De Mexico*".

Jessica slowed to let the car go in front of her. Ahead of her was a dump truck carrying a dozen men wearing safety vests in the middle lane. A gap opened in the right lane, and she slipped into it, placing the dump truck between her and the car. Glancing over, she saw Sarah staring at the back of the truck as if trying to see through it.

"Was that more police?" Sarah asked.

"Don't know." Jessica refocused on the road. "Might be private security or something." Jessica doubted it. It was most certainly a government organization. Maybe something like state troopers.

The rear bumper of the car come into view and Jessica realized the car was slowing down. She accelerated up, moving along the right side of the big truck to maintain cover.

Jessica could feel her heart beating in her throat. She gripped the wheel tighter in an effort to bring her trembling fingers under control.

There was a flurry of brake lights as traffic thickened and slowed at a major merge point. Two new lanes appeared to the right, leaving Jessica pinned in from all sides.

Frantically she scanned the road, searching for the car.

The two new lanes broke away again, rising to connect to the upper level. Reacting quickly, she signaled and squeezed into the right lane just as they separated. She breathed a sigh of relief as they merged onto the upper lanes. The traffic thinned slightly giving room to maneuver, and there was no sign of any police-like vehicles.

However, a new worry set in; how would she find Constituyentes from up here? Would they overshoot it? She searched for a ramp to take them back down to the lower level. After a nerve-wracking eternity, she finally spied one.

"Jess?" Sarah's voice rose in a squeak, catching Jessica's attention. She was looking in the side mirror.

Jessica glanced in the rear-view and watched as a motorbike carrying a uniformed person raced up behind them. When it was about three car lengths behind them, it slowed, matching their speed. The uniformed man brought one hand up to his face holding a small, black object which Jessica guessed was a radio.

"Does the entire Mexican police force work for the Templars?!" Sarah clenched her jaw and balled her fists.

"Not necessarily," Jessica responded. "At this point we could be on the radar for assaulting police officers, theft, murder—"

"What do we do?"

"Not stop and try to explain!" Jessica replied. They were just about to merge with the lower ring road again, and Jessica could see the '*Vigilancia*' car from earlier, its rear tire matched up with the front tire of the pickup. Jessica floored it, and the truck lurched forward with a roar.

They entered the road ahead of the car, which swerved to the middle lane to avoid getting clipped by the pickup. The car accelerated, while the bike took up position behind them.

"Constitution!" Sarah shrieked pointing up to the right. Jessica swerved in time to catch the exit bearing a sign labeled 'Constituyentes Pte' which crossed over to a two-lane street running parallel to the ring road. The accelerating car overshot the entrance and was now next to them on the other side of a low, concrete barricade. The bike was behind them. Jessica looked over and saw the car driver brake hard, looking backward. Evidently, he planned to reverse to the exit and resume the chase.

Another exit appeared on the right with a sign indicating Constituyentes Pte. Jessica turned, causing the tires to screech in complaint. Sarah flailed to grab anything to prevent her sliding into Jessica's lap. There was a rough jolt as they hit a speed bump going much too fast.

"You okay, Alyona?" Jessica glanced back at the grimacing girl.

"No," Alyona responded through clenched teeth.

"Sorry." Jessica winced and returned her attention to the road.

The exit straightened and merged with another multilane. Another sign bearing the name Constituyentes directed them to a sharp turn to make the exit on the right. The pickup swayed, threatening to roll, then they were racing along on a single lane with cars parked on the right. The road ended in an intersection.

Jessica's face fell as she recognized the road they had just left.

"What the heck?" she cried as she ignored the stop sign and turned back onto the road paralleling the ring road, navigating a break in the traffic flow.

"What do we do?!" Sarah cried.

"Try again," Jessica said with determination, forcing her voice to be calm.

Right again onto the exit, speed bump, then merge left. The police car was just ahead of her as he turned right onto the exit. Scanning the area, Jessica noticed a second exit after the one they had taken the first time and swerved to take it. This road went down and merged with Constituyentes Avenue. They entered a tunnel under a triple-stacked road above.

Traffic was moderately heavy, and the motorcycle kept pace but did not move to pass them.

"Oh shoot," Jessica exclaimed. "We're going the wrong way!"

"Are you sure?" Sarah cried.

"Yeah! We were going clockwise around the ring, we left it to the right, and then we just went under it. We're traveling away from the city center. We need to go the other way!"

Jessica glanced at the small curb separating the traffic in the other direction. The pickup could bump over it easily enough, but there was too much traffic to pull it off without causing an accident.

"Again?" Sarah groaned in frustration, looking out the driver's side window. The car was there again, racing to get ahead of the pickup and cut it off. To the right, a sign reading '*Retorno A Periferico*' pointed to an exit which appeared to drop down below the road.

Jessica read the sign out loud. "That has to take us back the way we came."

She stomped on the gas pedal, racing the police car next to her. Before she passed the exit, she slammed on the brakes, allowing the car to overshoot again.

The motorcycle rider realized what was happening too late. He braked hard and turned to the right in a futile attempt to avoid crashing, but collided with the back of the pickup with a dull thud. Jessica accelerated down the exit, passing under the avenue into the sickly yellow glow of overhead utility lights, then they were climbing back toward the light.

Jessica swerved, narrowly missing a large passenger bus as she merged into traffic heading back toward the city center.

"Okay, this should turn into Metro José Vasconcelos," Jessica said, recalling the final directions she had committed to memory that morning, "Then we need to split right toward the Mexico City Arena."

They whisked back under the ring road, swerving and threading their way through traffic. A moment later the avenue dumped onto another major road.

"I didn't see a sign, but this has to be it." Jessica followed the heavier traffic and moved to the right lane.

"Arena!" Sarah pointed to a sign labeled 'Arena Ciudad de Mexico'.

"Perfect," Jessica grinned, "Next is left to Reforma Centro."

"There!" Sarah pointed out a sign again, and Jessica swung left.

They were running parallel to what she believed was Metro Jose Vasconcelos, separated by a small curb punctuated with short trees.

"Are you kidding me?" Jessica raised both hands and slapped them against the steering wheel. The police car was there, beside them, running his lights.

"Plaza Melcho Ocampo is our next landmark!" Jessica shouted. There wasn't enough traffic to provide them cover. The police car slowed, parallel to them, and Jessica could see the passenger looking at her.

The curb between them widened, creating a small, grassy strip dotted with manicured shrubbery.

"There!" Sarah pointed out a sign to the right.

"Okay, next right," Jessica replied, "Then left, then right at the first three-way intersection after that."

They passed under a road, and the police car was separated from them by a concrete support. Jessica took the exit and glanced back to watch as the police car bumped roughly over the curb, tearing a bush out of the ground.

"Skip an intersection, then turn left!" Jessica recited the directions. The first intersection was a one-way going the wrong direction. Traffic was backed up on the cross-street, but fortunately there were no vehicles in the intersection. Jessica kept the pedal down and blasted through.

Glancing in the rear-view mirror, flashing lights came into view.

The second intersection was a one-way to the left. Jessica cut the corner, narrowly missing an inattentive pedestrian as she raced to slip into a hole in traffic in front of a subcompact car, whose driver honked his disapproval.

Jessica could barely contain her excitement. They were getting so close!

A pedestrian walking in the street jumped out of her way, waving his arms angrily.

"Use the sidewalk, ya moron," Jessica muttered.

She veered left around a slow-moving car, then right to avoid a vehicle pulling into the intersection. The police car was in sight again, and cars were clearing a path for it.

"Traffic lights!" Jessica called out, racing through the intersection on a yellow light. The police car was less than a half block behind them now.

She braked hard and turned onto the narrow one-way street to the right. The police car was nearly on them.

Jessica floored the pickup again, plowing through a flimsy portable barricade which had been set across the road.

To the left, two uniformed men stood near a tall, imposing solid steel gate. She swerved toward it, coming to a halt, inches from the metal.

Several men appeared from the doorway of what appeared to be a gatehouse, rifles at the ready. Jessica threw open the door of the pickup and jumped out, hands above her head. It was a risk—it was safer to stay in the vehicle with her hands on the wheel—but with the police car right behind, she decided to take a chance, rather than give the policeman the first word.

"Please don't shoot," she cried. "I'm an American."

"On the ground! Keep your hands above your head!"

Jessica dropped to her knees, and two men approached her. One forced her to the ground and restrained her hands while the other searched her for weapons.

"We were kidnapped," she said, when the pressure on her back relaxed slightly. "We escaped. Some of the police are working with them. We're Americans, please help us!"

"Back up!" someone shouted in Spanish.

"They're ours," a voice responded, "They killed some men and stole their truck!"

"I said back up!"

There was a pause. Jessica turned her head to see two Mexican policemen, pistols out but pointed at the ground, facing off with two Marines holding ARs which were not pointed at the ground.

"Please don't let them take us," she begged again, "we're American!"

"This one needs a medic!" someone said from behind her.

There were some shuffling sounds, then another voice said, "She's pretty banged up. We need a stretcher so we can move her."

"They are terrorists. You need to give them to us."

"They are staying here until I can check out their story. Now stand down! Holster your weapons!"

There was some angry mumbling, then she heard the slamming of car doors and the sound of an engine starting.

"Get her up," the same authoritative voice ordered, and Jessica was pulled to her feet, her hands bound behind her. A middle-aged man in a black uniform stood directly in front of her. He was solidly built, a full head taller than her, and he had a broad chest. His eyes were narrow slits, studying her. He held a pistol up to her face. "You want to tell me about this?"

"We took it from our captors," Jessica replied, "there's another one ..."

He held the second pistol up next to the first one. "What's your name?"

"Jessica, sir. Jessica Hansen."

Two men carrying a small stretcher jogged past her to the pickup. Sarah was led, hands bound, to stand beside Jessica.

The man turned his attention from Jessica to the men with the stretcher. "Take her inside. Have Jensen look her over and evaluate her treatment needs." He returned his gaze to Jessica. "My name is Colonel Levitt. I oversee security for the embassy. You want to tell me what's going on here?"

"It's kind of a long story," Jessica began. The colonel nodded. Then turned to another soldier, a younger woman with Hispanic features. "Lieutenant Dominguez, escort these two inside, and find a room to hold them with a posted guard. Find someone from staff who can get them some food and water."

"Yes, sir." Dominguez saluted and turned to Sarah and Jessica. "Follow me please."

"Captain Harding," the colonel continued as the girls followed Lieutenant Dominguez, "Assign a team to inspect the pickup. Bring it inside if it passes. Report anything suspicious to me immediately."

"Yes, sir."

"Miss Hansen," the colonel called as Jessica was entering the door into the compound, "I'll be along shortly to hear your… story."

Jessica stopped and turned. "Is there any chance I can call my parents? I haven't talked to them for weeks, they must be worried sick."

The Colonel nodded and glanced to the lieutenant again. "Get her a phone—supervised."

"This way please," the lieutenant addressed Jessica and Sarah, directing them through the doorway.

Jessica gazed over her shoulder once more to watch as Alyona was removed from the back of the pickup on the stretcher.

"They'll take good care of her," Lieutenant Dominguez assured her. Jessica nodded and followed the soldier through the doorway into the embassy compound.

Chapter Twenty One

"Hello?"

Tears flooded her eyes at the sound of her mother's voice. Jessica was seated at a utilitarian table—a three-foot by eight-foot slab of wood resting on sturdy metal legs—in the middle of a small, windowless room with sterile white walls. The office phone was the only object adorning the table.

"Hi, Mom," Jessica struggled to stop the tremble in her words.

"Jessie baby?" Her mother's shaking tone betrayed her own efforts to temper her emotions. "Honey, where are you? We were so worried. We haven't heard from you for so long. Are you okay?"

"Yeah, Mom, I'm okay, we ran into some trouble here, but we're okay now. We're at the US Embassy, in Mexico City." Jessica looked up to where Sarah stood at the far

"This compound you were taken to." The colonel returned his attention to the documents, thumbing over the top few pages. "You don't by chance recall any distinguishing features or landmarks?"

"Do you have a topo map?"

The colonel fixed his penetrating gaze on her again, his eyes narrowing ever so slightly. Jessica forced herself to hold his gaze in spite of her discomfort.

"Lieutenant," the colonel spoke, his eyes unmoving, "I need topographical maps of the Guerrero region."

"Yes, sir." The lieutenant saluted and left the room.

A moment later there was a knock at the door, and a young man in a suit peeked in. "I was told you wanted to speak to me, sir?" he addressed the colonel.

"I need sleeping arrangements for these two," the colonel indicated Jessica and Sarah, "with a guard detail. No local contractors."

"Yes, sir," the man replied, "I'll take care of it. Anything else?"

The colonel examined the two girls critically. "I imagine a change of clothes would be appreciated."

The young man sized them up. "I'll pass that request on to someone more qualified." He finally said, "What about meals and toiletries? How long will they be staying?"

"Working on that. I'll let you know when I do."

The young man nodded and closed the door.

Several minutes later the lieutenant returned with a stack of maps. "Where do you want to start?" she asked.

Jessica scratched her head. "Actually, I guess I probably need to start from a road map. Mexico City or south-ish of it."

The lieutenant selected a map and unrolled it, laying it out on the table in front of Jessica. Jessica began working her way backward in her mind, tracing the route that matched her recollection. She was able to work back to Leticia's home town on the larger road map. Lieutenant Dominguez noted the coordinates and selected a topographical map for that region, which Jessica used to trace her way backward along the canyons and ridges, until she was satisfied she had pinpointed her base camp.

She was less certain of the trip prior to that. She had spent a few days around the cave, and she had sufficient time to become familiar with the area. Getting to there had been under stressful conditions, with less time available to commit landmarks to memory. Working backward through each event, she identified matching details near her best approximations of direction of travel and distance covered each day. Finally, she dropped her finger onto a spot on the map.

"Right around here," she said, meeting the colonel's gaze.

The colonel looked at her for several seconds. "Where are you from?"

"Utah, sir. A small farming town."

"Farm girl," he grunted. He turned to the lieutenant. "Get on the horn with Inspector Hidalgo. Speak to him directly—no messages. Tell him we want to arrange a joint reconnaissance mission. Tell him to arrange a face-to-face with me. Through you, no other points of contact."

The lieutenant saluted, gathered the unused maps and left the room.

It was evening by the time everything was finished. The colonel had arranged two adjacent rooms in the neighboring hotel: one for Jessica and Sarah, and one for a detail of three Marines assigned to guard them. Jessica let Sarah have the bathroom first, after seeing the dreamy look in her eyes when she saw the bathtub.

An hour later when Sarah finally emerged, Jessica was asleep on top of the bed covers of one of the queen-size beds.

Chapter Twenty Two

A tap at the door woke the girls just after sunrise. Jessica slowly opened her eyes, reluctant to leave the gentle embrace of the clean sheets and soft mattress. She didn't remember actually getting under the covers, but now that she was there, she was in no hurry to leave.

A second, slightly louder tap confirmed Jessica's suspicion that ignoring the knocking would not work. Jessica rose from the bed with a yawn, stretched and shuffled to the door.

"Hello?" she croaked, her voice still thick with sleep.

"Lieutenant Dominguez, ma'am," came the familiar voice. Jessica opened the door.

"Sorry to rush you," the Marine apologized. "Colonel wanted you up at first light, back in the compound within the hour."

Jessica nodded. "We'll get dressed."

"Breakfast will be here in ten minutes. I will be just outside if you need anything."

Shutting the door, Jessica spun on her heels. Sarah sat on the edge of her bed, blinking up at her.

"What time is it?" she asked.

"Time to get ready." Jessica ran a hand through her tangled hair. "I'm going to jump in the shower."

Jessica took a quick shower and slipped into the new underwear and clothes supplied by an aide from the embassy who had stopped by briefly yesterday afternoon to take sizes, and then rushed away with a great deal of enthusiasm. There were a few options, and Jessica suspected the aide had rather enjoyed the opportunity to go on a shopping spree for them. Jessica selected a pair of faded blue jeans and a long, navy peasant top, with embroidery on the front.

Sarah was already dressed when Jessica emerged from the bathroom. She wore a light-blue, flowing, knee-length summer dress with a pleated waist. She twirled in it like a little girl, and she kept running her hands over the fabric, feeling the cleanness of it.

"Breakfast is here." Sarah pointed to the trays of food on the table: a tortilla topped with eggs and salsa, some slices of avocado, and some sort of sweet bread.

Jessica picked up one of the pieces of bread and examined it, nibbling on it tentatively.

"They're called *conchas*," Sarah said as she prepared to take a bit of tortilla. "Lieutenant Dominguez says they're really good dipped in hot chocolate."

"Jess," Sarah said, swallowing. "Do you think they'll let us go home today?"

Jessica sighed. "I hope so. I don't think they'd keep us here for very long, but..." Jessica looked out the window longingly, "with two governments involved, who knows?"

"I hope Alyona's okay."

"I'm sure she is." Jessica placed a hand on Sarah's knee. "She's a fighter."

Sarah's eyes saddened. She looked down at her lap. "I miss Meredith."

"Me too." Tears stung Jessica's eyes.

A knock came at the door.

"Yes?" Jessica called, standing and brushing away the tears.

"If you're ready, we should get back to the embassy, ma'am," Lieutenant Dominguez said from the other side of the door.

"Just one more minute." Jessica turned to face Sarah again. "Ready?"

Sarah nodded. "Let's go."

They opened the door to find the lieutenant waiting with a detail of four Marines in battle dress.

"Is everything okay?" Dominguez asked after looking at their faces.

Jessica managed a smile "We're okay."

The lieutenant studied her for a moment, then led them down the hall to the elevator.

"What's that plan for today?" Jessica asked as the elevator descended.

"We are to take you back to the embassy and report to Colonel Levitt," Dominguez replied, "I'm afraid I can't tell you anything more than that."

"Oh, I see," Jessica smirked, "Top secret, clandestine stuff eh? Cloak and dagger? Black-ops mission?"

Dominguez smiled, but remained professional. "I am sure the colonel will have details regarding the agenda for the day. This way please." She gestured into the lobby as the elevator doors opened.

"Hey!" a voice called as they crossed the lobby. "Is this the *gringa* who stole my truck?"

The Marine detail formed up around the girls as a young man approached, two other young men following close behind.

"My friend was using my truck, and you killed him and took it! You owe me a truck!"

"Step aside, sir," one of the Marines said.

"You step aside, *señor,*" the young man sneered, puffing out his chest. "She owes me a truck."

"How much ya pay for it?" a rich baritone voice asked.

Jessica furrowed her brow, the voice seemed like it should be familiar to her, but how could she know anyone here?

"What?" The young man seemed both surprised and a little annoyed that someone was interrupting him in his moment of bravado.

"The pickup? How much did you pay for it?"

Jessica's eyes went wide as the tall, lanky figure of Uncle Ben came into view. He was a quintessential cowboy, in denim jeans, plaid shirt, an open denim jacket, and worn cowboy boots and hat. He walked with the long gait of a man who had spent his life stepping around manure in a pasture. His permanent squint and wrinkled, weathered skin spoke of years spent herding cattle from horseback in the high deserts of Wyoming. A bit of salt and pepper hair could be seen just below his hat, a match in color to the thick handlebar mustache. His partially concealed mouth, like his eyes, seemed fixed in a state of perpetual amusement.

Jessica wanted to cry out for joy, yet she forced herself to remain composed and kept her feet firmly planted as Uncle Ben walked past and toward the young man. Technically he wasn't her uncle, he was her father's uncle, but he had been 'Uncle Ben' to Jessica her whole life.

"Who are you?" the young man demanded.

"I'm the guy that's asking you how much you paid for your wheels, son."

"I paid fifty thousand pesos for it, cowboy! What business is it of yours?"

Uncle Ben whistled. "Fifty thousand pesos. And she's the one that took it?" He pointed toward Jessica without taking his eyes from the young man.

"Took and destroyed it. She smashed it up, painted it crazy colors... She wrecked it."

"She vandalized your truck? Now that is a shame," Uncle Ben said, sounding appalled.

"Here you go," a softer, more tenor voice said, out of sight behind the tall cowboy.

Jessica's heart leaped and tears pooled in her eyes. She would have bolted toward the sound had it not been for the Marine detail keeping her corralled.

"What's this?" The young man was caught off guard.

"Twenty-five hundred American dollars," the soft

voice replied, "About fifty thousand pesos, to replace your pickup."

The boy stood holding the stack of money, his mouth agape. The face belonging to the soft voice now came into view as he turned and walked toward Jessica.

"Daddy!" Jessica shoved through the Marines, wriggling through a gap and breaking free to rush and leap into her father's arms, tears freely flowing down her cheeks.

"Hey there, Jess," he said, wrapping her in a fierce embrace. He kissed her cheek, then he pressed his own cheek against hers. It was comfortingly warm, smooth, and soft. Uncle Ben accused her dad of having won the genetic lottery. In all her life she could never remember him ever seeming to age. His features seemed timeless. He had a full head of dark hair with a light curl, framing a serious face with a perpetual hint of a tan.

"I am so glad to see you." Jessica broke the long silence, reluctantly releasing her grip. She turned to face Uncle Ben.

"Hey there, Droopy!" he said, his eyes twinkling. Ben was fond of nicknames and had given her many. One of the earliest was 'Miss Droopy Diapers,' owing to her frequently roaming around as a toddler with a very wet diaper hanging down to her knees. Droopy was the short version he had settled on, since her mother threatened him with bodily harm the one time he had tried out 'Double-D' as an abbreviation.

"Hey, Uncle Ben." Jessica smiled, then embraced the gruff old man in a warm hug, enjoying both the sound and feeling of his deep, throaty chuckle.

"What are you doing here?" Jessica asked.

"Your mamma called us as we were getting ready to board a plane to come looking for you," Uncle Ben replied, "She told us where you were, and since we already paid for the tickets, we figured we might as well use 'em. We managed to get the tickets changed to a red-eye into Mexico City, rented a car, and found a hotel room as close to the embassy as we could. Figured we'd stroll over and check on you this morning. Nice of you to save us a walk."

"Do you know who I am? Do you know who my father is?" The young man had found his voice again.

"No, sir, I don't," Jessica's father replied, his voice even and unemotional. He never raised his voice, never got excited, never got flustered. He was steady; he was a rock, a firmly rooted tree, an anchor in the storm.

"You think she'll get away? My father will find you! He'll find her! He'll come and he'll take her. He'll make all of you pay!"

"I don't know about any of that," Jessica's father began, his voice unchanged, "but if your father comes to my home, I'll have to kill him."

There was no hint of threat in his voice, no anger or fear, not even the slightest trace of emotion in his face. It was spoken as a statement of undeniable fact—an inevitable, foregone conclusion, like stating the sun would set.

The young man stared at Jessica's father uncertainly, his boldness tempered by the unflappable man.

There was a flurry of sound at the doors, and the colonel and a dozen more Marines entered the room, guns at the ready, causing no small amount of panic among the few other individuals milling about the lobby.

The new arrivals placed themselves between the three young men and Jessica, forming a protective line.

"What seems to be the trouble?" the colonel asked.

"Miguel!" a voice snapped, "What are you doing? Why are you bothering these poor people?"

Sarah gasped and grabbed Jessica's arm, squeezing it tightly. Jessica took Sarah's hand and placed herself between Sarah and the voice.

"Gentlemen, my apologies." He was a handsome man with a broad smile and perfect teeth. He was smooth and charismatic—regal even. His eyes were alert and exuded a warmth, yet Jessica sensed it was a false warmth. She could see the hidden danger in them. He was followed by four large men with unblinking eyes in dark suits. Quiet men. Dangerous men. Jessica gripped Sarah's hand tighter.

"You'll have to forgive my son," the man said, "Youth can be overdramatic sometimes."

"No harm done," Colonel Levitt replied guardedly.

"So, these are the girls I heard about?" The man's voice took on a concerned tone. "These are the wild, party girls that killed a man and took his truck on a joy ride?"

"That's one story." Levitt's face was as unreadable as his voice.

"Ah, of course they tell a different story, no? Such a shame." He feigned regret. "I guess the courts will decide, no?"

"Perhaps," Levitt responded, "several options are being evaluated."

"*Señor.*" The man looked shocked. "Surely you're not suggesting that America will ignore Mexico's right to administer justice?"

"I'm sure they will come to a reasonable decision which will be acceptable to most." Levitt still didn't blink.

"Oh, *señor.*" The man smiled and shook his head slowly. "I don't think you understand the gravity of your situation."

"Are you planning to enlighten me?"

The man's gaze darkened. As if on cue, his four bodyguards moved forward ever so slightly. It was a move meant not so much to provoke a response, as it was to intimidate. The colonel seemed unimpressed. He continued to stare at the man.

The two groups stood, staring each other down, for what felt like ages. It reminded Jessica a little of old Western movies—right before the big gunfight. She glanced around, trying to decide the best place to drag Sarah for cover.

Jessica heard a hiss and a pop from somewhere behind the leader of the Templarios, followed by a sharp slap. A small cloud of red mist erupted directly behind his head. He screamed and clutched the back of his head.

"I'm shot!" he screamed, "I'm shot! My brain!"

His four bodyguards turned and drew guns, searching for the attacker. Some Marines moved to provide cover for Sarah, Jessica, her father, and Uncle Ben. Several other Marines trained their weapons on the Templario bodyguards, while the rest formed up and moved in the direction the shot came from. The handful of bystanders in the lobby were screaming and running in every direction, seeking cover or an escape.

"Lower your weapons," the colonel barked at the Templarios.

"It's not blood!" shouted Uncle Ben, "It's just paint."

It took a few moments for this to sink in for the rest, but as it did the tension lessened.

A minute later, the scouting group returned from around a corner holding a piece of pipe with a tank on the end.

"An improvised paintball gun," Uncle Ben observed, making no effort to conceal a smirk of admiration.

"There was writing on the wall in spray paint above where this was lying on the floor," one of the Marines informed the colonel.

"What does it say?"

"*No intocable.*"

"Not untouchable?" The colonel frowned.

Uncle Ben threw a questioning glance at Jessica's father, who turned a much more subtle, questioning gaze to her.

She shook her head imperceptibly then she froze, eyes widening in comprehension. She scanned the room, looking for a familiar face.

"Does that mean anything to you?" the colonel asked, fixing a hard stare on Jessica.

"No," Jessica responded, feigning innocence. The colonel continued to stare at her. Finally, accepting that she wasn't going to change her answer, he shrugged it off.

"And you two are?" Colonel Levitt turned his attention to the two men.

"Jared Hansen. Jessica's father. This is my uncle, Ben."

"She invited you here?"

"No, sir, we were already on our way here."

Colonel Levitt inhaled deeply, his jaw clenching.

"Well, let's move this reunion to a less public location." He barked a series of orders, assigning one group of Marines to secure and scout the area, and another group to escort the girls and the two men away from the Templarios and to the embassy.

Chapter Twenty Three

"What'd he mean about the courts deciding?" Jessica asked Colonel Levitt once they were settled in at the embassy again. The colonel narrowed his eyes as he stared at the walls of the conference room.

"There's a group protesting in front of the embassy, demanding that you be turned over to the Mexican courts to be tried for murder."

"Protestors?" Jessica widened her eyes.

"It's why we brought you in the way we did this morning; to avoid the mob."

"I don't understand." Jessica shook her head.

"Best we can tell, a small group showed up early this morning. A woman was crying to a local television crew about a group of rich, psychotic American girls who lured her poor, sweet son into a trap, got him drunk, murdered him and stole his friend's pickup truck. The story brought in the usual group of anti-American, anti-capitalist malcontents screaming for justice, demanding that America stop interfering in Mexico's affairs, and protecting rich American criminals."

"But it's not true," Jessica protested.

"We believe the woman is on the Templar payroll—an actor. The rest are... professional protestors, people with too much time on their hands and not enough sense to use that time productively. Comisario Perez made an appearance as well. Promised to get justice for the underprivileged victims."

"But he and the Templar leader are cousins!" Jessica gripped the arms of her chair until her knuckles were white.

"Distant cousins," the colonel corrected. "There's nothing to suggest the two communicate."

"So what does this mean for the girls?" Uncle Ben placed a hand on Jessica's shoulder from where he stood behind her.

"It means the bureaucrats are going to spend a few days negotiating, looking for a way for everyone to save face. I'm sorry. It means you are likely going to have to stay here for a while. Under our protection of course."

Uncle Ben took a seat. "I got nowhere pressing to be."

"Forgive me, sir," the colonel said, "but we won't be able to extend that hospitality to you. You'd be largely on your own, in questionable territory."

Uncle Ben chuckled softly, his eyes twinkling. "I appreciate your concern, colonel, but I think you'll find me rather less skittish than yer gangster."

The colonel shot an appraising glance at Uncle Ben. "I suppose you are right. I assume you're not one to take firm suggestions from authority figures either."

"No, sir." Uncle Ben smiled, but determination shone in his eyes.

The next several hours were spent in the confines of their assigned embassy accommodations. Occasionally someone would check on them, making sure they were comfortable, but most of the time it was just the four of them. Jessica and Sarah recounted their ordeal, while the two men listened intently.

Uncle Ben told a few tall tales from his youth to pass the time, and to take the girls' minds off things. He was just wrapping up a story about him and some of his cousins losing a tractor in a nearby lake as teenagers, when the door burst open. Colonel Levitt and several uniformed Marines entered.

"Do any of you have anything you need from your hotel rooms?" the colonel asked.

"Nothing we can't afford to leave," Jared said.

"We didn't have anything to begin with," Jessica answered.

"There's been an unexpected turn of events," the colonel continued. "A video from a camera phone turned up, showing Comisario Perez and Gonzalo Rodriguez having a conversation in a restaurant."

"What? I thought they never communicated."

"It appears someone tricked Perez into thinking Rodriguez wanted to talk to him. It hit the news feed this evening, people are in the streets in force demanding

Perez's head. Our sources suggest the president is taking a personal interest in dealing with this. At any rate, this will almost certainly end any talk of indicting you two, but it's hard to know what Rodriguez might try."

"You think he might have people here too?" Uncle Ben asked.

"Not that I can prove."

"So we're gonna make a break for the border?" Uncle Ben smirked.

"We have a military transport flying some Marines back to the States tonight. We worked out the logistics to get you on with them, then transfer you to Hill Air Force base. That's a bit north of home for you, isn't it?"

"A bit," Jared confirmed, "but we can arrange a ride from there."

"They have room for the four of you, but they are leaving now, so we need to get you on your way."

"But what about Alyona?" Jessica asked.

"Arrangements are being made for her as well, she will be transported to a hospital—States-side. The destination has yet to be finalized, but she is already en route for air transport. I will keep you posted as to her status."

Uncle Ben stood and made a grand sweeping gesture. "By all means, get us on our way then."

The video was dark, but the man sitting at the table was easily recognizable as Gonzalo Rodriguez, leader of the Templarios. He was sitting at a table with another well-dressed man, eating and discussing something.

One of the Marines in the truck taking them to the airstrip had pulled up the video on his phone for Jessica and Sarah to watch. The video was taken with a phone, and the angle suggested it was shot by someone seated at a nearby table, with the phone held low.

Comisario Perez walked into the shot, looking sweaty and nervous. He strode to the table.

Gonzalo looked up; his face showed no sign of recognizing Perez. "May I help you?"

"You wanted to see me." Perez furrowed his brow, "You said it was urgent."

"You idiot!" Gonzalo gritted his teeth, "Why would I want to meet with you? Especially in a public place? Get out of here before someone sees you!" A look of realization crossed Gonzalo's face. He scanned the room, and the video went black as the camera was tucked into a jacket.

"Someone has a camera." Gonzalo's voice could still be heard. "Find it!"

The video ended, and Jessica returned the phone to the Marine.

"So pretty safe to say whoever took the video got away safely." Jessica tried to keep the concern out of her voice.

"It's been all over the news," the Marine spoke excitedly, "This might be the chink in Rodriguez's armor we've been looking for."

"Really?" Jessica asked.

"I've been down here a couple times in the past year, working with local law enforcement," the Marine explained, "We provide training and assist in joint operations to help take down drug operations, and more recently we've been assisting with efforts to break up some of the human trafficking rings. We've known Rodriguez was deep into both for a while, but we haven't been able to make anything stick."

"Because of Perez," Jessica interjected, "his cousin."

"Seems so, ma'am. We knew he had to have connections, just didn't know how to find them or prove them. Now it's public knowledge, and people are riled up about it. If the president doesn't act fast, Perez and Rodriguez will wind up in the cemetery instead of the prison."

"Way to go, Jess!" Sarah grinned. "Your very own revolution."

"What?" Jessica whipped her head around to look at Sarah. "I didn't do this!"

"You inspired it," Sarah persisted. "Miss Untouchable."

Jessica could feel the flush in her face.

"What's this?" the Marine asked Sarah, "You saying she's the spark the started the fire? Come to think of it," the Marine grinned at Jessica, "You do look a trifle warm."

"Oh, stop!" Jessica rolled her eyes, as the other two shared a laugh.

They arrived at the airstrip and boarded the waiting aircraft. The wheels had barely left the ground before both girls were fast asleep.

Chapter Twenty Four

Jessica awoke early. It was early August—four months since the spring break ordeal. She dressed in running clothes and was out just before the sun cleared the mountains. It was good to be back home. She felt a little bad for her brother Joseph, who had enjoyed his own room for mere months before being rather abruptly returned to the shared bedroom with Sam. She hadn't planned on moving back. She had intended to get a job, and maybe even take an extra class over the summer, but after everything that had happened, going home felt like the right thing to do.

Summer at home had been good therapy. She easily slipped into a familiar routine, which helped establish a feeling of normalcy. She woke up early, went for a run, helped her brothers and sisters with their morning chores, and worked with the horses.

The funeral was hard. Meredith's body was located, recovered, and returned to her family a week after Sarah and Jessica left Mexico. Meredith was an only child, and her parents were overwhelmed with grief. Jessica's parents went with her to the funeral, which helped. She drew from their strength as she stood by the graveside, their arms around her a safe harbor.

Jessica's parents had followed Alyona's progress, and as soon as it was permitted, they made arrangements for Alyona to move to the farm, where they managed her recovery over the months as fractured ribs mended. Colonel Levitt had managed to fast-track her for a green card, and Jessica's mother had become her coach in working toward citizenship. Jessica's father offered her room and board in exchange for helping on the farm once she was well enough. Alyona had eagerly accepted and was quickly adopted into the Hansen family. She was increasing her workload as her ribs permitted, and her time on the Hansen farm had removed much of her cynicism.

Jessica cut her run short, making a quick five-mile loop and then returning to help her mother with preparations for the large family barbeque planned for that evening in celebration of Emily's sixth birthday. Extended family and several close neighborhood friends would be attending, and Sarah was driving down that morning to be there as well. There were plenty of preparations to be made. Chairs and tables were to be set up on the lawn. Decorations were to be hung, a cake needed to be decorated, and there was a full-page list of salads and side dishes to be prepared.

She showered and ate a quick breakfast of eggs collected from the chicken coop, a toasted slice of freshly made bread covered with raspberry jam her mother had canned last fall, and a handful of strawberries she had picked before she came into the house after her run.

"Good morning," Alyona greeted as Jessica was just finishing her last bite of toast and gathering her dishes to be washed in the sink.

"Hey, Alyona!" Jessica responded cheerily. "How are the ribs doing today?"

Alyona grimaced. "So-so."

"Overdid it a little bit yesterday, huh?" Jessica chided her good-naturedly.

"Perhaps a little."

"It's okay to leave the heavy lifting for my brothers," Jessica said. "Get yourself better before you try to impress them."

"I'll keep that in mind." Alyona rolled her eyes.

The phone rang.

"I'll get it!" shouted Emily as she raced into the room and grabbed the phone.

Alyona chuckled. "She's very excited for her birthday phone calls, no?" Emily had taken an instant liking to Alyona, which Alyona had reciprocated. "Speaking of which, what is plan for today? What you need me to do?"

Jessica pointed to a large bag of potatoes resting against the wall, "Probably first thing this morning will be to peel and boil potatoes, so we can get them chilled and ready for a potato salad."

"What time is Sarah arriving?"

"I think she said around one or two. She had a couple things to tie off at work this morning."

"She's working too much."

"Yeah," Jessica sighed, "I think she keeps herself busy to keep her mind off things. She doesn't go out with her old friends like she used to, and I don't think she's made many new friends yet. Still kinda keeping to herself."

"It's difficult," Alyona offered. "But she's strong."

"Yes," Jessica smiled, "It'll take a little while, but she'll get through. She's gonna stay through the weekend. She even suggested the three of us go camping—if you're up to it."

"Jessie?" Emily interrupted, her face wrinkled in confusion, "I think it's for you."

"Who is it?" Jessica asked.

"Umm... I'm not sure. She talks funny. I couldn't really understand her. Maybe it sounded like she said she was lettuce?"

Jessica frowned. "Okay, Thanks, Em."

She took the phone, and Emily skipped away.

"Hello?" Jessica said tentatively.

"Hello?" came a familiar voice, "This is Jessica? Jessica Hansen?"

"Leticia?" Jessica said in surprise.

"*Si*," came the happy reply.

"Holy cow. Leticia! How are you? How did you find me?"

"Oh, was so hard! I called too many people. I am so glad I finally found you."

"How's your family?" Jessica leaned against the counter.

"We are all very good. We are home again. Do you know how are the other girls?"

"They're good. Alyona is here, with my family and Sarah is gonna be here this afternoon, if you want to talk to them."

"Oh," Leticia hesitated, "maybe not just now."

"I understand." Jessica twisted a loose strand of hair around her finger. "I think they have forgiven you, if that helps any."

"*Si, gracias.* Me and my brother, we are talking about coming to America for a vacation, maybe we can see you then?"

"I'd like that, but wait, your brother? As in the one your mother disowned? And you said you are home again?"

"*Si.* Los Templarios are gone. My brother Nicolas, he got the people to chase them away. He made a video that got the leader to go to prison. My mama is very proud of him," Leticia said, the pride also evident in her voice.

"Nicolas?"

"*Si*, Nicolas. He told me to say hello to you and to thank you for being his… how you say… muse? *Musa* is muse?"

"*Si*," Jessica replied, smiling, "Wow, that's crazy. Nicolas is your brother. Well, give him a hug from me next time you see him. It's so good to hear things are going okay for you."

The two girls talked for a while, catching each other up on the events since they went their separate ways. They agreed to talk again in a week, and to make plans to meet in the fall, then they said their goodbyes.

Smiling, Jessica walked to the kitchen where Alyona was peeling potatoes.

"So," Alyona spoke without looking up, "Leticia found us. I would have guessed Rodriguez would find us first."

"He's in prison."

"Really?"

Jessica nodded. "His cousin too. It sounds like the Templarios are history."

Alyona looked up. "How did that happen?"

"You remember Nicolas? The guy at the gas pump?"

"The one you suspected shot Rodriguez in the hotel lobby?"

"Yep. Turns out it was him. He also got the video in the restaurant, and then he organized the local towns to run the Templarios out."

Jessica filled Alyona in on the rest of the story as they peeled potatoes, then placed them in a pot of water on the stove to boil.

"So, they are maybe coming to visit then?" Alyona asked as they started working on making a vegetable tray.

"I think so," Jessica said, "Will you be okay with seeing her again?"

Alyona paused to take a deep breath. "Yes. Like you said, she was trapped, she had dilemma with no good answer."

"So… forgiven?" Jessica peered up through her lashes.

Alyona nodded. "Forgiven."

The birthday party was enjoyably chaotic, with cousins and friends playing loudly and older family and friends swapping tales till the late evening. Once everyone else was gone and the mess cleaned up, Jessica, Sarah, and Alyona relaxed on the back porch, looking at the stars.

"So," Sarah started, "Are you coming back to school this fall, or are the two of you going to hide out on the farm forever?"

Jessica chuckled. "There is nothing wrong with staying on the farm. My parents would probably prefer to keep me closer, but yes, I am planning on coming back to school. Alyona got her acceptance letter today too."

"Roomies then?" Sarah asked.

"Roomies." Jessica grinned.

Sarah cheered and clapped her hands. "I picked a major," Sarah said after another pause, "I've decided to go into nursing."

"Good for you. You'll be great."

"What about you two?" Sarah asked.

"I am thinking about studying criminology," Alyona said, "I've met some people who work with a group that helps to rescue people from groups like the Templarios. I think I will like to do that."

"Wow. I bet you'll be amazing!" Sarah turned to Jessica. "How about you?"

Jessica shrugged. "I'm not sure yet."

"You should go into politics," Alyona said.

"Politics?" Jessica asked doubtfully.

"You inspire people. You would be an excellent President of the United States."

Jessica laughed. "I'm not sure how to take that."

"It's actually a pretty good idea, Jess," Sarah spoke

earnestly, "you really do bring out the best in people, you inspire people, and you're practical and smart."

"Let's see if I get through the next semester before we go making big plans," Jessica said.

Sarah gazed at the sky and sighed. When she returned her focus to Jessica, her expression became serious and a little sad. "I have something to confess. I told you I'm doing okay, but I'm not really. I'm not sleeping very well. I jump at every noise. I don't go out anymore, and I've turned down every offer for a date. I have nightmares a lot and..." A tear rolled down her cheek.

"It gets easier with time." Alyona placed a hand on Sarah's knee. "Don't try to deal with it all by yourself. You have friends. Talk to them."

"That's right." Jessica reached over and took Sarah's hand in hers. "We got through it together, and we'll get through it together. We aren't gonna let one rainy day take away the rest of our sunny days, are we? We'll get back to school, we'll stay up too late playing games and telling stories, and we'll find some nice boys to hang out with."

Sarah laughed, "Whatever you say, *Polkovnik*!"

Jessica lay on the ground, looking up at the most beautiful sky she had ever seen. The stars were unbelievably bright, and there were so many of them. The grass was the perfect temperature, and it was softer than down. The gentlest of breezes blew just enough to rustle the leaves in the trees. Nearby a merry little stream bubbled and gurgled happily over the rocks.

"Hey, Grandma-great," Jessica said. She knew she was there, without looking.

"Good evening," Grandma Dalton said. She was in her rocking chair knitting. "Lovely night, isn't it?"

"I haven't seen you in a while, wasn't sure if you'd left or not."

"Oh, I keep pretty busy, but never so busy that I can't check in on you, dear."

"Was it you that... helped Sarah that night?"

"Helped her? I don't know that I was much help, just let her know she wasn't alone. She's a strong girl. Been through a rough patch, but she'll blossom again. Just needs a little sunshine and water."

"Well, thanks for being there."

"I'm always here, child." Grandma Dalton spoke matter-of-factly, but Jessica could feel a deep affection in those words as well.

"So, any advice for me?" Jessica asked.

"Advice on what?"

"What I should do next."

Grandma Dalton set aside her knitting and looked Jessica in the eye. "You have a gift for leading people, Jess. Don't shy away from the opportunity when it arises."

"What?" Jessica chuckled. "Are you saying I should run for President?"

"The best leaders don't always lead from the front, dear."

"So, what should I do?"

"Child, I'm here to help you now and then when you need it, but I'm not going to run your race for you. Don't worry so much, keep the faith, and hold your course. Trust yourself. You've got a good heart and a sharp mind. You know how to take care of yourself, and you know how to help others. Just keep learning and doing good when the opportunity presents."

Jessica looked back up at the stars, lost in thought.

"Jessica?"

"Yes, Grandma-great?"

"I'm proud of you."

Jessica smiled and closed her eyes. "Thanks, Grandma."

Acknowledgments

Special thanks to the many friends and family who provided encouragement and counsel in this endeavor.

Thanks also to Timothy Ballard (who I very nearly had the chance to meet in person while I was wrapping up my first draft), and the members of Operation Underground Railroad, who work tirelessly to bring attention to – and strive to end – the continued existence of human trafficking.

Most importantly, a special thank-you to my dear wife, who sacrificed so many hours and personal plans, put up with the clickety-click of the keyboard and the glow from the screen in the middle of many nights, and through it all encouraged me to keep going, allowing me the time to pursue this dream of mine. I Love you.

About the Author

Edwin Philips is an IT professional with delusions of becoming an author. He grew up in the United States, in rural Idaho, where he made a hobby of collecting hobbies (computers, cycling, falconry, role playing games….).

He currently resides in Utah, where he works in IT to support his family, and in his spare time he tries to write stories he hopes others will find both entertaining and inspiring.